BOOK ONE IN THE RECKLESS SERIES

Reckless HOPE

NYSSA KATHRYN

An NW Partners Book
Cover by Deranged Doctor Design
Developmentally and Copy Edited by Kelli Collins
Line Edited by Jessica Snyder
Proofread by Amanda Cuff and Jen Katemi
Cover Photography by Madison Maltby Photography

❀ Created with Vellum

Every man she's ever known has hurt her...until him.

Life hasn't been kind to Harper Rain. In fact, so far, it's only proven the one person she can rely on is herself. But when all her efforts to escape her family fail, she takes the last desperate option—run.

With little more than a few dollars to her name, she ends up in the small town of Misty Peak. The first person she meets is a tall mountain of a man...whose kindness is only outshone by his captivating smile.

As a former Delta Forces soldier, the urge to protect others is in Cody Walker's genes. So when a woman walks into his bar in the middle of a storm—with only a backpack and a black eye—ignoring her isn't an option.

Trust doesn't come easy to Harper, so Cody starts by giving her a job. The more he gets to know the enigmatic woman, the more he's convinced that slowly working his way behind her shields is well worth the effort.

Unfortunately for them both, time is a luxury they can't afford. Harper's pursuer is catching up, and if they can't have her, no one can...least of all Cody.

ACKNOWLEDGMENTS

Thank you to everyone who helped make this story what it is. To my team of editors and proofreaders—Kelli, Jessica, Amanda and Jen— you're wonderful to work with and such professionals.

Thank you to my ARC team and readers. I love that you love my stories; you always push me to write the next one.

And to my family, you're my world. My reason. And you inspire me every day to work hard. I wouldn't be able to do this without you.

CHAPTER 1

Harper Rain leaned forward, squinting as she tried to see through the thick raindrops. They hit the windshield in quick succession, so fast the wipers barely had time to clear them. Of course, it didn't help that it was dark and there were almost no streetlights.

God, how was anyone supposed to see in this weather?

She checked the time. One a.m.

So, five hours. She'd been driving for five freaking hours from Hamilton, Alabama, to wherever the heck she was now, through town after town, and she felt every one of those hours. Each had bled into the next, but she hadn't dared stop.

She blinked, trying to remain awake. Her eyelids had been growing heavier for the last hour.

Dammit. She needed to pull over soon. To stop and rest. But where? She didn't even know where she was. Her phone had died two hours ago, and she'd left her charger at home with about a million other things she needed.

A familiar panic crawled around her chest, digging into her bones.

Alone. She was completely and utterly alone, in God knows where, with barely any possessions or money.

Her pulse stuttered, her lungs desperate for oxygen.

You're fine, Harper. Just breathe.

She'd been alone and in crappy positions before, and she'd always fought her way out of them. This was no different. Hell, she was good at being alone. She'd had to be.

She took the next exit and turned onto what looked like a main street. Businesses bordered both sides of the road, but every one of them looked closed. Not a surprise. It was early morning, and even though it was a Friday, this looked like a small town. Places weren't open late in small towns.

There had to be some type of accommodation, right? Somewhere she could rest for a bit. A cheap motel, perhaps. Yeah, she definitely needed cheap.

Her heart clenched at the thought of her bank balance.

Gone. Her money was *gone*. Every dollar she'd worked so hard to save over the years. The money that would have helped achieve her dream.

A part of her wanted to cry, but she'd already shed too many tears, and what would more of them accomplish?

So instead, she clung to the anger. Anger at her family for taking *everything* from her. Bleeding her dry while only caring about themselves. Also, anger at herself for not realizing that she should have run long ago.

When her lids began to fall again, she pinched her right thigh, the small sting propelling her eyes open.

Should she give up and sleep in her car? She'd freeze her ass off.

Suddenly, a building with a hint of light poking through the window came into view. Hope warmed her chest. Were they open? Was there someone in there who could direct her to a motel?

She pulled her Camry over in front of the business before leaning forward to read the sign.

Meridian. A bar?

Well, if anywhere was going to be open at one a.m. in a small town, it was a bar.

Before getting out, she flicked the visor mirror down, cringing at what she saw. Dark circles shadowing both eyes and bruising around the left one that was already going a purplish-blue shade.

Great.

Quickly, she rummaged through her handbag and pulled out her small pouch of makeup. It was probably pointless to try to look presentable, what with everything that had happened today and all that she'd lost. But every other action she'd taken tonight had been pure instinct, and so was this.

She flinched as she patted concealer over the bruising, then cringed when she was done. It still looked terrible, and to be fair, the dim lighting didn't help. But at least it didn't look any worse.

With a quick breath for courage, she pushed the car door open and stepped into the storm. Immediately, heavy rain soaked her shirt.

Crap, it was cold!

With her head down, she sprinted to the door, all but falling inside the building. Warmth immediately slipped over her skin. But so did the quiet. Was the place empty?

It was a large room, with a bar to the left and a couple of pool tables beyond it. Booths pressed against the opposite wall, and tall tables were scattered throughout the space between.

Harper took another step inside, the eerie quiet ringing through her ears. "Hello? Is anyone here?"

Silence. Maybe they were closed and forgot to lock up?

Her gaze caught on a notice on the bulletin board attached to the wall just inside the door.

Bartender Job Available:

Forty hours per week. Must be available evenings and weekends.

A job… *She* needed a job. Hell, she needed a lot more than that, but a job would be a great start. She'd never worked in a bar before though. And even if she did have bartending experience, she couldn't settle here. She didn't even know where *here* was, but five hours from her family wasn't far enough. She needed ten, fifteen hours between them at least, and even then, they'd probably still feel too close.

Another flyer was pinned next to the job announcement.

Misty Peak Sky Walk—opening soon.

Misty Peak…was that where she was? She knew of the small town. It was in East Tennessee and sat on the edge of the Smoky Mountains. She'd only heard of it because it was a tourist hub.

She nibbled her bottom lip and turned. What did she do now? Wait? See if someone else came in? Leave?

A shudder coursed down her spine at the prospect of getting back into her car and sleeping there. She hated the cold. She could layer her clothes on top of her, but would that be enough? And what if someone broke in?

She ran her fingers over the wooden edge of a table. "Hello?"

Again, nothing.

There was an open doorway behind the bar that presumably led to the kitchen. There was also a closed door beside that, and a shadowy hall she assumed led to a bathroom.

She moved toward the closed door and was about to knock when she noticed it was actually ajar. Carefully, she pushed it open. An empty office. Papers were piled up on a desk in the center of the room, and cabinets sat to either side against the walls. The desk held what looked to be a half-finished mug of coffee and an empty plate with crumbs.

A photo on the wall caught her attention. Two smiling parents and six kids—five boys and a girl. The kids were young, and they looked happy.

Something twisted in her belly…because she'd never had a

family like that. Parents who'd made her smile. Siblings who looked at her like she was a blessing rather than a burden.

"Hey."

She gasped and spun at the deep, gravelly voice. Then she looked up, way up, at the mountain of a man who stood in front of her. He was huge, and not just in height. He wore a shirt that stretched tightly over his thick biceps and chest. Then there were his eyes…they were a beautiful light blue color, like the ocean when you saw to the sand at the bottom.

"I'm sorry! I, um, didn't hear you come in." The words stumbled over each other, and she wanted to slap her forehead. Man, what was she doing in the guy's office in the first place? He had to be pissed. "I called out a couple times but no one answered."

Instead of looking angry, the man almost seemed…intrigued?

* * *

CODY WALKER STUDIED the woman in front of him. Her long brown hair fell over her shoulders, dripping, presumably from the storm. She wore what looked like work slacks and a white shirt and heels. The top clung to her chest like a second skin, to the point he could see the intricate details of her lace bra.

But what really had him looking closely was the bruising around her left eye. She'd tried to hide it with makeup, but either she was terrible at applying the stuff or she'd done it in the dark, because it did nothing to hide the injury.

Anger lit his veins. He knew what a black eye caused by a fist looked like, and someone had definitely hit this woman. A guy? A boyfriend? A *husband*?

Fuck, that made him angry. It was a man's job to protect a woman, not hurt her.

"I was in the alley feeding Tommy." He was careful to remain exactly where he was so he didn't scare the woman. He knew his size could be intimidating, and she wasn't a local to Misty Peak. She didn't know she was safe with him.

Her brows tugged together. "Tommy?"

"He's the alley cat. We've tried to bring him in but he refuses to be domesticated, so we feed him outside every night."

Actually, Tommy was now quite demanding about his daily meals. Cody often didn't get around to feeding him until he finished his shift, something Tommy had become accustomed to, and he'd go so far as to scratch the back door and make loud protests until he got someone's attention each night.

Something flashed in the woman's eyes. A small hint of amusement, perhaps? "That's nice of you."

"I'm a nice guy. Although my brothers would try to convince you otherwise, but they can be dicks." He grinned, enjoying the small lift of the corners of her lips. "My name's Cody Walker, by the way. I'm the owner of this bar."

"Harper Rain."

Harper...it suited her. Pretty and feminine but not overly common.

"You're not mad that you found me in your office?" she asked quietly.

"No. There's a storm outside, and you're clearly from out of town. You came in here looking for help, right?"

Relief flickered across her features. "I did."

Her black eye only told part of the story. Was she searching for help in the middle of the night because she was running from whoever had hit her? Was there an asshole not far behind?

She cleared her throat. "I was wondering if you knew of a motel in the area where I might be able to stay for the night?"

He frowned. There *was* a motel, but it was on the outskirts of town and dirty as hell. No way was he sending this woman there. He'd wonder all damn night if she was okay, and then he wouldn't sleep.

"Ali Stapler has an inn with a few independent cabins. She'll be closed now, but I could give her a call and see if she has something available?"

"An inn?" she asked quietly. "That would be expensive, right?"

So, she was short on money too. An abused young woman, caught in a storm in the middle of the night, in a town she didn't know, who didn't have money. How much more vulnerable could she get?

"Ali doesn't charge too much, just one of the reasons everyone loves her. Give me a second and I'll call her."

Hope flickered in her eyes, and she nodded.

Pulling his phone from his pocket, he turned and pressed on Ali's name in his contacts. The woman was middle-aged and motherly. He hated waking her at this hour, but if anyone would understand, it was her.

She answered on the third ring. "Cody, honey, it's late. Is everything okay?"

"I'm sorry, Ali. I kind of have an emergency. There's a girl here, just showed up at my bar, who needs a place to stay." He lowered his voice so his words didn't travel to Harper. "I think she may be in trouble."

"What kind of trouble?"

"I'm not sure. She's alone, short on cash, and has a bruise on her eye. I was wondering—"

"Of course." There was a new hardness to Ali's voice. "I have a spare cabin. I'll go get it ready for her."

"Thanks. Her name's Harper."

"Harper. Okay. A warm bed will be ready for her when she arrives."

He hung up and turned to see Harper's arms wrapped around her body in a defensive gesture, her gaze on the photo of him and his family.

"That's been up on the wall for a long damn time," he said.

Her gaze swung back to him. "Is it your family?"

"It is. My mother, father, and five siblings, all as annoying as the next."

"You look happy." Her voice was quiet, almost wistful. Then she frowned. "Sorry. Does Ali have a spare room?"

"She does. I'll drive you."

Harper was shaking her head before he'd finished speaking. "I can drive myself. I have a car."

The muscles in his forearms flexed. "I'd prefer it if you let me take you. Or at least follow me to make sure you're safe. It's late, you don't know this town, and the storm's pretty wild out there."

She shook her head vigorously. "I'm okay. I've been driving through the storm for hours. Another few minutes won't hurt."

He was tempted to tell her it only took a second for something to go wrong in a storm like this. But she probably wouldn't appreciate the warning. "Okay. To get there, drive straight down this road and turn left at the end. There'll be a big sign that says Ali's Cabins, then a long driveway."

"Straight, left, Ali's Cabins. Got it."

He still didn't like letting her go alone. It went against every protective instinct inside him. "Do you have a phone? I can give you my number in case you get lost."

She cringed. "It died, and I need to buy a new charger."

Jesus. He bit back a curse, hating the situation she was in. Moving around her, he didn't miss her small intake of breath as he brushed her shoulder. He pulled his charger from the wall. "Would this fit in your phone?"

"Yes, but I couldn't—"

"Take it." He reached for her hand and set the charger in her palm. Awareness swept up his arm like a wildfire. Damn, her skin was soft. In a gentle voice, he told her, "Charge your phone in your car on the way."

"Are you sure?"

"Absolutely. I have a spare upstairs."

Her mouth opened and closed before she nodded. "Okay. Thank you. I'll return it—"

"No need." He turned to his desk, found a loose scrap of paper and scribbled his number onto it before handing it to her. "Text or call if you need anything while you're in town."

She took the piece of paper tentatively, staring at it like it held a question she didn't know the answer to, before finally looking up. "Why are you being so nice to me?"

He frowned at the question. Were people not *usually* nice to her? Something about that made a vein throb in his temple. "Why am I helping a young woman who walks into my bar, soaking wet and clearly needing help? Because I'm not an asshole." Maybe that was it. She was used to having assholes in her life.

She swallowed. "Well, thank you, Cody Walker."

He followed her out of the office toward the door, but before she could step outside, he slipped his fingers around her upper arm. "Wait—"

She flinched, and he immediately pulled his hand back. What the hell? He hadn't grabbed her tightly. In fact, he'd barely touched her. "Sorry, did I hurt you?"

She shook her head quickly. Too quickly. "No, I'm okay."

He didn't believe her for a second, but he let it go. Instead, he went back to the office and grabbed a sweatshirt before returning and holding it out to her. "Here."

"I have clothes in my car."

"I don't have an umbrella down here, so I'm giving you this to hold over your head as you run through the rain. It will keep you dry."

"I can't take your sweatshirt."

"You can return it tomorrow." Honestly, he wouldn't care if she kept it. But a part of him wanted to see this woman again.

He thought she'd argue. So when she nodded and slipped the sweatshirt from his fingers, he was surprised as hell.

"Thank you." She turned toward the door, but before pulling

it open, she looked at him one last time. "For everything. It's been a while since I've met a good person."

His chest twisted. He'd really like to meet these not-so-good people in her life and give them a piece of his mind. "Stick around, and you'll find plenty more in this town."

She offered a small smile before slipping out of the bar and into the storm. And for some damn reason, he already couldn't wait to see her again the next day.

CHAPTER 2

*L*oud knocking pricked at Harper's sleep, pulling her to consciousness. She groaned and rolled onto her belly, tempted to lift the pillow and shove it over her head.

Man, she was tired. Like a deep, sunk-into-her-bones kind of tired that made her want to curl farther into the warm bed.

At the beat of silence, Harper sighed. Good, they'd gone.

Then the knocking sounded again.

Goddammit.

With a humph, she climbed out of bed, her avocado nightshirt dropping to her thighs as she moved to the door of the cabin. The place was small and wooden and cozy. One open space for the kitchen, dining area, and bed, with a small separate bathroom. The second she'd stepped inside last night, she'd been swept up in the warmth of a burning fire.

Bliss. Absolute bliss, and exactly what she'd needed.

She peeked through the peephole to see Ali, the cabin owner, on the other side of the door holding a tray of food. The woman had been here to greet her when she'd arrived last night and had been the very definition of kind and nurturing.

Harper pulled the door open, and immediately, Ali's smile shifted to a gasp as her gaze swept over Harper's face.

Oh, God, she hadn't even thought to look in the mirror before opening the door. Was her hair all over the place? Her day-old makeup smudged? Heck, if there was even any makeup left after that rain last night.

Ali recovered quickly, straightening where she stood and offering a half smile. "Good morning, honey, sorry to wake you. I tried to wait as long as I could. I've brought you breakfast."

Harper's gaze shifted to the tray of food in Ali's hands. "Oh, you didn't have to do that." She stood back so the other woman could pass. "But thank you. Do you know what time it is?"

Ali stepped inside and set the tray on the counter. "Ten."

Ten? She'd slept in until *ten a.m.*? Christ, she really had been tired. She was a six a.m. waker. Always had been, even on the days she wasn't due into the office. Yesterday had really wiped her out.

"I've brought you some toast, homemade jam, sunny-side-up eggs, and freshly squeezed orange juice. Oh, and a coffee."

Harper's jaw dropped. "That's so kind of you, but honestly, just allowing me to check in so late last night was everything."

"Well, the cabin is yours to rent for as long as you need. And breakfast is included in the nightly rate."

It was like she'd stumbled across the town with the nicest locals she'd ever met.

"Thank you. I'm not really sure what my plans are yet." Like… no clue. If she was honest with herself, she was probably still in a bit of shock from the day before.

Sympathy flashed over the woman's face, as if she knew everything Harper wasn't sharing. "Why don't you start with today. What are your plans?"

Her gaze shifted to the sweatshirt she'd hung over the back of a chair. "Just to return Cody's sweatshirt to him."

Ali's eyes warmed. "That boy's a good one. You stumbled into the right bar last night."

"Do you know him well?" She bit her bottom lip, not sure if she was prying with the question, but frankly, she hadn't been able to get his ocean-blue eyes out of her head all night. She was pretty sure she'd even dreamed about him.

Gah.

"I've known that boy since he was a baby. The whole family, actually. Although, he was gone for a while. Only got back less than a year ago."

She tilted her head. "Gone?"

"He was a Delta Forces soldier. All the men in his family have served. Two of his brothers, Lock and Jace, are still in the military. Cody came back to help his dad and sister with the bar. Kayden came back around the same time, and Eastern only a few months ago. Of course, their daddy's passed away now, and their sister moved to Idaho."

Harper's brows flickered, the picture of the happy family flashing back into her mind. "That's so sad."

"He was sick for a while. A beautiful man though. It's no wonder he raised beautiful kids. Beautiful and dangerous, that is." She laughed. "Okay, I'll leave you to it. My number's on the fridge, so don't hesitate to call if you need anything. There's also the number for some local businesses, like the coffee shop, some take-out places, and Sugar and Spice."

"Sugar and Spice?"

"You have to visit. Mrs. Sandler runs the place, and she sells the most spectacular cupcakes and drinks. Her chocolate swirl cupcakes are to die for."

That made Harper smile. She did have a sweet tooth. "I'll have to pay her store a visit before I leave."

"You really should." Ali paused, a small frown creasing her forehead. "Before I go…if you're thinking of staying for a while, I should mention…we've had a little trouble recently with a local firebug."

Harper blinked. "A firebug?"

"Some dreadful person has been setting a few fires around town. Not to worry, really. We have a great fire department here, and the sheriff is working overtime to find the culprit. But the last one was less than a mile away from the cabins, so I just thought it prudent to mention."

"I'm glad it's being handled."

Ali moved toward the door. Before stepping through it, she stopped and turned. "Remember, there's no rush to leave. Stay as long as you like. You're very welcome here."

Harper's chest tightened. Welcome…something she'd never felt with her own family, let alone strangers.

When the door closed behind Ali, Harper headed to the bathroom. As she entered the little room, her gaze caught on her reflection, and her feet ground to a stop.

Holy shit. No wonder the older woman had gasped when she'd seen her. The bruising around her left eye was so dark, it looked like she'd literally gone over it with black paint.

Jesus Christ.

Tentatively, she reached up and touched it, flinching at the flicker of pain.

Memories of the previous night came back to her. Of the empty bank balance. The explosion of anger when she'd gone to her mother's house. And the rage of her brother.

She'd run. Left her apartment. Her job. Everything she'd known to get away from them both.

She shuddered and turned away, quickly peeing before returning to the bedroom.

With a sigh, she lifted her phone from the bedside table. Even though she'd charged it on the way here, she'd turned it off before bed because, yeah, she was scared about what she'd find.

Sure enough, there were five missed calls from her brother

and several messages. Messages asking where she was. When she was coming back. Calling her a coward.

She didn't let any of them affect her. She'd heard it all before. Instead, she blocked his number and switched off her phone again.

Done. She was *done* with them.

* * *

"Boy, you are not doing that right."

Cody's lips twitched as he turned to look at Barry. The man had aged over the years, with new lines around his eyes practically every day and plenty of white hair. None of that had affected his ability to judge every little thing Cody did.

"I'm curious—did you tell my sister she organized the bottles wrong too?"

"Of course not. That girl could do no wrong."

Yeah, he'd heard that before. To be fair, his sister had worked with his dad and Barry at this bar for years while he'd been in the Army. Cody had only been back a year. "Well, old man, you're about to witness real efficiency."

Barry scoffed, but there was a hint of a smile on his face. He was currently Cody's only other bartender, and he also worked in the kitchen. They didn't serve much, just fries, burgers, and a few appetizers. But it just being the two of them here…that was a problem. They needed more staff, but in the small town of Misty Peak, that wasn't easy to find.

"When are you hiring more help?" Barry grumbled as if reading Cody's thoughts. "We can't keep going with just you and me. If someone gets sick, we're screwed."

Cody grimaced as he continued to restock the alcohol. "Kayden will fill in if we need him. And I'm working on it." Although, his older brother Kayden was pretty busy working at the Misty Peak Visitors Center, as both a tour guide and on the search and rescue team.

"How?" Barry asked.

"I've put out the word around town that I'm looking for someone."

"Because that worked so well for you last time."

Cody's back teeth ground together at the thought of his last hires. Thieving assholes.

Barry sighed. "Look, son, I'm just reminding you that you might be a helluva soldier, but you can't run this place without staff."

Cody opened his mouth to tell the old man they'd find someone, when the door to the bar opened and Vanessa walked in.

He barely held in a groan, while Barry cursed under his breath before disappearing into the kitchen. Yeah, she wasn't exactly a crowd-pleaser.

"Cody." She leaned across the counter, her generous cleavage on full display. "How are you?"

"I'm fine. What do you want, Vanessa?"

She pouted. "Don't be like that. We said we'd remain friends."

He laughed but the sound was humorless. "No. *You* said we'd remain friends. My silence should have told you I had no interest in being friends with the woman who cheated on me with my high school best friend."

Her brow pinched. Only for a moment, then it cleared. "*Ex*-best friend. You haven't exactly been close to him since school."

Did that change anything? It had still been a kick in the gut. "Last chance, Vanessa. Tell me what you want or get out."

"Fine. I have to host a work luncheon. You know we take turns, and this month, it's mine. It was supposed to be held at Sugar and Spice, but *Mrs. Sandler* just informed me she can't host anymore. No reason given. The coffee shop can't take us. And my place is too small. So…"

Vanessa worked in marketing at an injectables office, where clients—and staff—got all sorts of fillers.

He laughed. "You're shitting me, right? You want me to host your work luncheon at my bar?" Had the woman lost her goddamn mind? Why she thought he would do her any favors was beyond him.

"Cody—"

"No." He turned and grabbed the box opener, using more force than necessary to open the blade.

"It's scheduled for two weeks from now, and everything's already been organized."

"Sounds like your problem, Vanessa." He grabbed a bottle and slotted it above the bar.

"Cody, please!"

He made the mistake of looking at her. There was a sheen of tears in her eyes.

"You don't owe me anything," she said quietly. "And I didn't want to ask, but so much hasn't gone to plan these last few months. Georgie passed away. Mom's been sick."

Georgie the Pomeranian had been her world. And her mom had been sick on and off for years with the onset of dementia. She hit him right where he lived—he understood the pain of a sick parent.

She swallowed. "Please? I can't lose my job. I haven't been there for that long, so I need to do a good job with this. One favor, and I promise I'll never ask again."

Jesus Christ. He couldn't believe he was doing this... "Send me the details and what you need me to do."

Her eyes widened, and she gasped lightly as she grabbed his hand over the bar. "Thank you! Thank you so much, Cody. You're such a good person."

Too damn good. He was only doing it because of the sick parent part. His dad had been sick for years before he'd finally passed, while his mother's sickness had taken her a lot faster. Neither were losses he'd wish on another person, no matter how much he disliked them.

She stepped away from the bar. "I'll message you tonight."

Great. Something to look forward to.

She'd just left the bar when his oldest brother, Kayden, stepped in, his brows drawn. "What was *she* doing here?"

"You don't want to know. You already finished for the day?"

Between leading hiking tours and his SAR responsibilities, Kayden generally worked long hours. He was damn good at his job, which was handy, seeing as so many tourists came here, only to get lost in the forest. The only thing Kayden lacked was patience.

His brother shook his head. "We spent hours looking for these tourists this morning who decided they didn't need a guide or a map. Finally found them, and they weren't even apologetic or grateful."

"Damn. That's a new level of stupidity." He set a glass in front of Kayden and poured some whiskey.

"Not new, but definitely stupid." His brother lifted his glass. "You seen Eastern today?"

Eastern was their younger brother and the only other sibling currently here in Misty Peak. He'd recently left his career as a Navy SEAL to come home to his daughter.

"Nope. He's too important for us now that he's sheriff."

Kayden laughed as the door to the bar opened yet again, and Harper walked in. The second Cody's gaze fell on her, his lungs tightened. Last night, she'd looked young and lost and vulnerable. Today, in her skintight jeans and navy T-shirt, hair dry and falling over her shoulders in soft waves, she looked fucking radiant.

"Harper." Shit, why did his voice sound so high-pitched?

She gave him a small smile as she moved to the bar. "Hi, Cody."

Kayden frowned as he looked between them. A beat passed before his brother cleared his throat. "My brother's clearly lost his manners. I'm Kayden."

He held out his hand, and for some reason, Cody didn't like the idea of his brother touching her, even if it was just a handshake.

"Harper." Her voice was soft, almost lyrical. She turned back to Cody and placed his sweatshirt on the bar. "Thank you again for lending this to me last night. And for saving me."

Kayden's brows shot up, but Cody ignored him, giving the woman his full attention. "Glad I could help. You get to Ali's Cabins, okay?" He already knew the answer to that because he'd called Ali, needing to know Harper had gotten there safely.

"I did. She was lovely, and the cabin was comfortable and warm."

"Good."

Her chest rose as her eyes flickered between his. Shit, what was it about this woman that drew him in so much?

"Well," she finally said, "I guess I should go."

She turned and took a few steps, and hell if every part of him didn't want to vault over the bar and tug her back. He was on the verge of doing just that when she suddenly stopped and turned, uncertainty in her eyes.

"Sorry. Before I go, I, um, wanted to ask about your job ad." She glanced at his corkboard, then back at him.

"You need a job?"

"Well, I don't have any experience working in a bar. I work in an office." She cringed. "Worked. I'm sorry, I shouldn't have asked."

She spun and was out the door before he could reply.

Shit.

He ran around the bar and after her, ignoring the questioning look from his brother as he pushed outside. He caught her partway down the block.

"Hey."

She stopped and turned. "Cody—"

"The job's yours."

Her eyes widened. "But I don't have any experience and you don't know me."

"I'll show you the ropes. I'm a great teacher." Was he? Who the hell knew? He just didn't want this woman to leave. "And I don't need to know you to know you'll do a great job."

"Are you sure? Because I'm clumsy and drop things all the time. I get muddled when people give me too many instructions, and I can be a hot mess when I'm stressed, and I've heard working in a bar can be stressful, and I don't want you to do anything that—"

"Harper."

She finally stopped, her expression one of embarrassment.

"You would be doing me a favor," he said. "Even if you're just clearing glasses from tables. I'm desperate. Please. Take pity on me and take the job."

She sucked her bottom lip between her teeth, and he almost lost his damn mind with the need to tug it out. "Are you sure?"

"Yes." Hell yes.

"Okay. Thank you."

Relief slid through his veins, and he had no fucking idea why. He didn't even know the woman, but he knew he wanted to see her again. "Great. Wear black. Arrive at four and I'll show you the basics before it gets busy."

Her brows shot up. "Four today?"

He chuckled. "Yeah. Is that okay?"

"Yes. Of course. Thank you."

"You got it, Storm."

She frowned. "Storm?"

"You showed up in a storm, drowned in water…seems fitting."

She held his gaze for another beat, giving him a small smile before turning and heading down the street.

He returned to the bar, unable to hide his own small smile of satisfaction as he moved straight back to the bottles he was stacking.

"Is that something else I shouldn't ask about?" Kayden asked when Cody gave him nothing.

"Yep."

CHAPTER 3

"*A* Bud, please."

Harper gave the man on the other side of the bar a small smile, hoping it said *I know what I'm doing*, when really, she had no freaking clue. "You got it."

She turned and grabbed a glass before looking at the beer taps. Bud…Bud…where was the—

There you are. She pushed the glass against the tap and filled it before sliding it across the bar.

The guy put some money down, then lifted his drink. "Thanks…"

"Harper," she finished for him.

He smiled. "Thanks, Harper."

This time, she beamed at him. There. See? She could do this. She may have zero experience working in a busy bar, but she could serve beer like she'd done it a million times before. Fake it till you make it. That was the saying, right?

Of course, she'd rather have gotten on the road the second she'd woken that morning to put more distance between her and her family, but she'd realized her serious lack of funds wouldn't have taken her much further. This was as good a place as any to make a few bucks before leaving again.

"Good work, missy."

She turned and grinned at Barry. He'd introduced himself when she'd arrived at the bar a few hours ago, and she'd instantly loved the older man. He was kind and funny and great at putting Cody in his place.

"I feel like I'm getting the hang of this."

"It's like you were born to work in a bar." He bumped her shoulder before moving back into the kitchen.

As Barry passed Cody, her boss's eyes flashed to her from the other side of the bar. Immediately, one side of his mouth lifted, and he winked.

Her mouth went dry, and for a moment she had to remind herself to breathe. He'd been nothing but patient with her as he'd shown her the basics of the job. She'd never experienced that type of kindness before. Sure, her last boss, Ivy, had been friendly enough. But Cody was…something else.

She turned away to serve the next customer. The place was busy—certainly busier than she would have expected for a small town like Misty Peak, but it was a Saturday night, after all.

About half an hour later, while she was filling a glass with whiskey, she felt heat at her side. Then warm breath in her ear as Cody whispered, "You doing okay, Storm?"

A shudder coursed down her spine.

He'd called her that more than once, and she swore it rolled over her skin every time, feeling more intimate. But God, she needed to *not* fall for the guy. She wasn't here to stay. She was only at the bar to earn a little money before getting farther away from her family.

"Yeah, I'm doing okay. I mean, no one's thrown their drink back at me yet, but the night's still young."

He shook his head. "I wouldn't allow that in my bar and my customers know it. You're safe here."

There was something about the way he said the word *safe*, in his deep rumble of a voice, that made her breath catch in her throat. Instead of answering with words, she nodded.

He was about to walk away when she touched his arm. "Cody, before I forget…I've had some issues with my, uh, bank account these last few days. I was wondering if you could pay me in cash until I get the issue sorted?"

She barely held in the cringe. Damn, she sounded as shady as she felt.

His brows tugged together. "Sure." He seemed to consider his next words for a moment. "If you need help with anything else, you can tell me."

She swallowed, a part of her wanting to lean on someone and share all her problems. But she'd only just met Cody, and he'd already helped her so much. "I'm okay. But thank you."

There was a flash of something that looked oddly like disappointment on his face before he nodded, bumped her shoulder, and headed off to serve the next customer.

She took a breath—a huge get-it-together breath—before grabbing a tray and moving out to the floor. You'd think clearing the tables would be her favorite part, seeing as she didn't need to work out where each bottle was located and how to work the register. But in reality, it was a lot harder to balance a dozen glasses on a tray at once.

She'd just lowered the tray to an empty booth when a whistle sounded behind her.

"I see Walker hired some new ass."

She tensed and straightened. When she turned, she saw four men standing around a tall bar table, all with eyes on her.

Okay, maybe Cody was wrong about *all* the people in this town, because the way the guys looked at her definitely didn't make her feel *safe*. She'd been the one to serve them when they'd arrived, and even then, she'd thought the way they looked at her was…less than friendly.

"Excuse me?"

"He's obviously changed tack, Travis," one of the guys said with a smirk, as if she wasn't even there. "Didn't get what he wanted from you or Dayne, so thinks a woman will be a better fit."

What the hell was he talking about? She wanted to ask, but not as much as she wanted to ignore them and get back to the bar.

She turned back to the table and filled the tray. She'd just straightened and turned again when suddenly a big chest was in front of her. Travis, maybe?

"What's your name, sweetie?"

Sweetie? This guy had to be kidding. "It's Harper. Excuse me, I need to get these glasses to the bar." She stepped to the side, but the guy mimicked the action, blocking her way.

"I'm Travis. Trav to my friends. I actually worked here for a while."

Her brows rose. Cody had hired this jerk? That surprised her. He really must have been desperate.

Travis lowered his head so his mouth was close to her face. Too close. "Word of warning, Walker might seem nice at the start, but he's an asshole, and if you're smart, you'll stay the hell away from him."

"Thanks for the warning." She wanted to add that the only person she felt the need to *stay away from* was this guy. But maybe he saw it on her face, because when she stepped to the side, he blocked her yet again, this time also grabbing her upper arm, causing a glass to tip to the side on the tray. "Hey—"

"You don't believe me?"

"Let me go. *Now*."

He lowered his head again. "Why? So you can run back and tattle to that asshole behind the bar?"

"Hey!"

Her breath caught at the angry voice behind Travis. It was

deep and laced with the threat of violence. They both looked up as Cody stepped toward them, his eyes on the fingers around her arm.

"What the fuck are you doing, Travis?"

The guy laughed, but the sound was all wrong. "Walker. It's nice to see you again, man. It's been a while. Since you accused me and Dayne of stealing and kicked our asses out of here, right?"

Cody took another step forward. "Release her arm."

"Or what?"

"You really want to fucking know?"

There was a dangerous beat of silence, where the air was almost too thick to breathe. Was this Travis guy really not going to heed Cody's warning? Because it *had* been a warning, and anyone with a lick of brains would listen. Cody was a head taller than Travis. Hell, he was a head taller than everyone, and even in the dark bar, you could make out the thick muscles beneath his shirt.

Her heart began to rattle at a faster pace, panic rising in her chest that a fight was about to break out. But then Travis released her arm, and Cody immediately shifted in front of her.

"Now get out," he said in a low, icy voice. "All of you. And don't come back."

One of the guys rose from the table. "Cody—"

"I'm serious, Dayne. You have no business coming in here after what you did."

Another laugh from Travis. "Screw you!"

Harper's breath caught. She was sure Cody would throw a punch in retaliation. But he didn't. Just fisted his hands and watched the four men leave his bar.

It wasn't until they were outside that Cody turned and looked at her. "Are you okay?"

She nodded quickly, even though she felt unsteady as hell. "I'm fine."

"What did he say to you?"

"That I shouldn't work here." Though in more *colorful* words.

Cody's fingers slipped around her arm right where Travis's had touched her. But while Travis's hold on her had been tight and threatening, Cody's was gentle, almost soothing.

"I'm sorry."

* * *

CODY LOOKED at Harper for what had to be the fiftieth time that night. They'd just seen out their last customer, and she was collecting glasses from the tables while he cleaned behind the bar. The memory of Travis touching her and blocking her way played over in his mind.

Fuck, he hated that guy. He couldn't believe he'd missed the jerk entering the bar.

Despite the incident though, Harper had impressed the hell out of him tonight. Her first time working in a bar and she hadn't missed a beat.

Barry patted his shoulder as he passed. "Good hire. I'm glad you listened to my advice, boy."

Cody rolled his eyes. Of course, Barry was taking credit for this.

"I'm sorry about Travis," Cody said quietly when Harper returned to the bar.

Her eyes widened and she shook her head. "It's not your fault."

He could have laughed. He'd just told her she was safe in his bar, then what happened? One of his customers and ex-employees grabbed her. "I didn't even see him and his friends come in. If I had, I would have sent them straight back out."

She took a cloth and wiped down the bar. "They stole from you?"

His muscles tightened. He still hated thinking about the way they'd abused his trust. "Yeah. They hadn't been working here for long. I had a bad feeling when I hired them, but I ignored it because Barry and I really needed the help. Then money started going missing from the till, and a few weeks later, they were caught red-handed."

She cringed. "I'm sorry."

"It was my fault for not listening to my gut."

A small smile curved her lips, and for a moment he stopped what he was doing and just stared like a starstruck moron. *Fuck.* She was gorgeous anytime, but when she smiled...the woman could bring the toughest man to his knees.

"What does your gut tell you about me?" she asked.

"That you're trustworthy. That you're a hard worker." And that she needed help. Not that he'd be saying the last part out loud.

"You're right. I would never steal from you, Cody." She turned and moved back to the floor to retrieve more glasses. Still, he struggled to take his eyes off her.

He was screwed.

When all the tables were clear and the bar clean, he grabbed a can of cat food from beneath the bar. "Ready to meet Tommy?"

Excitement lit her eyes. "The alley cat? Sure. I love cats. They're probably second on my list, after cupcakes."

"You like cupcakes?"

"I would sell my right kidney for a good one, most days."

He laughed. "My sister's the same. Told me once that if she died before me, it was my job to make sure she was buried with all her favorites."

Harper laughed and the sound was lyrical. "I think I'd like your sister."

They headed toward the back door. "Have you ever had a cat?" he asked.

"No, I didn't want to get one until I bought a place, in case I had to move in a hurry." The second the words were out, she cringed, like she hadn't meant to say the last part.

Interesting. So she'd known she might need to run from something. "Is that what happened last night? You had to leave in a hurry?"

She gave a small nod.

What was this woman hiding? Or better question...what was she running from? She'd done a good job of covering the bruising on her eye with makeup tonight. If he hadn't seen it last night, he might not have known it was there.

"Come on." He pushed outside into the alley and, sure enough, Tommy was waiting for him. "Hey there, Tom Tom, you ready for dinner?"

The black cat purred, rubbing against his legs as Cody crouched and emptied the food into a bowl. "Tommy, this is my new bartender, Harper. If you're nice to her, she might just feed you too."

Harper knelt down beside him. "Hey there, honey."

The softness in her voice had his chest clenching. She reached out and scratched Tommy's head as he ate. Immediately, he purred again, pushing his head into her hand.

"He likes you," Cody said quietly.

She looked up and grinned. It was wide and uninhibited. "I like him too."

She was so close he could smell the floral fragrance scenting the air around her. See the specks of hazel in her brown eyes despite the darkness. Even though he barely knew the woman, he itched to lean forward. See if she tasted as sweet as she smelled.

Then her gaze shifted over his shoulder—and she gasped.

He shot to his feet and glanced down the alley, but there was nothing there. He turned back to Harper, who was also standing. "Did you see something?"

"I saw..." She stopped and frowned, then shook her head.

"Nothing. It was a shadow, probably another cat or wild animal. Sorry. I guess I'm a bit jumpy."

He took another look over his shoulder before touching the small of Harper's back. "Come on. Let's get back inside."

CHAPTER 4

*H*arper measured out the Campari, then the gin, followed by the sweet vermouth. She waited until she'd put the orange peel in the glass to stir it and push it across the bar to Barry. Then she held her breath and watched as he lifted the glass to his mouth and tasted the drink.

His face gave nothing away, to the point that nerves fluttered in her belly.

Finally, the glass hit the bar again. "Girl, that is a *good* Negroni."

"Really?"

He leaned forward and touched her hand. "You're going to dazzle the pants off this town."

She grinned at him because, well, if nothing else in her life was going the way she'd planned, she would at least be able to make a good cocktail, right?

"Barry! No hitting on my new bartender."

Her heart thumped at Cody's voice, and she turned to see him walk in through the back-room door, carrying a big box. His white T-shirt was tight, the material stretching across his biceps as it always did, and with the box in his hands, those muscles were rippling.

Holy dry mouth…

Tonight would be her fourth evening working at the bar, and for some reason she'd thought that after a few days, this little infatuation with the bar owner would go away. Okay, not little. Big, huge, mammoth infatuation.

But nope. It seemed familiarity did not have that effect on her. Not even a little bit. If anything, her attraction had intensified. Not only was the man hot as hell, he was sweet and attentive and protective, and she had no idea how to deal with any of that, because no other guy in her life had ever been treated her that way. Certainly, no previous boyfriend.

Cody grinned at her. "Be careful of the old man. He has a thing for beautiful women."

Her lips parted, a small puff of air sucking into her chest. Beautiful? The gorgeous man was now calling her beautiful?

"Who are you calling an old man?" Barry grumbled, taking another sip of the drink. "I could run circles around you, boy."

Cody laughed. "You could try, but I wouldn't recommend it. You might break a hip."

Harper bit back a grin. The two men did nothing but bicker. It was quite entertaining.

"Keep dreaming, son." Barry stood, lifting the cocktail as his gaze returned to Harper and softened. "And good work, Harper. You're a keeper."

He moved into the kitchen.

"I like him," she said quietly, her thoughts slipping out of her mouth.

"Me too. But don't tell him that—it'll go to his head."

She chuckled and walked over to the box he'd just opened, helping him pull out the bottles. As their arms grazed, it took a lot for her to not react, when in reality every part of her felt hot from the burn of his skin.

That had been happening a lot over the last few nights. Sometimes his hand or hip would brush hers while working the bar. Sometimes he'd lean close to grab something over her head. And every time, she scolded herself for wanting him. Although, in all fairness, she was human and he was…well, he was ex-special forces with a sweet side no one expected, least of all her.

"Hey, wait here. I got something for you."

Her gaze shot up at Cody's words. "For me?"

It was a stupid question, there was no one else in the room. Didn't stop the shock though.

He laughed. "Yeah, Storm, for you. Give me a sec."

He disappeared into the kitchen just as the bar door opened and the most beautiful woman Harper had ever seen stepped inside. She wore three-inch heels, which just elongated her already long, toned legs. Skintight jeans that hugged every curve, and a tight red top that accentuated her ample breasts. But it was her face that really had Harper pausing. Beautiful, high cheekbones, long lashes with perfectly applied makeup, all framed by her long, thick black hair. The woman could run for Miss America.

The smile on the woman's face fell when she saw Harper, her feet pausing partway across the room. "Who are *you*?"

Okay, she may be beautiful, but she wasn't so friendly if her frosty tone was anything to go by. "Hi. I'm Harper."

The woman started moving forward again, but her steps were slower now, her eyes assessing. "And what are you doing behind the bar, Harper?"

Harper's brows rose. Who *was* this woman?

"Got it!"

They both looked toward the kitchen doorway as Cody stepped behind the bar. He stopped when he saw the woman. "Vanessa. What are you doing here?"

Vanessa's gaze shifted from Cody to Harper, then back to Cody. "I came to talk to you about the work luncheon."

"I thought we already did that." Cody continued forward, only stopping when he was beside Harper, where he placed a small box onto the counter.

Vanessa's gaze shifted to the box, a frown creasing her brow before she looked up again. "I had some more things to run past you."

"What things?"

She cleared her throat. "Can we talk about it in private?"

Okay, Harper knew when she wasn't welcome. She started to walk away, but Cody touched the small of her back, sending an immediate blast of awareness up her spine.

"This is Harper, my new bartender. She'll be present at the luncheon, so she'll need to know any and all details about the event."

There was a slight narrowing of Vanessa's eyes, but she recovered quickly. Was she an ex? It wouldn't surprise Harper. Cody was gorgeous. The woman was gorgeous. They'd make a lovely couple.

"Well," Vanessa finally said, straightening just slightly. "My boss has added a couple of people to the list, so with more guests, I was thinking I'd arrive a bit earlier. Maybe ten?"

"That's fine."

Did Cody's thumb just graze her back?

"And I have a small list of things I'd love Barry to cook, but I'll also bring some pre-lunch snacks."

"Barry can do that, and I'm fine with you bringing in snacks."

"I was also wondering if you could be on hand to make drinks. I just love your Negronis," Vanessa continued, leaning across the bar, her overpowering floral perfume heavy in the air.

"Yeah, we can make whatever. Barry was just teaching Harper this morning, so we're all set."

Her lips pursed, but she nodded.

Harper shifted away from Cody's touch, lifting a couple bottles from the box and starting to put them on the shelves as the two continued to talk details. Nothing Vanessa said sounded like it was *that* important, or at least, it could have been texted or emailed. Was this just an excuse to see Cody? She didn't blame the woman. Who wouldn't want an excuse to spend time with him?

It was twenty minutes later when Vanessa finally stepped away from the bar. "Thank you, Cody. I so appreciate you doing this. You're making my life just a bit easier with your kindness."

Even though Vanessa said the words in a sweet, I'm-kind-of-flirting-with-you voice, Cody gave her a quick nod. "Happy to help."

She turned to look at Harper. "It was nice to meet you."

That was almost laughable, because the hard expression on her face in combination with the cool in her voice told Harper it was actually the opposite. "You too."

When she walked out, Harper peeked at Cody. He was still looking at the closed door, his knuckles white around the counter. She nibbled her bottom lip, considering what to say or whether to just remain quiet.

In the end, she stepped closer to him. "Are you all right?"

He looked at her, blinking as if he hadn't even realized he'd been staring at the door. "Yeah. We used to date, but she cheated on me with my best friend…right around the time my dad died."

Jesus. "Cody! That's awful. And you're letting her host a work luncheon here?"

"Yeah. I'm a glutton for punishment."

Maybe. Or maybe he still had feelings for her. "I'm sorry."

He lifted the small box from the counter. "Here. This is what I grabbed from the back before she came in. I picked it up for you today."

Tentatively, she opened the box to find the most delicious-looking cupcake inside. It was vanilla, with pink icing and half a strawberry on top.

"You said you liked cupcakes."

Her gaze lifted. "So you bought me one?"

"So I bought you one."

The beats of her heart stumbled over one another. Would it make her look completely pathetic if she revealed that this was one of the sweetest things a guy had ever done for her? One of the sweetest things *anyone* had ever done for her? "Thank you."

"You're welcome. It's from Sugar and Spice. Everything's amazing there." He squeezed her arm before moving away.

Man, she needed to hurry up and make some money and get out of here, because something told her *not* falling for Cody would be one of the hardest things she'd ever done—and she'd done some seriously hard things.

He'd just stepped into the kitchen when her phone vibrated from her back pocket. She pulled it out and immediately felt the blood drain from her face.

Unknown number: Did you block my number? Mom and I have something important to tell you. Answer me.

She was so caught up in the text from her brother that she didn't hear Cody step back into the bar. When he touched her arm, she gasped, almost dropping the cell.

"Hey, you okay?" he asked, voice gentle.

She clicked out of the message and pushed the device back into her pocket. "Of course. I'm going to take a five-minute break to devour this cupcake, if that's okay?"

His brows were drawn but he nodded.

She walked away, needing a few minutes to collect herself. Why wouldn't her brother leave her the hell alone? All she wanted to do was get away from them. He and their mother had already taken everything from her. Could she not have some peace for just a small fragment of her life?

* * *

SHE WAS QUIET. Too quiet. They were halfway through the shift, and she'd barely said two words to him. He'd already asked her half a dozen times if she was okay and always got the same damn answer…that she was fine.

Yeah, he didn't believe her for a second. Something had rattled her. Something that even Mrs. Sandler's cupcake couldn't make better.

"Stop staring, brother."

He glanced at Kayden, who sat at the bar, beer in hand. "I'm not staring."

"You sure as hell are, and there's no way she hasn't noticed. You'll scare her away."

"What are you even doing here? I thought you were spending the night with Eastern."

"He's meeting me here."

"Great. So I have to put up with both of you tonight?"

Kayden smirked at him. "We love how excited you are to spend time with us." He lifted the beer to his mouth. "Have you heard from Nylah?"

The tightness in his chest loosened at the mention of his twin sister. She'd moved from Misty Peak to Cradle Mountain, Idaho, a few months ago. That's where she'd met Liam. Cody had been skeptical about him at first, but after spending time with the guy, he knew the relationship was real. "Yeah, she called a few nights ago. She's really happy."

It was about damn time. She'd sacrificed too much of her life here, in this bar, helping their dad while Cody and his brothers had been serving in the military.

Kayden nodded. "Yeah, I spoke to her this morning. I'm glad she's doing so well."

Barry stepped up beside him. "Kayden. Talk some sense into your brother. He's agreed to host Vanessa's work luncheon here at the bar."

The fuck did he have to bring *that* up for? "Thanks, Barry."

Kayden looked at Cody like he'd lost his mind. "She cheats on you with your best friend and you're *helping* her?"

"She came in here basically crying, telling me she had no one else and her Pomeranian died and her mother's sick."

Kayden shook his head. "Not your problem."

"Thank you," Barry sang before moving away.

What was he, the angel of trouble?

Kayden tilted his head. "Cody—"

"I know. It's a one-time event, and once it's done, it's done."

Kayden raised a brow. "Until the next thing pops up. Even after she cheated on you, she wanted to keep dating, remember? And she uses every excuse she can find to be around you, even while flaunting her relationship with Miles. Doesn't it piss you off?"

"It did." His gaze rose to Harper. "But I don't really care as much anymore."

In fact, he cared more about Miles's deceit than Vanessa's.

Kayden followed his gaze before shaking his head. "Just ask her out already."

What the hell kind of universe was Kayden living in? He couldn't just ask out his new employee.

Before he could respond, Eastern sat beside Kayden at the bar. "Ask who out?"

"The beautiful brunette on the floor, Cody's new hire."

Eastern turned to look at her.

Cody rolled his eyes. "Yeah, good, let's all stare at her. That will make her feel real welcome. Won't scare her at all."

Eastern shifted his attention back to Cody, a smile on his face. "She's pretty."

She wasn't pretty, she was beautiful, but no way was he saying that out loud to his annoying-as-hell brothers. He'd never hear the end of it. "She showed up here in the middle of the night needing somewhere to stay. Came back the next day asking about the job."

The humor on both his brothers' faces dropped.

Eastern leaned forward. "She's running from something."

Yeah, they knew. "My thought too. What, exactly, I don't know." But he sure as hell wanted to find out.

When Harper returned to the bar, she went to pass him but he touched her arm. "Harper."

She looked up, smiling at him, and fuck if that lift of her lips didn't gut him. "You've met my brother Kayden, but I want to introduce you to another brother of mine, Eastern. He's also the town sheriff."

Her brows shot up. "The sheriff?"

"It's nice to meet you, Harper." He gave her a smile that would appear easy to anyone else. Cody knew better. His brother was already trying to figure her out.

It wouldn't happen. Not yet. She kept her cards too close to her chest.

"You too."

She kept moving down the bar to serve a customer, and Cody's gaze rose to scan the room. He'd been doing that a lot since Travis, Dayne, and their friends had visited the other night.

"Looking for Travis?"

Cody's attention swung back to Eastern. "You a damn mind reader?"

"No. But I heard about the altercation."

"From who?"

"A few locals. People talk in Misty Peak."

Yeah, he knew that. Secrets never stayed secrets for long in a small town.

"The asshole touched her," Cody growled between gritted teeth, knowing his brothers would know who he was talking about.

Kayden's knuckles whitened on the beer bottle. "Why the hell did he do that?"

"To warn her about me. That I'm not the good guy I appear to be." Both his brothers cursed. "She told him to release her, and he didn't. I intervened."

"Good," Eastern said. "I would have too. Just...be careful around him."

Cody's eyes narrowed on his brother. "Why? Is he more than just a thieving jerk?"

"I'm not saying that. Just that Travis and Dayne like to cause trouble, and they probably did that the other night specifically to get a rise out of you."

Well, they'd certainly done that.

Cody's gaze found Harper again. "If he messes with Harper, I don't give a fuck if he's trying to get a rise out of me or not, I'll come down on him so hard, he'll know never to come back."

CHAPTER 5

"You mean to tell me you're single? That's madness."

Harper chuckled. It was the end of the night, at the end of an even longer week. All the customers had left, except Archie Jader, an older man who was in Meridian basically every night. Usually, he only had a couple of beers. Tonight, it seemed he'd been overserved. Maybe he'd been alternating who he got drinks from.

"No," she finally said. "What's madness is that some people spend three hundred dollars on a toaster. Me being single is the opposite of madness."

He frowned like he couldn't make sense of what she'd said. "My toaster broke a long time ago. They cost three hundred dollars now?"

She heard a muffled laugh from behind the bar. Cody was cleaning while being zero help in getting Archie out. "No, most don't, just the pretentious ones." She tilted her head. "So, no toast for breakfast for a while?"

"Breakfast? Who eats breakfast?"

She bit her bottom lip to curb the grin. The man might be drunk, but at least he was a happy one. "Okay, Archie, it's time to go. I need to get home for some beauty sleep, and I can't do that with customers still here."

"Beauty sleep?" He rose to his feet, immediately tilting to the side. She grabbed his arm in an attempt to steady him. "You get any more beautiful and you'll stop traffic."

"You're a real charmer, you know that? Are you sure you don't need me to call anyone?"

"I've been doing the two-minute walk home for years. I'll be okay." They were halfway to the door when he stopped, and she wasn't sure if he intentionally leaned into her or was just unstable. "Although, if a certain pretty lady would like to walk me home, I wouldn't object."

A throat cleared behind her. "All right, Casanova, time to get home. I've ordered you a car." Cody slipped Archie from her hold.

"A car?" Archie frowned. "I don't need a car."

"Well, it's here to take you home anyway, and I'm going to make sure you get into it."

He sighed. "Just like your sister, always making sure people are okay. Your parents raised you kids right."

"They did okay."

As they stepped outside, Harper returned behind the bar, wiping down the counter. Once that was done, she went into the back storage room and reached up for a box of beer on the top shelf. It was only when she shuffled it to the edge that she realized her mistake.

Heavy. *Far* too heavy. But it was too late. The box started to tilt and she cried out, already scrunching her eyes for when it fell on her face.

Suddenly, fast footsteps sounded and her name was shouted before warmth permeated her back and strong arms reached over her head, taking the box from her fingers.

She froze briefly, then turned to see Cody standing close behind her, concern on his face.

He lowered the box to his feet, his muscles flexing, before straightening. "Are you okay?"

"Yeah, sorry, I didn't realize…" How heavy it was? That was stupid. Of *course* a case of beer was heavy. "I shouldn't have attempted to lift the box."

"If that had fallen on you…" A muscle flexed in his jaw.

"I'm sorry."

"I'm not angry, just worried."

She hadn't expected worry. Maybe because not a lot of people had worried about her throughout her life.

Silence trickled by, each second falling into the next. In that quiet, she became very aware of how close he stood. How it was just the two of them and it would be so incredibly easy to do something she shouldn't.

Without her permission, her eyes lowered to his lips. Suddenly, every part of her wanted to do something she'd never done before—take a chance on a man who was still basically a stranger.

She lifted her gaze back up to find Cody's eyes had darkened.

Oh, God, what was she doing? She couldn't kiss him. He was her boss. He was helping her out while she hid from her family and saved money to keep running. Because she *was* running…and would eventually *keep* running.

She stepped back, her ass colliding with the shelves. "I, um, should be getting home now."

Before he could respond, she turned and walked—or more accurately, ran—back into the bar. She grabbed her bag from the office and was about to step through the bar door when warm fingers wrapped around her upper arm, the touch gentle but firm.

She stopped and glanced over her shoulder.

His blue eyes were still intense, like the ocean in the midst of a storm. "Hey. You sure you're okay?"

No. She was far from okay. She was crushing on a man she

absolutely shouldn't be. "Yes. I'm fine. Closed tomorrow, right? I'll see you Tuesday?"

He nodded slowly. "I'll see you Tuesday."

For a moment, she wanted to just pause time and get lost in those beautiful eyes. Argh. She needed to stop. Stop staring and dreaming and wanting.

She turned and pushed outside, heading straight toward her car. She was halfway down the street when a flicker of something caught her eye. She stopped. The movement had come from right beside a car parked on the other side of the road. Was someone there?

Something cold slithered over her skin, and she sped up her steps. The second she was behind the wheel, she locked the doors, her heart beating so hard in her chest she could almost feel the rattle of her ribs. It had probably been nothing. But when you were running, everything felt like something.

The drive home felt too long even though it wasn't long at all. She forced herself to forget the shadow, but then Cody's blue eyes immediately took their place. The heat that had cascaded off his body. The way his thumb had caressed her skin in his hold.

When she finally got home, she climbed out of her car and moved to the cabin door. She frowned and slowed when she saw muddy footsteps on the small porch.

Whose were they? Ali's?

Her gaze shot around the area, another chill sweeping over her skin before she shoved her key into the door and pushed inside. Immediately, the warmth from the fire slid over her chilled skin. Ali always started it before Harper got home, and it was a godsend when she returned after a late shift.

Quickly, she moved into the bathroom and set her phone on the counter. The second she stood beneath the stream of water in the shower, she forced her mind off the muddy footprints, but again, her imagination betrayed her and flicked back to Cody. His two brothers had popped into the bar again tonight, and just like Cody, they were a million feet tall with broad shoulders and chiseled jaws.

How was it that one family could produce so many good-looking men? And not just that, they all looked at her like they saw far too much.

Was it the former soldiers in them?

For a moment tonight, she'd thought Cody might kiss her. Or at least that he wanted to kiss her. But that was crazy, right? He dated model-looking women like Vanessa, while Harper was... well, she was ordinary.

By the time she'd finished in the shower, Harper had basically convinced herself that Cody *had not* been looking at her like he wanted to kiss her, and he *did not* feel that way about her.

She wrapped a towel around her body and glanced at herself in the mirror. The bruise on her left eye had almost faded, but the memory of how she'd gotten it certainly had not.

"We're family. What's yours is mine, right?"

She shuddered and turned away at the memory of her brother's words. Lifting her phone, she saw two missed calls and a text, all from an unknown number. She didn't bother to read the text, instead just deleting it, knowing it was Ross telling her to answer his calls because he had something to discuss.

Did he really think she was interested in *anything* he had to say after their mother had wiped out Harper's savings and he'd struck her?

She wasn't surprised her mother hadn't tried to contact her. The woman had been emotionally absent most of her life, finding more meaning at the bottom of a bottle than she had in her daughter.

Harper was walking out of the bathroom when another text came through, this one from her old boss, Ivy.

Ivy had always been good to her, giving her a job when she'd never been in an office in her life, and allowing her to work her way up to executive assistant. And then Harper had just…left her, with nothing more than a text to say she was quitting.

She cringed.

Ivy: Hey, Harper. I just wanted to check in and see how you're doing. You left in such a rush. I'm not angry, just worried.

Harper: I'm so sorry I left like I did. I'm doing okay.

Ivy didn't know about the mess that was her family. Harper had always been careful to keep that information locked away.

Ivy: I care about YOU, not that you left in a rush. Are you safe?

Harper: I am. I promise.

Ivy: Okay. Well, your last paycheck is going into your account this week. I wish you all the best.

Her last paycheck? She'd almost forgotten. And God, she could use that money. But she still hadn't opened a new account, and if her work deposited the money into her old account, and her mother saw it before she did…

Harper: I'm sorry to ask, but could you mail a check for me to cash instead? I know it's old school but there's an issue with my account that I haven't sorted out yet, and I haven't opened a new one.

The three dots popped up, then disappeared before Ivy's response came through.

Ivy: Sure. We can do that. Just let me know where to send it.

She nibbled her bottom lip, a part of her not wanting to disclose that information, but she really did need the money. And Ivy wasn't associated with her family.

Harper: Meridian—it's a bar in Misty Peak. Thank you so much.

She included the mailing address, then put the phone on the dresser. As she pulled on her avocado nightshirt, her phone vibrated again. She expected to find another message from Ivy.

Cody: Hey. I just wanted to make sure you got home safely.

Her mouth went dry. She'd given him her number on her first shift, just in case they needed to get in contact with each other, but this was the first time he'd used it.

She nibbled her bottom lip and started typing a message, only to delete it. Then she tried again.

Oh, for Christ's sake, he's just your boss.

Harper: Home safe and sound. Thanks for checking in.

Send. There. Done. She'd kept her cool. Hadn't given away that she'd been thinking nonstop about him and the almost-kiss that couldn't possibly have been an almost-kiss.

Her phone vibrated.

Cody: So...tomorrow. Any plans?

Why was he asking? Didn't people usually ask that question if they wanted to hang out? Did he want to hang out with her?

He texted again before the crazy thoughts could completely take over.

Cody: Because if you're not busy, I was thinking I could show you around town. I could even show you the mountains.

Her jaw dropped. He *did* want to hang out. Oh, Jesus. She should say no, right? Keep her distance from the locals because her time here was limited?

But then why did she want to say yes so badly?

Ha. She knew the answer to that. The same reason she'd looked at his lips tonight and hadn't been able to get them out of her head since.

She was about to respond when a noise sounded outside. The creaking of a wooden board...on the porch? Was it Ali?

Slowly, she walked over to the door and looked through the peephole. Nothing. She was about to turn away when she heard it again. She stopped and frowned. This time when she went back, she opened the door to look out. Even though she didn't see anything, unease slid over her skin. Because it almost felt like there were eyes on her.

Her mind flicked back to the muddy footprints.

"Hello? Is anyone here?"

Nothing. Nothing but the eerie silence of the night.

Quickly, she closed and locked the door, her pulse suddenly

beating too fast. She was still standing with her back to the wood when her phone vibrated in her hand.

Cody: Hey...you there? Everything okay?

She needed some good in her life. There was no harm in letting Cody be that good, even if it was just for a little bit...right?

Harper: I would love for you to show me around town tomorrow.

CHAPTER 6

$\mathcal{C}$ody turned into the parking lot in front of the Misty Peak Visitors Center. He'd picked up Harper and she'd been quiet the entire drive, despite his attempts to make conversation.

Because they'd almost kissed last night? Fuck, the moment her eyes had landed on his lips, he'd been a second away from crashing his mouth onto hers…but then she'd stepped back.

"So," he started as he pulled into a parking space and turned the car off. "This is the Misty Peak Visitors Center. There's a café, a small eco-center, the start of a few walking trails, where you can use maps or a guide to take you through the mountains, and they're just building a skywalk."

"I saw something on your noticeboard about a skywalk."

"Yeah. It looks like it's going to be pretty awesome, but it's not finished yet."

"That's okay, a walk through the mountains sounds great. Do you think we'll see your brother?"

"Probably, the man basically lives and breathes these mountains." He undid his seat belt. "He'd either be taking tourists for a guided hike or rescuing some unlucky soul who has to endure his wrath."

She chuckled as they climbed out. "His wrath?"

"Oh yeah. Kayden works in search and rescue but has zero tolerance for people who get themselves lost by their own stupidity."

"I see." They moved toward the entrance of the center. "So if we get lost, we'll be the unlucky souls who have to endure his wrath."

"We won't get lost. I know these mountains like the back of my hand. They were my backyard growing up. You're safe with me."

An emotion flashed through her eyes. Surprise, maybe? He'd used that word a couple of times around her, and each time, she reacted the same. Had no one told her she was safe before?

He touched a hand to the small of her back. "Come on, Storm. Let me dazzle you with my town so you never want to leave."

She gave him a small smile as he bypassed the entrance to the visitors center and led her toward the start of a trail.

When they stepped onto the path, a small shudder rolled down her spine.

"Cold? Need my sweatshirt?"

"No, thanks. But I'm glad you told me to grab mine."

"Yeah, the trees shade a lot of the sun, but trust me, the walk's so beautiful it's worth it."

"I do...trust you."

Something about her words twisted his gut. For some reason, he *wanted* this beautiful, intriguing woman to trust him.

Over the next hour, Cody led Harper down the trail, pointing out different trees and plants. Telling stories about the area. Something that really got him was that when he talked, she truly listened. He hadn't dated Vanessa very long, but she'd always seemed distracted when he spoke, either with her phone or something else around her, and she rarely asked follow-up questions.

When he spoke to Harper, she asked intelligent questions and looked at him like he was the only person she heard. And damn, but that did something to him.

He loved these mountains. The fresh air. The smell of nature. Even the sound of running water from the stream and the low hum of the wind.

"It must have been amazing, growing up with this as your backyard," she said quietly.

He nodded. "We were pretty lucky."

"Do you see your mom often?"

He stepped over a log. "My mom passed away when I was eight. Breast cancer."

She stopped. "Oh…I'm so sorry. You mentioned you lost your dad, but I didn't know about your mom."

"It's okay. It was a long time ago." They continued walking but at a slower pace. "It rocked the family, but we created a new normal after that."

"Still, I'm sorry." She took his outstretched hand to step over the log. "Losing both your parents must have been so hard."

"When Dad was diagnosed with lymphoma, I was in the military. I wanted to come home, and so did my brothers, but both he and Nylah insisted we stay. She took care of him, and Kayden and I returned shortly before he died."

"Nylah being your sister?"

"Twin sister."

Her brows shot up. "You're a twin?"

"I am. Although, if you ask her, it's not that fun. I'm both overbearing and overprotective."

Something he couldn't identify crossed her face. "As much as sisters say they don't like that, I'm not sure it's true. Even the most independent woman at some point wants a protector in her corner."

He guessed this woman had never had a protector. "I always suspected she secretly loved it. So…you know all about my family. What about yours? Parents? Siblings?"

Immediately, her expression shuttered, the easy expression on her face disappearing. She looked off into the path in front of them as she answered. "An older brother and mother, but we're not close. My father's alive but I haven't seen him in about eight years."

He frowned. There was so much more to that story, and he wanted to push. To learn everything there was to know about this woman. But she wasn't ready to share. Was it her family she'd run from? And if so, why? What had they done to make leaving her only option? Was it one of them who'd given her the black eye? He'd assumed an ex because in his family, no one would ever do that to one of the others, but not everyone had a family like his.

"I'm sorry to hear that, Harper. I'm not sorry you landed here in Misty Peak, though. Was leaving home to come here difficult?"

A bitter smile flitted over her face. "No. It's funny really, how we carefully construct a life for ourselves, but given the right motivation, we can leave it so easily."

He had so many questions. And every time Harper spoke, he thought of a dozen more. He opened his mouth to ask one of them—but a couple of men rounded a bend, coming toward them.

His back teeth ground together at the sight of his high school best friend, Miles.

"Cody," Miles said, as he and his friend stopped in front of him and Harper. "It's good to see you."

Was it?

"This is Jack."

His friend dipped his head while Miles's gaze shifted to Harper. He waited for Cody to introduce him, but when he didn't, he introduced himself. "I'm Miles. An old friend of Cody's."

As if sensing the tension, Harper only offered a smile that didn't quite reach her eyes. "Harper. I work at the bar."

Miles's brows shot up. "Really? That's great." He shifted his attention back to Cody. "You were looking for help, right?"

"Right." Cody put a hand on the small of Harper's back, not missing the way Miles's gaze followed the move. "We'd better get going."

"Okay. I'll see you around," Miles said, watching as they walked away.

It wasn't until they gained some distance down the path that Harper spoke. "That's Vanessa's partner, isn't it?"

The woman was either a mind reader or just really perceptive. "Yeah, and my best friend once upon a time. It's stupid, but *his* betrayal actually hurt more than hers." Maybe because he'd suspected Vanessa wasn't a great person, and he'd been about to end things between them anyway. But Miles...Miles had always seemed like a genuine friend.

Harper's expression softened. "It's never stupid to expect more from the people we love and feel hurt when they break our trust."

She sounded like she spoke from experience. "I think you're right."

Their eyes held for another beat before her phone rang from her pocket. It had done that a few times today. Someone was trying hard to get in touch with her, but she didn't seem interested in answering.

She canceled the call, but immediately it started ringing again.

She cursed under her breath before looking up at him. "Do you mind if I take this? Otherwise, they'll just keep calling."

"Go for it."

* * *

HARPER STEPPED AWAY FROM CODY, moving off the path and into the thick trees. She didn't go too far, but she also didn't want Cody to hear what she had to say.

When she felt she was a safe distance, she finally answered the call. "What do you want, Ross?"

"Ah, my pretentious baby sister finally answers."

Her jaw clenched. "Guess my *not* answering wasn't hint enough. Or hell, my leaving town wasn't hint enough. *Leave me alone.* I don't want anything to do with you *or* Mom."

"Does that mean you don't want to know what my news is?"

"No, I don't! I don't want anything to do with either of you. You've done enough. You stole my money. My sanity. You're toxic. I just want you to stay the hell away from me."

He laughed, but the sound was twisted and ugly. "Okay. Well then, this is going to bring me even more joy than I thought it would. Dad's out."

Her muscles locked, a deep chill sweeping over her skin and through her veins. "What do you mean, Dad's out? He has another two years of his sentence to serve."

"A combination of good behavior and overcrowding. It's why Mom emptied your shared account, so she could redo some things around the house. Get her hair done and buy some new outfits."

Her breathing became jagged and uneven. "It wasn't a *shared* account. It was my money, and she stole it from me."

"Whatever. Her name was on the account, so she took what she had access to."

The anger turned her vision red, so many words and emotions seeping to the surface, threatening to break free, but she locked them away. "Well, you've told me, now leave me alone." She hung up before her brother could respond.

Out. Her father was out.

Her mother and brother were nothing compared to him. He'd been arrested when she was fifteen, but even before that, she'd known to stay the hell away from him. He didn't just abuse alcohol, he took drugs—the heavy stuff. And when he did, he was violent.

With the huge quantity of drugs that had been found in his possession the night of his arrest, combined with the assault charges, he'd received a ten-year prison sentence.

A wave of panic rolled over her as she remembered the last time she'd been in her father's presence. The panic weaved up her throat, threatening to choke her.

No. She couldn't lose it now. Not here.

He didn't know where she was. None of her family did. And not only would he not be able to find her, he'd have no reason to look. Her mother had already taken her money. She was safe.

With a deep, calming breath, she turned and headed back toward the path, a million emotions rolling through her mind, threatening to break free. She hadn't visited her father once in prison, despite pressure from her mother and brother to do so. As far as she was concerned, they should have locked him up for longer. Thrown away the key.

She made it about ten feet when she stopped and frowned. Wait…had she gone the wrong way? Where was the path? She walked a few steps to the right. God, everything looked the same. No wonder they needed a SAR team here.

She walked about twenty feet before stopping again. No. This was definitely the wrong way. She lifted her phone to call Cody, only the signal bar was down to one.

Dammit. It was like the entire freaking universe was against her today.

She growled—yes, actually growled—as she stomped through the forest. At some point, she vaguely thought she should probably feel fear over her current predicament, instead of the anger surging through her body. But honestly, was it not enough that her mother had *robbed* her and her brother had *hit* her? Now her drug-addict father—who'd made a habit of hurting his family—

was out of prison! Getting lost in the woods was a vacation in comparison.

She wanted to yell. To scream. To throw her fist in the air and ask the universe why she couldn't have been given one, just *one*, half-decent family member.

She was so busy cursing her family that she didn't see the tree root. Her foot caught on it, and she yelped as she tumbled to the ground, her ankle scraping across a broken branch in the process.

With a quick glance, she saw blood slipping down her ankle. Crap.

"Harper!" Her head shot up as Cody ran toward her and dropped to his knees. "Are you okay?"

"Yeah, it's just a scratch." She watched as he lifted her foot, his brows tugged together as he inspected the gash. "It's fine. How did you find me?"

"When you didn't come back, I tried calling but it went straight to voicemail. I heard you cry out."

She cringed. "Sorry. I didn't mean to move so far from the path."

He looked up at her, the concern shifting to something a bit gentler. "Are you sure you're okay?"

Her breath caught. Was he talking about more than the cut? Could he see every ugly secret she was keeping locked away from him?

"I am now," she whispered, more truth to that statement than there should have been.

Before she realized what he was doing, he slid his arms around her back and knees and lifted her against his chest.

She gasped and grabbed onto him. "Cody, it's okay. I can walk!"

"I need to get you back to the center so I can treat the cut."

She opened her mouth to tell him that she was fully capable of getting there with her feet on the ground, but he was already moving, his impressive muscles flexing against her side.

Cody walked quickly, and they reached the deck behind the center just as Kayden was stepping out.

"Hey…everything okay?" His gaze shifted from her face to her ankle.

She nodded quickly. "Just a scratch."

"We're just gonna use the first aid kit," Cody said.

"Yeah, go for it."

Cody slipped past his brother. There were two doors off the deck, one which led to the room with the desk they'd walked past to enter the mountains, and another, she wasn't sure.

He stepped into the entry, which was basically just a large space with a desk to one side and the front entrance on the other side of the room. There was also the small eco center opposite the desk.

A girl looked up from the desk. "Cody. Is everything okay?"

"Hey, Pixie. Yeah, I'm just taking Harper into the back room to treat a cut."

"Okay. Linda's not in there, so it's free. Let me know if you need anything."

Cody carried her into the back office and lowered her to a couch before grabbing a first aid kit from a cabinet. She was quiet as he knelt in front of her and rolled up her pant leg, his touch gentle as he swabbed the wound.

"I'm sorry I didn't find you faster."

He was apologizing to *her*? "It's my fault. I should have just stayed on the path."

"Why didn't you?"

She nibbled her bottom lip. "I guess I was scared someone would overhear the conversation."

"Someone being me?"

Bingo.

"Would that have been so bad?" he asked when she didn't answer.

"Yes." The one honest word slipped from her lips before she could stop it.

He put a small bandage over the wound before looking up. "Why?"

"You've been so nice to me. But if you knew how much of a mess my life was, you'd run." More truths she probably shouldn't be sharing. Had she hit her head as well as scraped her ankle?

"You think I scare that easily?" he asked.

"No. I think my life's that much of a mess."

His hands went to her thighs, and her body tingled as if he were touching bare skin. "I won't run. We may have just met, but I feel something for you, Harper. And when the day comes where you feel comfortable enough to tell me, I promise I'll do everything in my power to help you."

The air stopped moving in her lungs. It just…stopped. If she'd thought she'd dropped a bomb with her honesty, it was nothing compared to his.

He tilted his head. "Can I ask you to just tell me one thing?"

Right now, with his hands on her thighs and his face so close, she'd probably tell him her entire life story if he asked. "Sure."

"Are you in danger?"

In danger… Had she ever felt anything *but* in danger with the family she'd been born into? "Right now, I feel safer than I've ever felt in my life." It wasn't really an answer to his question. But it kind of was.

CHAPTER 7

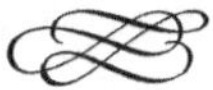

"**W**hat in the ever-loving hell is this? It looks like Barbie threw up in here."

Cody emptied ice into a bucket and looked at Barry. "If I never see pink again, it will be too soon."

It was everywhere. Pink balloons. Pink bows on the chairs. Vanessa had even carried in a two-tier pale pink frosted cake with pink macarons on top. It looked less like a work luncheon and more like a party.

"If I never see *Vanessa* again, it'll be too soon," Barry said in a voice so low only Cody heard.

He elbowed the older man, although he wasn't disagreeing.

"Cody!"

Barry groaned at Vanessa's voice. "Good luck," he muttered under his breath before moving into the back room.

Vanessa leaned over the counter. "People are arriving. Would you be able to set out the pre-lunch snacks?"

"Sure. Do you always have balloons and cakes at work luncheons?"

"We're a fun company, and it also happens to be two people in the office's birthdays. I'm trying to make a good impression." Her gaze shifted around the bar. "I notice Harper isn't here. It's just you and Barry?"

The words had just left her lips when the door to the bar opened and Harper stepped in.

His world fucking stopped when he saw her. Every. Damn. Time. Even just in jeans and a tight black tee, the woman looked so damn beautiful she took all his attention.

Since their day in the mountains a week ago, something had shifted between them. Their gazes held for a beat longer than they used to. Conversations felt more meaningful.

Harper crossed the bar, her gaze moving around the room. "This looks great."

Vanessa gave her a tight smile. "Thank you." She turned back to Cody. "Snacks?"

"I'll get on it."

"Thank you."

As Vanessa walked away, Harper put her bag in the office, then rounded the bar. "Sorry I'm late," she said quietly.

"That's okay. Is everything all right?"

"Yeah. Everything's fine."

He traced the shadows under her eyes with his gaze. "You look tired."

"I just didn't sleep well last night."

He reached out and grazed her arm. "If you're not okay, you can—"

"Cody, I'm okay."

He opened his mouth to tell her that he wasn't sure that was true, but Vanessa's voice cut through the quiet.

"Cody—please. I *really* need those snacks."

"Go," Harper said quietly. "I'll get started on drinks."

Before he could respond, she slipped around him, and fuck if he didn't want to just tug her back. He grabbed the platters of food from the kitchen. They also had some hot food prepped and waiting in the oven.

He set the first platter in the center of the table, and when he turned, an older woman who had way too much filler in her lips stood in front of him. "Hi, Cody. I'm Olivia. It's so nice of you to host this luncheon for us."

"Happy to help."

He went to step around her, but she touched his arm. "Before you go, my daughter Jenny has just returned home from college. She's single."

Jesus Christ. "I've really got to get back to the food, Olivia." He glanced up to see Harper watching him, a ghost of a smile on her face.

He tried to step away again, but for the second time, the woman blocked his way. "She's a nurse and loves animals, especially birds. She has two blue jays and a mourning dove. I could give you her number?"

"Thanks, but I'm not looking to date."

This time he stepped to the side so quickly the woman didn't have time to stop him. When he returned to the bar, Harper looked a second away from dropping to the floor in a fit of laughter.

"You think that was funny?" he asked.

"It's not *not* funny." She grinned at him. "It's a shame you're not looking to date, because Jenny sounds great. You could have built quite the aviary."

"I'm not looking to date *Jenny*. Someone else could convince me."

Her smile slipped, and a number of emotions passed through her expressive eyes. Surprise. Desire. And maybe just a bit of fear. For some reason, she was scared of their connection. Why? Because it was so intense? Because she had a bad history with men?

"Harper!" Her gaze shot toward the kitchen at the sound of Barry's voice. "Can I get some help?"

"Sure." She glanced back at Cody, but the smile was well and truly gone. "I'll, um, go help in the back."

As she walked away, it was *his* turn to smile. Because he intended to get to the bottom of whatever was going on. And he also intended to break through her walls and gain her trust.

The next couple of hours were a mix of women eating, drinking, and talking business. Well, mostly business. He was pretty sure he heard a fair bit of gossiping as well.

When he wasn't needed out front, he went into the office and tried to stay busy with a couple of things just to give himself space to breathe. Before long, footsteps sounded outside the door, and for a second, he thought it might be Harper. It wasn't.

Vanessa stepped inside and partially closed the door. "Wow, being in here brings back memories."

Was she talking about when he'd try to work and she'd sit on his desk and attempt to distract him? Before the cheating, of course. Because nothing else had happened in this room. "Is everything okay?"

"Yes. I just want to say thank you again for letting me host this event in the bar."

"You've already thanked me."

She stepped closer, starting to step around his desk. "I know. But after what I did to you, you could have said no."

He *should* have said no.

"I never meant to hurt you, you know." This time her voice was lower, almost sultry. "Cody—"

He stood quickly. "I need to get back out there." And get away from *her*. The two of them being alone in here felt too intimate.

He moved the opposite way around his desk to open the door and step out. Harper looked up from behind the bar, a small smile stretching her lips when their gazes collided. The smile slipped when her gaze fell behind him—right on Vanessa as she followed him out of the office.

* * *

Was she overthinking this? Sure, Cody and Vanessa had been in his office alone, and yeah, she'd looked smug as hell when she'd strutted out. That didn't mean anything had happened. And even if it did, that was none of her business.

It was just…confusing, because Cody had been giving off all kinds of signs that he was interested in her.

Yes. That's why she was out of sorts. Because she was confused. *Not* because she was jealous that the two of them had been alone in his office doing God knows what.

She walked into the kitchen and started loading the dishwasher. She felt Barry's eyes on her before he spoke. "Everything okay?"

"Yeah, of course. It's fine. Absolutely fine. I mean, people can do whatever they want, right? It's not like we can predict how people will act, or wish for certain behaviors. And even if people *did* act the way we wanted, a part of us shouldn't want that. We might even be scared of it. Because hope can be a terrible thing. Hope makes us believe something good is possible when sometimes it just isn't. And I just—"

Barry touched her arm. Christ, she hadn't even heard him come toward her.

"I'm not following much of what you're saying," he said gently. "But I can tell you with a hundred percent certainty that hope isn't always a terrible thing."

"How do you know that?"

"Because I'm a wise old man who's been given the gift of hope a few times in his life."

Gift. Barry saw hope as a gift. Whereas whenever she'd hoped for anything, it had been ripped away so violently she'd been scared to ever hope again.

She opened her mouth, not exactly sure what was about to come out, only to stop at *his* voice.

"Harper."

Her heart jumped, and she looked up to see Cody standing in

the doorway of the kitchen, his beautiful ocean-blue eyes boring into her.

"Can I talk to you?"

"Of course." The words came out too quickly and far too high-pitched.

Barry cleared his throat. "I'll, uh, go see how the luncheon's finishing up."

Cody waited for Barry to leave before crossing the room. He did it slowly, like he was afraid he'd scare her off. It kind of felt like when an animal stalked its prey.

She was his prey.

"Everything okay?"

"Yes." Another word that came out too quickly.

"Good. Because I've made my intentions clear."

She swallowed. "Your intentions?"

Three more steps and he was right in front of her—touching distance. "I like you, Storm. In an every-time-I'm-close-I-want-to-kiss-you kind of way. In a take-all-my-attention-when-you're-in-the-room kind of way."

Her lungs malfunctioned. "But you just met me."

He brushed some hair from her face, and his touch was like a bolt of electricity. "I know. It's crazy. But I've always been a fan of crazy."

"You're not real." He couldn't be, right? He was one of those fictitious men in Hallmark movies who made all the right decisions and said all the right things.

"Then what am I?"

"I don't know. But we can't...I mean, I don't even know how long I'll be here."

That didn't seem to deter him. "Maybe this could convince you to stay."

Slowly, so slowly she had all the time in the world to pull away, he lowered his head.

When his lips touched hers, she just...stopped. Stopped

breathing. Stopped thinking. And she let his soft lips smooth out all her resistant edges.

Almost of its own volition, her body leaned into him, and his arms slipped around her waist, tugging her closer. When her breasts pressed against his hard chest, she sucked in a surprised breath, and he took the opportunity to slip his tongue inside her mouth and taste her.

She groaned, her fingers sliding up his chest. God, he tasted good. She wanted to lose any remaining part of herself in the kiss.

She probably would have if it wasn't for the gasp that sounded from the door.

Quickly, she pulled away to see the back of someone as they left the room. Maybe Vanessa. Maybe someone else. In that moment, she didn't really care. His kiss was all she could think about.

She glanced back at him to see he was looking at her like she held the answers to the world's questions.

"I like kissing you," he whispered.

The beats of her heart did that speed-up-and-stumble-over-each-other thing. "I like kissing you too. But I don't know if that was smart."

"Then what was it?" When she didn't respond, he lowered his head to her ear and whispered, "I'd call it magic."

CHAPTER 8

Harper had one question. Just one. Why did Cody have to have everything? Sure, maybe give him a kind personality. And hell, throw in a sense of humor. But sweet, intelligent, sculpted like a God, *and* a million feet tall? Surely it wasn't fair to the other men in the world *or* to her.

She grabbed another glass and ran a towel over it, trying like hell to think about anything but him. Trying not to *look* at him.

It was almost closing time, and it had been another busy night. Not that she'd really noticed. Cody had taken up far too much of her attention.

They hadn't talked about the kiss they'd shared yesterday. And every time they were alone, and she thought he might bring it up, she ran. Yes, literally *ran* from the room like she was being chased by a pack of dogs.

Gah.

She was being a coward. But the kiss had been hot and heavy and not like anything she'd experienced with anyone else. Which wasn't necessarily a good thing when she had no idea how long she'd be here.

She kept waiting for Cody to show her a flaw. There had to be *something*. Everyone had a flaw, but so far, nothing. She hadn't been lying yesterday when she'd told Barry that hope was dangerous. She didn't want to hope that this town could be her new beginning. That Cody might actually be interested in her *and* a good guy. Because what if none of it panned out?

A woman stepped into the bar, the expression on her face as far from a smile as possible as she crossed the space and lowered onto a stool on the other side of the bar.

"Hi. Scotch on ice, please." Her voice was quiet and almost completely devoid of emotion.

Harper frowned as she pulled out a glass and scooped some ice into it. "Coming right up. Is everything okay?"

"Nope. Not even close."

Harper poured the drink and pushed it across the bar. "I've had a few bad days lately myself. They suck. But everyone in this town has been wonderful at making me feel better. Hopefully they can do the same for you."

The woman laughed, but the sound was almost bitter. "Unfortunately, I am *not* a crowd-pleaser around here." She shot back the Scotch, swallowing the hard liquor in one gulp.

"Want to talk about it?"

For the first time, the woman looked up and met Harper's gaze. "You're new here."

It wasn't a question. "I am. Cody took pity on me and gave me a job. Are you a local?"

"I was. But I left about five years ago when my dad..." She shook her head. "It's complicated. But I left."

"I know complicated families. I have one. Family is supposed to make life easier, but that was never the case for me."

Understanding crossed the other woman's face. "Yeah. Me neither."

"I'm Harper."

"Matilda. But people call me Tilly."

"Well, Tilly, if it's a friendly face you're after, I'll always offer you one in here."

For a second, Harper almost thought she saw a sheen of tears in the other woman's eyes. Was she that desperate for someone to be kind to her? Had others in this town really been so terrible? "Thank you."

"Harper, I—" Cody stopped beside her, his gaze shifting across the bar. "Tilly. What are you doing here?"

"Just getting a drink." An awkward, drawn-out silence passed before she spoke again. "Is that okay?"

At Cody's hesitation, Harper looked at him. Was he really going to say no?

When the silence stretched, she nudged him in the shoulder.

"Of course," he finally said, but it didn't come out easily or sound as warm as usual.

What was going on here? Had Tilly done something to the locals of Misty Peak?

"We're just closing up now though," he added.

Harper looked around and, sure enough, there was no one left in the bar.

Tilly set money on the bar and stood quickly. "I'll see you both around." She nodded at Cody, and when she looked at Harper, there was a small lift of the corner of her lips before she turned and left.

The second she was gone, Harper turned to Cody. "What was that?"

"What was what?"

"Why did you hesitate when she asked if it was okay that she was here?"

"It's—"

"Cody, I need your help in here," Barry called from the kitchen before he could finish.

He gave her a lopsided smile. "Saved by the old man. I'll be back."

Harper turned toward the door, but the woman was already gone. With a sigh, she pulled out the full trash bag from behind the bar and grabbed a can of cat food.

She heard Tommy the second she stepped outside. He came straight over to her and rubbed against her legs.

"Hey, boy. Have you been waiting for me?"

She'd been feeding him a lot lately, because, well, why *wouldn't* she want to come and have a pat and some cuddles with the friendly alley cat?

Setting the trash bag beside the cat bowl, she lowered to her haunches. The small can had barely been opened and Tommy was already trying to get his head inside.

"Hang on, buddy. I need to get it into your bowl first." She chuckled as she emptied the can, and he immediately purred and hunkered down to eat the food. She scratched his head. "Maybe one day you'll let Cody take you home. I think he'd be a good cat dad."

In fact, she'd come to the conclusion he was probably good at everything.

With a shake of her head, she rose to her feet and moved to the dumpster. She'd just dropped the bag in when a quiet noise sounded behind her. She started to turn—

Rough fingers clenched her hair, yanking her head back.

She screamed and her assailant shoved her into the brick wall beside the dumpster. Her head collided with the surface, and a burst of pain blasted through her skull.

The attacker's head lowered and a deep voice said something, but the buzzing between her ears was too loud and she couldn't make out what they were saying. It wasn't just the buzzing that distracted her though. It was the pain in her head. The heat of the person's body, pressing her own to the bricks, causing claustrophobia to crawl through her veins.

She couldn't think. Could barely breathe. It brought back all the memories of being a kid and having her father intimidate and hurt her.

The panic was starting to suffocate her when a door opened, then a loud, angry voice boomed. "Hey! What the fuck are you doing?"

Suddenly, she was released. Her knees caved and she dropped to the ground. Heavy footsteps pounded the ground, growing distant...then warm hands touched her arms before she heard Cody's deep, calming voice.

"Harper! Are you okay?"

She looked up, holding his gaze like it was the only thing keeping her conscious. She tried to nod but was almost certain her head didn't move.

She wasn't okay. Not even close.

* * *

CODY WANTED TO HIT SOMETHING. No, not something. He wanted to find the asshole who'd shoved Harper against the wall and drive his fist into the jerk's face.

He'd bruised her. Hurt her. Scared her.

He lowered Harper onto the desk in his office, then immediately turned to search through the cabinet for the first aid kit. He'd already texted Eastern before carrying Harper in here. The station wasn't far, so he wouldn't take long. But it wasn't enough, dammit!

The asshole who'd attacked her had gotten away. Cody could have chased him, but he couldn't make himself leave her. Barry had given chase, but despite the old man's boasting about his stamina, he hadn't been able to catch the asshole.

He returned to the desk and grabbed an antiseptic wipe. Gently, he patted the cut on her forehead, his gaze moving back to her wide eyes. "I'm sorry I didn't get to you in time."

She looked at him, a small frown creasing her brow. "It's not your fault. You saved me."

"You shouldn't have needed saving. You certainly shouldn't have gotten hurt. Not outside my bar. Not when I was so close."

He was still dabbing the cut when she cupped his cheek. "Cody. Don't take the blame for someone else. Someone attacked me. And if you hadn't gotten to me when you had…" She stopped, her chest rising with a deep inhale. "I don't know what would have happened. But I don't think he would have just left. Thank you."

He wrapped his fingers around the wrist of the hand cupping his cheek, needing to touch her. To feel her pulse beating beneath his fingertips. "I'm glad you're okay."

The door behind him opened and Eastern walked in, a deputy close on his heels.

Harper's hand dropped.

"Hi, Cody. Harper." Eastern's voice was all business. "It's nice to see you again, although I'm sorry it's under these circumstances. This is Deputy Cally, another officer from the station. Cody said you were attacked in the alley behind the bar?"

She nodded. "Yes, but I don't know if I'll be much help. I didn't see his face."

"That's okay. How about you tell us what happened."

She took a breath, her chest rising and falling. When she didn't say anything, Cody slipped his fingers through hers. Her gaze flashed up at him before switching back to Eastern.

"I went out there to feed Tommy and took a bag of trash with me. I'd just dropped it into the dumpster when I heard something behind me. I started to turn but someone grabbed a handful of my hair and shoved me against the wall beside the dumpster."

Cody's muscles tensed, and it took too much goddamn self-control to stay exactly as he was. To not show on his face the absolute fury that was alive inside him.

Her brows creased together. "He said something, but I

couldn't make out his words because my ears were ringing. Then Cody came out and he let me go."

Eastern nodded while his partner took notes. "Size? Frame?"

"Big," she said quietly. "Cody may know more. He probably got a better look."

"About six-two. Wide shouldered and built." His fingers tightened around Harper's hand. "It was dark, so that's all I got."

"That's helpful. Harper, do you know anyone who may want to hurt you?"

Her eyes widened. Only a fraction and only for a second, but it gave her away.

Yes. Someone *did* want to hurt her. But then, Cody already knew that because she'd already *been* hurt. She'd walked into his bar with a goddamn black eye the first night he'd met her.

"No one who knows where I am," she eventually said, not exactly answering the question. "I don't know if this is anything, but about a week ago, there were some muddy footprints on my cabin porch and some noises outside."

Cody's chest clenched. What the fuck? "Why didn't you say anything?"

"It may be nothing. It could have been Ali. She usually starts the fire in my cabin shortly before I get home at night. Or someone staying in one of the other cabins. Or hell, a wild animal."

Yeah…or it could have been the person who'd attacked her tonight.

Eastern looked like he wanted to push, but he didn't. "We'll look into it. A car is already patrolling the streets for anyone skulking around. We'll also have a car do some rounds near the cabins. In the meantime, don't go into any alleys by yourself. Try to stick to busy areas while out around town, and don't walk alone at night."

"Okay." Her voice was low, almost defeated.

"Do you have a way to get home?" Eastern asked.

"I brought my car."

"No," Cody said.

At the same time, Eastern said, "Not a good idea."

Harper frowned.

"After a head injury, you shouldn't be driving. At least not tonight." Eastern looked at Cody. "No signs of a concussion?"

Cody shook his head. "But I'll still drive her home. Unless you want to stay here."

Her brows shot up. "Here?"

"I have a spare room upstairs."

She was shaking her head before he'd finished speaking. "I can't do that."

"You can, because I'm offering."

She swallowed, but Cody could already see he wasn't going to get his way on this one. "I appreciate the offer, but I'd rather stay at the cabin. Ali's close, I have your number if I need you, and I'll keep the doors locked."

He ground his back teeth together. "Fine. But I'm at least driving you home."

"But how will I get to work tomorrow?" she asked.

"You won't."

She gave him a look. "Cody, you need more than just Barry."

"I'll be fine." He had to be, because there was no way this woman was working tomorrow after her attack tonight. She needed rest. Harper looked like she wanted to argue, but he shook his head. "It's not a fight you'll win, Harper. Come on, I need to get you home."

He slid an arm around her waist and helped her off the desk. He met his brother's gaze before stepping out, silent communication passing between them that Eastern would make this a priority.

And his brother knew the bar well. He'd close up.

Cody's knuckles were white against the steering wheel as he drove to the cabin. The trip was quick and silent. When he reached her place, he was out of the car and around to her side within seconds, sliding an arm around her waist as he helped her inside. He scanned the area. It seemed quiet, but there were so many damn places someone could hide. Fuck, he hated that.

The cabin was small but comfortable, with touches of warmth in the form of throws and rugs, and a fire that was already blazing, which he now knew was Ali's doing.

Harper lowered to the edge of the bed.

"Are you okay?" he asked quietly.

"In a twisted way, it's kind of funny." She ran her hands over her face, her actions contradicting her words.

"What is?"

"I leave one bad situation, only to fall smack-dab into another. I told Barry, hope is dangerous. You start wondering if this is it. This is the peace you were hoping for. Your happy place. And *boom*—the world shows you differently."

He crouched in front of her and gently pulled her hand from her face. "Hey. Look at me, Storm."

She did. She raised her eyes, eyes that held far more sadness than they should. "Hope is never bad. In fact, I would argue that it's as vital to us as the air we breathe. And when things don't pan out, that hope just twists and changes into something new."

Her brows flickered. "You're not like anyone I've ever met, Cody."

"I have a feeling that's a good thing."

"You have no idea." The whispered words barely reached his ears. Slowly, her head lowered, and she touched her lips to his. The kiss was soft. Gentle. A short graze of her mouth. Yet, he felt it like she'd devoured him. Changed him.

He nibbled her bottom lip, and when her mouth opened, he slipped his tongue inside, tasting her.

Damn, she was sweet. And her quiet moan was like a melody for his ears alone.

When they separated, he touched his forehead to hers. "I don't want to leave you."

"I'll be okay."

"But will I?"

Her expression softened. "Thank you for tonight. And for every night before this one since we met."

"I'm starting to realize…I'd do anything for you."

CHAPTER 9

Cody pushed into the Misty Peak Sheriff's Office and headed straight for Eastern. His brother was sitting behind his desk, a deep frown set into his brow. That wasn't unusual. His brother had been a Navy SEAL and took everything seriously, especially the safety of others.

Though, *no one's* safety was more important than that of Avery, his eight-year-old daughter. The kid was the center of his world, although he wasn't with her mother anymore.

Eastern looked up. "Hey. Thanks for coming in."

Cody lowered to the seat across the desk. "Is everything okay? You look tired."

Dark circles shadowed his eyes. That wasn't unusual for his brother either. But it also wasn't great.

"Yeah, I'm fine."

Cody didn't believe that for a second. "Eastern. It's me. What's up?"

There was a brief pause while Eastern ran his fingers through his hair. "It's Jaime. She left."

Cody straightened and leaned forward. "What do you mean, she left? Did she take Avery with her?"

"Nope. I had Avery for the weekend, and Jaime just never came to get her. When I called, she didn't answer, but she sent a text a day later to say that she's gone away because she needs a *break*, and she's not sure when she'll be back."

Anger shot through Cody. "A break from *what*? Her daughter? Being a mother?"

"That's a damn good question. One I'd love to know the answer to." Eastern dropped his head into his hands. "I haven't told Avery. Fuck, she's *eight*, man. How do I tell her that her mother left town and I don't know when she'll be back? *If* she'll come back?"

"You think she's gone for good?"

"I don't know. Since I got back to town, she's made a few references to how she can finally do some of the things she wanted to do with her life, now that I'm here. But I never thought that meant leaving."

"I'm so damn sorry. But Avery will be okay because she has you, and you're a great dad." The best.

"There's more."

Fuck, what more could there be?

"Avery's been telling me about Jaime's…drinking."

Cody narrowed his eyes. "Drinking?"

"Yeah. Apparently, she was drinking a lot—to the point she was passing out at night. Avery was getting to school late. Some days being sent without lunch and clean clothes."

"Shit! Man, I'm so sorry." Cody felt awful. He'd had no idea. Jaime had barely let him visit his niece. He'd tried. Hell, he'd texted the woman almost daily when he first came home. Asking to see her. Speak to her. Spend even an hour with the kid to give Jaime a break. But she'd refused his help. Kayden's too.

Because she knew they'd see her problem?

Eastern looked up again, pain crossing his face. "It's my job to protect her. She's my kid, and I didn't see what was going on. I hate myself for that. I would have come home earlier. I would have looked into things, made sure she was safe."

"Hey." Cody leaned forward. "You're here now. And you aren't leaving her."

"You're right. And I'm documenting everything. Making sure that if Jaime *does* return, she'll have to fight me to get Avery back *period*. I want full custody. And I'll get it." He sighed and shuffled some papers around his desk. "But that's not why I asked you to come here."

Eastern pulled out a piece of paper and pushed it across the desk. Cody lifted it and frowned at the printed news report. It featured a guy named Rodney Rain, who was released early from prison on good behavior after serving most of a ten-year sentence.

Cody quickly skimmed the article.

The night of Rain's arrest, neighbors heard a scream from his home and called police. Upon arrival, police found the fifty-six-year-old in a drug-fueled rage after having physically assaulted his wife, son, and daughter. The fifteen-year-old daughter was sent to the hospital for immediate medical attention. Rain was convicted of drug possession and aggravated assault.

He glanced up at his brother, who looked as solemn as Cody felt. "Is this…"

"Harper's father," Eastern finished for him, confirming his thoughts.

"That son of a bitch," Cody growled. "He sent her to the hospital?"

"And now he's out. I found it when I was filing the report last night and did a quick search on her."

Every muscle in Cody's body felt tight. No wonder she struggled to trust anyone. She'd been hurt by one of the few people who were supposed to protect and love her.

He dropped the news report before it was crushed in his hand under the weight of his fury.

Eastern leaned forward. "I know she implied that the people who might want to hurt her don't know she's here, but information is easier to get than we think."

"He may have found her."

"Yeah. And while her mother and brother chose not to testify against him, *she* did. And it was her scream that got the police to their door that night. I'm sure that's something he's thought about for the last decade."

His mind flicked to Harper, alone in that cabin. Suddenly, all he wanted to do was go to her. Make sure she was safe and protected. "Thanks for looking into it." Cody was about to rise, but he paused. "Can I do anything to help with Avery?"

Eastern shook his head. "Not right now, but I'll let you know if that changes."

* * *

Harper groaned as she rolled onto her belly. The dull throb from her head beat into her eyes. It felt like a hangover, but worse.

Gently, she prodded her forehead, only to wince at the shot of pain. Nope. No drunken night here. Just an ordinary, got-thrown-into-a-wall kind of evening.

She rolled to her side and lifted her phone, noticing a missed call from Cody.

Thank God he'd been there last night. If he hadn't walked out when he had…

No. She couldn't think about that. She didn't know what that guy had wanted—maybe to attack her, maybe to rob her. Either way, it hadn't been friendly.

Slowly, she pushed up and set her feet on the floor. At least her cabin was warm. It was just one of the things she loved about this place. Ali always came in and lit a fire for her while she was at work, and it kept the cabin warm all night. That lady was an angel.

When she stepped into the bathroom and saw her reflection in the mirror, she cringed. Just when the bruise from her brother had faded, this happened. Great.

Leaning forward, she inspected the blue-and-purple bruising that bordered a small cut. Memories of Cody's gentle touch last night skittered through her mind and had her breath catching. The way he'd cleaned the wound with such care. Looked at her like he was going to tear down the world to protect her.

She wanted to let him in. She wanted to trust him, trust that this thing between them could become permanent. But God, it was too hard. Everyone she'd trusted before had hurt her. Her father had been an angry, aggressive drug abuser. Her mother had been a drunk who'd never protected her a day in her life, then stole from her. And her brother was quickly turning into another version of their dad.

She still remembered the days immediately after testifying against her father. Her mother's drinking had worsened, and she'd cried like Harper had taken something precious from her. And Ross…he'd become a monster. Just like her father. He'd looked at her with so much hate, like *she'd* been the one to beat all of them, not him.

No one saw the fifteen-year-old who was hurting and in need of comfort and love and support. Or if they did, they didn't care. They just blamed her for her father being sent away.

She took a deep breath. That was why she'd cleaned offices until the full-time assistant job had come up in the same building. And the second she'd been able to afford it, she'd gotten an apartment one town over and started working toward her goal of saving for the home she'd always dreamed about.

That was her mistake though, wasn't it? One town over hadn't been far enough. Because they'd always wanted something from her. Another piece. To drag her down to exactly where *they* were. Her mother had constantly gone to her for alcohol money. And when she said no or tried to block her mother's calls, her brother took over, harassing her with calls and texts and ultimately showing up at her door until they got what they wanted.

The knock at her cabin door had her jolting in fear, almost thinking she'd brought her bad memories to life. She took a deep breath and calmed her racing heart.

Ali, she assumed. Had to be Ali. No matter how many times Harper told her she didn't need to, the woman often came with a tray of breakfast in the morning.

Harper stepped out of the bathroom and crossed the cabin. She didn't bother to change out of her cat nightgown or brush her hair. The woman had seen it all before.

She opened the door—and the ready smile for her landlord dropped from her face.

"Cody!"

He held the tray that Ali usually brought, his eyes narrowing slightly at the bruise on her temple before he covered the frown with a smile. "Good morning, Storm. I hope you don't mind, I intercepted the breakfast tray from Ali on my way here. If you're wondering how, I just dazzled her with my smile and wit."

She opened and closed her mouth. "I…I'm not changed."

His gaze shifted to her spaghetti-strap sleep shirt, which was so short he'd almost be able to see her ass when she turned.

Shit. Why couldn't she wear nana pajamas, with big baggy shirts and pants that reached past her ankles?

Discreetly, she tugged at the base of the gown.

When his eyes returned to her face, he tilted his head. "I like what you're wearing. But then, I have a feeling you'd look good in anything."

Oh, he was a charmer. "Even a paper bag?"

"Especially a paper bag." One side of his mouth lifted. "How about I get your breakfast ready while you shower and change?"

He was doing nothing to curb this super-sized crush she had on him. Hell, what was she talking about? It was way past a crush.

"Sure, but on one condition?"

"Anything."

"Share breakfast with me? I don't want to eat alone."

That tilt of his lips deepened. "How could I say no to that?"

She stepped back, and when Cody moved inside, she realized he took up all the space. He'd been in here last night, but she'd still been in shock from the attack. Now, he was all she could focus on. His broad shoulders. His tree-trunk arms.

She wet her lips as she closed the door. "I'll just go get changed."

"Take as long as you need," he replied, setting the tray on the counter.

Even though he wasn't looking at her, her skin tingled as if his eyes were glued to her body as she rushed to grab clothes and move to the bathroom. She took the quickest shower of her life before throwing on yoga pants and a T-shirt. When she stepped back into the room, the smell of eggs and bagels wafted through the small cabin.

"Ali stopped by while you were in the shower and delivered even more food," Cody said with a smile as he glanced up. "I guess I looked hungry, and she took pity on me."

Harper crossed the space between them, her gaze brushing over the eggs and bacon Cody had set out on the table.

"Cody…what are you doing here?" She hadn't meant to ask the question, the words just fell out.

He paused from where he was taking glasses from the overhead cabinets. When he turned, he looked at her with so much intensity that her lungs felt like they were decompressing. "I needed to check you were okay."

"I'm okay."

He stepped closer, and that one step ate up all the space between them. When his hands went to her hips, she felt his touch seep through her clothes and into her skin. "I'm just going to mention this one more time, and if you say no, I'll drop it…but know that the offer is always there."

She frowned but remained silent.

"The second room in my apartment over the bar has a lock on the door. It's comfortable. It even has some feminine touches, thanks to my sister. Plus…I'd feel better if you were there, with me."

He thought she should *live* with him? He was already in her head and all she thought about; imagine if she woke up to him every morning. Breathed in his deep, masculine scent every night…

"Cody, you don't need to do that."

"I know. I want to. I want you safe."

"It was probably just a crime of opportunity. I'm sure after seeing you, they won't be back."

He looked at her like he didn't believe her. Like he knew all her secrets, even the ones she kept locked deep inside her. "I like you, Harper. A lot. And I will be whatever you want me to be. The friend. The boss. The protector. I'll move as slow as you need, but I know—and I think you do too—that this always ends the same way."

She swallowed, and it took a few tries to get the question out. "And how's that?"

"You and me, together."

CHAPTER 10

*H*arper walked down the street toward Sugar and Spice. She should probably be consumed with thoughts of the attack a couple nights ago, oddly coinciding with the fact her father was out of prison. But she wasn't. Instead, all she could think about was Cody.

She nibbled her bottom lip. She'd rested yesterday and most of this morning, and she told Cody she'd be back at work this afternoon. Not that he'd liked that. The man had basically growled at her that she needed to take more time off, but she couldn't. Not with his bar being so understaffed. He was training another person this coming week, but even that wouldn't be enough.

And maybe there was also a small part of her that wanted to go to work because she wanted to spend the evening with Cody, even if it was just at the bar.

Okay, not a small part of her. A big, mammoth, couldn't-get-the-guy-out-of-her-head part.

Sweet dough scented the air before she'd even reached the store, making her speed up her steps. If Cody didn't already make her want to stay in Misty Peak, the cupcake he'd given her from Sugar and Spice would.

She stopped in front of the store, her gaze catching on the display of cupcakes through the glass. Oh God, as well as cupcakes there were glazed donuts and cookies and a million other amazing-looking baked treats. Maybe this wasn't a good idea, because Harper and sweets could be a dangerous, addictive combination.

The second she pushed inside, her mouth watered. If she thought it smelled good from the outside, that was nothing compared to inside the shop. And not only did it smell amazing, but the place was all fun pastel colors. There was a counter to the side and several tables for customers.

Her gaze caught on the coffee machine. Okay, this was definitely her favorite place on Earth.

She was so busy taking it all in, she almost missed the customer at the counter. Tilly. She had a wide smile on her face as she spoke to the older lady behind the counter. She looked nothing like the defeated woman who'd walked into the bar the other night.

"Darling, don't let the haters get to you," the older woman said, leaning forward. "Anyone with half a brain knows you have a good heart."

Tilly's smile softened. "Thank you, Mrs. Sandler." She glanced over her shoulder, her eyes widening. "Hi. Harper, right?"

"Hey. Yes. It's nice to see you again, Tilly."

"You too."

"This place is gorgeous." She once again took in the array of baked goods.

"You haven't been here before?" Tilly turned toward the older woman. "Then you haven't met Mrs. Sandler, the talent behind these delicious treats and the reason people visit Misty Peak. Mrs. Sandler, this is Harper, Cody's new bartender."

Mrs. Sandler's brows rose. "You work with Cody? That's

wonderful! I'd heard he needed some help at the bar. That boy takes on too much work."

"He's actually doing me a favor," Harper said, lifting a shoulder. "He gave me the job when I had no experience and I desperately needed one."

"He has good instincts. Well, except when he hired Travis and Dayne. I could have told him they were bad news." She shook her head. "Anyway, what can I get you, dear?"

Tilly leaned closer to Harper. "The Oreo with buttercream frosting is amazing."

Her mouth watered just at the description of the cupcake. "Yes. One of those, please. And a coffee in a to-go cup."

Mrs. Sandler nodded. "I'll make both your coffees now. Have a seat, ladies."

Harper settled at the closest table, and Tilly sat opposite her.

"You look happy," Harper said before she could think better of it.

"Mrs. Sandler has that effect on me. Plus, she's never held the sins of my family against me like other members of the community."

Harper frowned. She wanted to ask what those sins were, but there was no way she actually would. They didn't know each other well enough for that, and she knew better than anyone that family issues were complicated and sometimes best left unspoken.

"I'm sorry I was so down and out the other night," Tilly continued. "It was my first day back in town and it was rough."

"That's okay. If you don't mind me asking, why return if people aren't kind to you here?"

The corners of her mouth lifted, but the smile was almost sad. "A few reasons. I own a house that was left to me. Also, this is where I grew up, so more than any other place, it *feels* like home. Plus, I just got a job here. One I've wanted since I was a kid.

Although, it's not public knowledge yet, and I have a feeling when it is, not everyone will be happy."

No place had *ever* felt like home to Harper. Even when she'd moved out of her family house and into her own apartment, her mom and brother had still been too close and poisoned it by dropping by too often, demanding things from her. The cabin was probably the closest she'd ever had to a real home. And wasn't that sad…

"I hope people come around."

"Me too."

The door to the shop opened, and Harper internally groaned at the sight of Vanessa. As usual, the woman looked impeccable, with her three-inch heels, perfect makeup, and skintight jeans. But even though Harper barely knew her, from what she'd seen, the woman didn't seem so perfect on the inside. How could she be when she'd cheated on a man like Cody?

Her eyes narrowed when they fell on Harper, but that was nothing compared to when she looked at Tilly. The anger was so evident, Harper could almost feel it.

"What are *you* doing here?" Vanessa growled.

There was a flicker of uncertainty in Tilly's eyes before she straightened in her seat, her features hardening like she was preparing for battle. "I've moved back."

"For good?" Vanessa's jaw dropped like it was the most shocking piece of information she'd ever heard. "Why? Because you want to steal even more from the hardworking people of Misty Peak? Because your family hasn't taken enough? Should I just take off my diamond ring and hand it to you now?"

"Vanessa!" It was Mrs. Sandler who spoke, her voice completely devoid of the gentleness of a few minutes ago. "Tilly never took anything from anyone. I'm almost finished with their orders and will be with you soon, but if you can't be polite, you need to leave."

Vanessa's lips pressed into a hard line, but she remained silent.

"Tilly, your iced coffee is ready," Mrs. Sandler said, her tone softer.

Tilly gave Harper a small smile, but it was strained and didn't quite reach her eyes. "I'll see you around."

Harper nodded, then the woman paid and collected her drink before leaving the store. Vanessa watched her the entire time as well, eyes digging arrows into Tilly's back.

God, what was wrong with that woman? Anyone could see that Tilly was a kind person. Maybe Harper didn't know the background of what had happened before she left town, but whatever it was, she was certain Tilly wasn't at fault.

When the door closed behind Tilly, Vanessa took out her phone and moved to stand at the counter.

Harper probably should have kept her mouth shut, but the quietly spoken words just tumbled out. "You know, it doesn't cost anything to be kind."

Vanessa snort-laughed, gaze remaining on her phone. "You just got here, what the hell would *you* know?"

"I know enough."

Finally, Vanessa looked down at her, one perfectly shaped brow raised. "You don't, actually." Her words were low, only reaching Harper's ears. "I bet you don't know that you're the rebound. Cody and I didn't break up that long ago, and when I say his heart was broken, I'm not exaggerating. He was *crushed* when I left him."

"Cheated. When you *cheated* on him," Harper corrected.

Her brows slashed together. "A rebound never lasts, because in the end, he'll always want what he can't have—*me*. And you? Well, you'll probably end up back wherever it is you came from. Where was that again?"

She shouldn't let the woman's words affect her. Still, they trickled through her carefully constructed walls and straight into her heart…because wasn't that her greatest fear? That she *would* end up back in the clutches of her family, and someone like Cody wouldn't stick around for someone as simple as her?

"Coffee and cupcake are ready, Harper."

At Mrs. Sandler's words, she forced herself to her feet, paying and thanking the older woman before stepping outside.

Vanessa's words were still rolling around in her head when she looked up and spotted Cody, Eastern, and a young child just down the street.

* * *

"UNCLE CODY, how old do I need to be before I can work at your bar?"

Cody bit back a laugh at Eastern's growl.

"Fifty," Eastern replied before Cody could.

Avery frowned. "Fifty? Uncle Cody isn't even fifty."

"Doesn't matter. They're my rules."

Cody shook his head. "The legal requirement is twenty-one."

Avery's little shoulders sagged. "That's *forever* away!"

"Why do you want to work at the bar?" Eastern asked.

"So I can save up for my snake and cookies."

Cody frowned. He knew the kid loved Mrs. Sandler's cookies, but a snake? "You want a snake? Like as a pet?"

"Yep." She nodded, her blond curls bouncing. "I want a red one with black bands, but Daddy says they cost a lot of money."

He looked at his brother. Bullshit. The snake wouldn't be that expensive, and even if the enclosure and everything needed to care for the snake was, his brother had money. He just didn't want one—and Cody knew why. Eastern may be a tough former Navy SEAL-turned-town sheriff, but he was deathly afraid of snakes.

"I know!" Avery just about shouted before Cody or Eastern

could get a word in. "I'll get a job at Sugar and Spice! I'm good at baking cupcakes and cookies. Sadie taught me."

Sadie had been Avery's nanny since she was a baby, while Avery was living with her mother. But when Sadie's partner had gotten a job in Atlanta, she'd moved with him. Cody hadn't known the woman very well, but he knew Avery loved her. Sadie was also Mrs. Sandler's granddaughter.

"You can ask Mrs. Sandler now," Cody suggested, receiving a hard look from Eastern.

They were nearing Sugar and Spice when the door opened, and Harper stepped out. Just like every other time he saw the woman, she made him feel like he'd been sucker punched, stealing every scrap of air in his chest.

"Who's that, Uncle Cody?" Avery whispered a bit too loudly. "She's looking right at you."

"Yeah, Uncle Cody," Eastern mimicked. "Who's that?"

"That," Cody said quietly as they closed the distance, "is Harper."

They stopped in front of her.

"Hey," she said as her gaze shifted between his eyes. "How are you?"

A hell of a lot better now. "Good. We're just heading to Sugar and Spice. You know my brother, Eastern, and this is his daughter, my niece, Avery."

"You're pretty," Avery announced.

Harper chuckled and crouched so she was on Avery's level. "Thank you. So are you. I love your curls. I've always wanted curly hair."

Avery beamed. "Thank you. Daddy says I have Grandma's hair."

It was true. Avery looked exactly like their mother.

"It's beautiful." Harper tilted her head. "Hey, I'm new in town. Could you tell me what the best cupcake is at Sugar and Spice?"

Avery's nose wrinkled. "Caramel popcorn. But I like the cookies. Mrs. Sandler has a triple fudge chocolate cookie that's my favorite. I'm not allowed to have it all the time because Daddy says the chocolate keeps me up all night."

Harper's grin was wide and radiant. "I think it would keep me up too. I'll try the caramel popcorn next time."

"Tell me if you like it!"

"I definitely will." When Harper rose, her gaze met Cody's again. "I'll see you later."

Avery yanked on Cody's arm. "Uncle Cody can walk with you. He always says it's safer to have company."

Harper's brows shot up. "Oh, that's okay. You guys were about to go into the shop, and I don't want to take him away from you."

"I don't mind," Avery said. "Uncle Cody can take me to Sugar and Spice tomorrow."

The sneaky kid. Any excuse for an extra visit to the bakery.

He ruffled Avery's hair before looking up at Harper. "I'll walk you to your car."

A frown creased her brow, and for a moment he thought she'd say no. Then she nodded. "Okay. I'd like that."

Cody gave Avery a hug before saying goodbye to his brother.

When he walked beside Harper, all he could smell was her sweet floral scent. "How have you been?"

"Since yesterday?" She grinned at him.

Yesterday being the day he'd gone to her cabin and basically begged her to take the spare room in his apartment. She'd said no, and he'd wanted to push. To tell her he knew about her father. That she needed some kind of protection.

Eastern had taken the call after her attack. She probably knew he would've looked into her background for any potential leads, would've learned about her father...but she hadn't said anything.

Maybe she didn't think it was information he'd share with Cody. But that news report Eastern had found—and the arrest— were matters of public record. He could ask her about her father. If she thought he was a potential threat.

No. He wanted her to bring it up on *her* terms. For her to trust him enough to talk about her family.

"Yeah, since yesterday," he finally answered.

"Good. I ate, slept, and watched *Seinfeld* reruns."

"You're a *Seinfeld* fan?"

"Oh, yeah. Kramer will always hold a special place in my heart."

Cody laughed. "I like Elaine and Puddy. Their relationship was so dysfunctional you couldn't look away."

Harper grinned. "Dysfunctional is definitely the right word for what they had." She handed him the paper bag in her hand. "Here, share with me."

"You're giving me part of your cupcake?"

"No, I'm *forcing* you to have *half* so that I don't eat the entire thing."

He took the bag and pulled off a chunk of the cupcake before popping it into his mouth. Then he groaned. "God, Mrs. Sandler makes a good cupcake."

"She does." There was a small pause. "I ran into Vanessa earlier." Then she cringed like she hadn't meant to let that slip.

Cody stopped and faced her. "What did she say?"

"How do you know she said something?"

"Harper…"

"Okay. She said that you're on the rebound."

He laughed, even though there was nothing remotely funny about it. "I'm not. I was actually on the verge of ending the relationship when she cheated on me. The only reason I hadn't already was because I had so much going on with my dad."

She nodded, her bottom lip disappearing between her teeth. Did she not believe him?

He stepped closer. "Harper, I dated Vanessa for just a couple of months. And the way I felt about her was *nothing* compared to what I feel for you."

She swallowed. "Really?"

"Yeah, Storm. You have me captivated. You have me thinking about you, and literally nothing else, all the time."

"But Vanessa's so beautiful."

Again, he could have laughed. Did she really not see what he saw?

He lowered his head. "No. *You're* beautiful." Then he kissed her, right there in the middle of the street, not caring who saw.

CHAPTER 11

Harper pulled up outside the cabin and leaned back against the headrest, just a hint of a smile curving her lips. Every time she'd glanced at Cody tonight at the bar, his gaze had collided with hers, like he felt her watching him. Was that possible?

A knock on the window had her gasping and looking up to see Ali standing on the other side of the glass.

The air whooshed from her chest as she grabbed her bag and climbed out. "Ali, hi. Sorry if I woke you by pulling in so late." Her house was half a mile down the road, so she shouldn't have, but she always felt guilty about driving by so late.

Ali shook her head. "Oh, no dear, you didn't wake me. I've been up for a while. I just came to tell you that the fire department left less than an hour ago. Do you remember that firebug I mentioned your first night here?"

She nodded.

"They set a stack of wood alight up here earlier today."

Harper's eyes widened. "Oh my gosh, are you okay?"

"Yes. I'd just gotten home from the store and called the fire department right away. All is fine. I just didn't want you to smell the smoke and worry."

Now that Ali mentioned it, the scent of smoke did tinge the air. "Thank you for letting me know."

"Of course. Everything okay with the cabin?"

"It's great. Although, I noticed you returned some of the money I left in your mailbox for rent."

"Because you left too much."

She shook her head. "No, I left—"

"Too much." She reached out and closed her hands around Harper's. "Dear, I don't run these cabins for the money. I run them to help my community. And you're part of that community now. I'll see you in the morning."

Harper's throat tightened as the woman walked away.

Community. She was being included in the Misty Peak community, something she never expected a few weeks ago.

After locking her car, she headed into the cabin. Immediately, that familiar calm swept over her. There was just something so comfortable about this place. Of course, it wasn't the white-picket-fence home she'd always dreamed about, but it was as close as she'd gotten so far.

She entered the bathroom and quickly stripped off her clothes before stepping into the shower. The warm water ran over her cool skin. Although, nothing warmed her like Cody's touch. Like his lips on hers. His breath on her skin.

She groaned as she tilted her head back, letting the water wash over her face.

When her phone vibrated from the bathroom counter, she turned off the water and stepped out to wrap a towel around her body before lifting her cell.

Cody: Did you get home okay? I heard there was a fire near Ali's Cabins.

The familiar tingle trickled over her skin.

Harper: There was, but it was taken care of. There's smoke in the air but it's not too bad. How did you hear about it?

Cody: Eastern texted me.

Of course he did. It paid to have a family member in law enforcement.

Cody: I'm glad you're okay. Get some rest.

Her heart thumped, and even after turning off all the lights and slipping into bed, Cody was still on her mind.

She was at the in-between-awake-and-asleep stage when something pulled her back to consciousness. What, exactly, she wasn't sure. A sound from outside? An animal?

She was just closing her eyes when she heard something again, this time louder. She shot into a sitting position. It wasn't just the noise that had her frowning. It was the strange light streaming through the curtains at the front of the cabin.

Then the smell of smoke that slipped into the room, thicker than when she'd gotten home.

What the hell?

Quickly, she climbed out of bed and moved to the window. The second she pulled the curtain back, her heart stopped.

Oh God…her car. It was on fire.

* * *

"You're saying she still hasn't made contact? Not even with Avery?"

"Nope," Eastern said, answering Cody's question as he lifted a glass of water to his mouth. "And I'm so mad at her that I can barely breathe most days. But Avery seems to be okay. And my neighbor, Mrs. Hanley, has been a lifesaver, taking up the job as her nanny and caring for her when she's not in school and I'm working."

Cody shook his head. The bar had closed about an hour ago, and he was having a drink with his brothers before Eastern started his night shift. He tried not to take too many of those, owing to his daughter, only when the office was desperate.

Cody was so damn angry at Eastern's ex. The woman had always seemed selfish, but this was a whole new level.

"Remember, you have us," Kayden said quietly. "I'll look after my favorite niece anytime you need."

Eastern grasped Kayden's shoulder. "Thank you, brother."

Cody sipped his beer. "Have you seen Matilda Taylor's back in town?"

Kayden's eyes narrowed. "What do you mean, she's back?"

"She came in here the other night. Didn't look happy, either."

Kayden scowled. "Of course not. After what her father did, and the way she and her mother skipped out of town so soon after. She should have stayed away."

Cody shared a look with Eastern. Out of all of his siblings, Kayden, the eldest, saw everything in black and white.

Eastern cleared his throat. "I think the key to what you just said is *what her father did*."

Kayden cocked his head. "You're telling me you think she didn't know? That she's had no contact with him since he robbed half the town?"

"I'm saying we don't choose our parents, and *their* crimes shouldn't become *ours*," Eastern explained, drawing his water to his lips.

"Yeah," Cody agreed. "And she might be different than her dad. Hell, the five of us are different from each other. Look at me, I'm chilled out and good-looking, while you two are neither of those things."

Kayden scoffed. "You forgot delusional."

"What's going on with you and Harper?" Eastern asked.

"Not nearly as much as I wish." His fingers tightened around the bottle. "I've been honest with her about my feelings, but she's hesitant. She doesn't seem to want to let me in or tell me about her family or what she's running from."

"Have you told her you know about her dad?" Eastern asked.

"No. And I don't know if that's the right decision or not, but I keep hoping she'll open up to me when she's ready."

Kayden lifted a shoulder. "Maybe she won't ever get there."

A vein throbbed in Cody's temple at that thought.

He was just lifting his beer again when Eastern's cell rang.

"Eastern speaking." There was a beat of silence, then his brother straightened, his gaze shifting to Cody. "Be right there." He hung up. "The firebug struck again."

"Twice in one day?" Cody growled.

"Yes—and this time they set Harper's car on fire."

Every muscle in Cody's body tightened. "*What the fuck?* Is she okay?"

"She's okay."

"I'll lock up for you," Kayden said quickly. "Go."

Cody grabbed his keys and strode straight to the door. The drive to Harper's cabin was a blur; she was all he could think about.

Was she scared? Was she *hurt*? Had the fire been set while she was sleeping?

A fire truck and firefighters crowded the open space outside her cabin. Once out of the car, it took him a moment to find her, and when he did, she was all he saw.

Her eyes were wide and her face pale. She stood beside Ali, who had an arm around her shoulders.

Harper frowned at him. "Cody?"

Without a word, he pulled her into his arms. He wasn't sure if he expected her to pull away or go rigid. She did neither of those things. She leaned into him, like she needed his touch as much as he needed to touch her.

When he pulled back, he cupped her cheeks and studied her face. "Are you okay?"

Eastern came to stand beside him.

She nodded quickly. "I woke when I heard something outside.

When I looked out the window, I saw the flames. I called the fire department, then Ali. I never saw anyone."

"You're safe. That's the important part."

Ali sighed. "I can't believe there've been two fires here in the same day." She looked at Harper. "I'm so sorry about your car, Harper."

Worry flitted across Harper's face, but she blinked like she was trying to keep the emotion at bay. "It's not your fault."

The next half hour was a mix of firefighters finishing their jobs and Eastern's team searching the area for any evidence of the culprit. When they were finally done, no words were shared as Cody followed Harper back into her cabin. It wasn't until the door was closed that she finally turned, arms wrapped tight around her waist.

"You don't have to stay," she said quietly.

"Well, I'd prefer you come stay with *me*. But if not, I'd like to sleep on your couch. It would be more for me than you. I won't sleep unless I know you're safe."

She opened and closed her mouth, but no words came out. He wasn't sure if it was the shock or that she really didn't have words.

He stepped closer. "You don't have to be brave anymore. You're safe to fall apart with me."

"My car was all I had." Tears gathered in her eyes. "I know that sounds stupid and shallow, but I left everything behind. My apartment, most of my clothes, all my stuff."

He gripped her hips. "Hey. The car wasn't all you had. You have *me*. You have this town and the community that comes with it."

She shook her head. "What if I need to run again? Now I have no way to do that!"

It was the first time she'd admitted that coming here was the result of her running. And the idea of her running again, but away from him this time, hurt so much it was an effort to keep the pain off his face. "We don't need to think about that right now. One day at a time. For now, you need sleep. I'll sleep on your couch and tomorrow we'll figure out how to move forward. Okay?"

She shook her head. "You don't have to do that."

"I do. I need to be close to you. Please let me have that."

The second of silence was heavy and beat into his chest. Then, finally, she nodded. "Okay. Thank you."

Thank fuck. He pulled her against him, all too aware of just how natural it felt to hold her. Like breathing. Also aware of the fact he didn't want to let her go.

CHAPTER 12

$\mathcal{C}$ody pushed a bottle of beer across the bar before taking the cash and putting it in the register. Every muscle in his body was tense, and his gaze continued to return to Harper. She moved around the room, lifting dirty glasses from tables. After waking up this morning, he'd made them breakfast in her cabin and tried again to convince her to move in with him. But no matter how hard he pushed, Harper just pushed back.

"Clench the bar any harder and you'll break the damn thing."

Cody dragged his gaze from Harper to Barry beside him.

Barry raised a brow. "Wanna talk about it?"

"Someone set her car on fire last night."

He nodded. "They did."

"And before that, she was attacked in the alley of this bar."

"She was."

"And now, she refuses to move into the spare bedroom in my apartment."

"Key word there—*your* apartment."

Cody's eyes narrowed. "Yeah, so? It's for her safety."

"Son, I may be an old man, but even I can see that woman's been hurt, and hurt people need slow. She needs time to trust.

Moving in with her boss, a man she basically just met, is not slow."

"I'm hardly a stranger. And I told you, it's for her safety. I wouldn't forgive myself if something happened and I could have protected her."

Barry leaned closer. "Then don't drive her away by pushing so hard."

Cody rolled his eyes as he moved to the next customer. "Hey, what can I—" He stopped when he saw the guy. "What are you doing here, Miles?"

His high school best friend swallowed, shifting on the stool uncomfortably. "Just here to get a drink. Is that okay?"

No. It sure as hell wasn't. He was already in a dark damn mood, he didn't want to serve the man who'd slept with his girl-friend. The man Cody had once considered a close friend.

Curse of being the only damn bar in town.

"One drink," Cody said through gritted teeth, knowing he was showing more mercy than he should. "What do you want?"

Disappointment flashed over Miles's face. "Any stout is fine."

Cody grabbed a glass and pushed it against the tap.

Miles cleared his throat as he leaned forward. "Look, Cody, we were friends once. I know what happened hurt that friend-ship, but with you moving on with Harper, I thought maybe—"

"First of all," Cody cut in, voice sharp, "Harper is not your business. Second, even if I were moving on with someone else, it doesn't change what you did—or the *timing* of when you did it."

"I know, but—"

"There is no *but*. Loyalty's important to me, something you're very aware of, Miles. And having *sex* with my *girlfriend* while my father was dying was not *loyal*. It's also not a friendship I'm inter-ested in mending." He pushed the beer in front of Miles and grabbed the money he left on the counter. "One beer, then you need to go and don't come back."

Miles scrubbed a hand over his face. "Okay, yeah. Sure."

When Cody saw Harper slip into the kitchen, he stepped away from Miles to follow. He stopped at the open door as she moved into the storage room.

"Stop calling me!" Harper's hushed tone just reached Cody. He inched forward. "I don't care. I don't want anything to do with you, Mom, *or* Dad. All you've ever done is make my life hell. I'm finally free of you, and you need to let it stay that way!" She hung up and turned, her face paling when she saw Cody standing behind her. "What are you doing back here?"

"I saw you come back. I wanted to make sure you're okay."

"I'm okay. It's just...my family. They're complicated." Her voice lowered. "They're not like yours."

He raised his brows. "Like mine?"

"I didn't grow up with parents who wanted the best for me or siblings who protected me."

He reached out and gripped her hips, tugging her into him. "What did you grow up with?"

Her chest rose on a deep inhale, her lips parting, and for a moment he thought she was going to tell him something important. Something that explained a bit about what she'd been running from. Then she stepped back, causing his hands to fall.

"I should get back out there."

Cody ran frustrated fingers through his hair, waiting a beat before following. He spotted Kayden at the bar and was about to move over to him when something across the room caught his attention.

Harper, trying to step past a guy—until his arm wrapped around her waist, tugging her into him.

What the *fuck*?

It was the last damn straw on his already shitty mood.

He rounded the bar and shifted through the crowd until he was in front of the asshole who held Harper's waist, shoving him hard in the chest. "What the hell are you doing?"

The man stumbled back, releasing her. Cody didn't recognize

the guy. Maybe a tourist from out of town. They got a lot of them here.

He had the balls to smile at Cody. Actually fucking *smile*. "We were just talking. I was asking this pretty lady if she's local."

Cody stepped so close, he could see the fucking pores on the asshole's face. "Even if that was your business, which it isn't, you don't grab a woman around the waist just so you can *talk* to her."

There was a small pause.

Harper touched his arm. "Cody, he's drunk."

"I don't care." Cody stared the guy down. "No one touches her."

The man raised a brow. "Really? So what if I do this?"

He reached around Cody toward Harper.

In one swift move, he grabbed the guy's wrist and twisted, pushing the asshole so he was bent over a table, his arm pinned with Cody at his back.

"Get the fuck off me!"

Cody lowered his head and quieted his voice. "You don't wanna play that game with me. I will fucking destroy you. Understand?"

The guy struggled and growled beneath Cody.

"Cody."

He ignored Kayden's voice, pulled the guy's arm higher, and this time when he spoke, he was louder. "Do you understand?"

"Yes! Yes, okay, I understand!"

"Good." Cody shoved him into the table before rising. "Now get out."

He waited until the guy rose and staggered from the bar before turning to face Harper. "Are you okay?"

She nodded quickly.

He studied her eyes, which were too wide, and face, which was too pale. She wasn't okay.

Gently, he placed a hand on the small of her back. "Come on."

He led her back to the bar, not caring that dozens of fucking eyes were on him.

* * *

HARPER WAS quiet as she wiped down the bar. The night was almost over and there were only a handful of customers remaining, most of whom Barry was taking care of. Cody had barely said a word since that guy had touched her. Well, since he'd pulled her into his office afterward to check if she was okay, and she'd just repeated that she was. She got the feeling he'd wanted more from her, but she wasn't a big sharer at the best of times.

She nibbled her bottom lip as she watched him behind the bar. He was so tense, his usual relaxed expression nowhere to be seen.

She was pretty sure this wasn't just about the guy who'd touched her, because even at the start of the night he'd been…off.

Her phone vibrated from her pocket, and she cringed, not sure if it would be her brother again. She had no idea why he was still calling her. He'd told her about their father. She had nothing for them. Why couldn't he just leave her alone?

She pulled out her cell to see it was Tilly. The woman had come in earlier and they'd exchanged numbers.

Tilly: What do you do when you can't sleep? Alcohol? Tylenol?

Harper laughed, and damn it felt good.

Harper: Well, for me, I find falling asleep to a book or a TV show on my phone does the trick.

Tilly: You're a good influence on me. Wanna meet for coffee tomorrow at Sugar and Spice?

Harper: I'd love that. Ten?

Tilly: Perfect. See you then. Message if you need a lift.

A lift…because her car was gone. She groaned. It was insured, but these things took time to process, and even when she received the money, she'd still have to source and buy a new car.

She shoved her phone into her pocket and moved across to Cody. "Anything you need me to do before close?"

"Could you just make sure the tables are clean?" His gaze didn't rise as he spoke. Then he moved past her into the office.

All right, that was it. She was done with the attitude.

She crossed the room to Barry. "Are you okay looking after the bar on your own for a couple of minutes?"

He looked up, his eyes moving to the office, then back to Harper. "Yeah. You go talk some sense into the grump."

That got a small smile out of her. "I'll try."

In the office, she found Cody facing the filing cabinets on one side of the room, his brows tugging together.

"Everything okay?" he asked without looking up.

"Funny, I was about to ask you the same question." She stepped farther into the room.

"I'm fine."

He went to move around her, but she stepped to the side, cutting him off. "You're lying. You're not fine."

He blew out a long breath. "What I'm not fine with is some out-of-towner wrapping his arm around you like he did tonight. What I'm not *fine* with is all the damn attacks you've had since getting to Misty Peak."

"Cody, tonight was some drunk idiot who grabbed me. A hazard of working in a bar. And each time before tonight, I've come out relatively unscathed."

He stepped forward, basically towering over her. "I don't like it."

"Me neither. But your brother and his deputies are looking into the incidents, and I don't think that guy tonight will be back."

"Move in with me."

She internally groaned. How many times had he asked that already? This morning, he'd asked her at least half a dozen times. "Cody, I told you I can't do that."

"You can. You just don't want to. Why not?"

"Because we're new and…I don't know. Are we even a thing?"

He laughed, and the sound was a little bitter. "We're definitely a *thing*. At least *I* think so. But…do you feel for me what I feel for you?"

Her lips parted, her heart wanting to give one answer, her head another. "Cody…"

His hands trailed up her waist. "It's an easy question, Harper. Do you feel for *me*, what I feel for *you*? Because I really like you. To the point you take up all my thoughts, even while I sleep."

She swallowed, a big-gulp kind of swallow. "You barely know me. If I told you the truth about me and the life I grew up in, it could change things."

"It would change *everything*…but not in the way you think."

He thought revealing her darkest secrets would change things between them for the better? That idea was as crazy to her as telling her the sun was purple.

When she remained silent, he sighed and dropped his hands, trying to step around her again.

She grabbed him and pulled his head down, plastering her mouth to his.

Immediately, he tugged her closer, his hard chest pressing against her soft. She moaned when he took over the kiss. Suddenly, she was turning, Cody lifting her onto the desk, then standing between her thighs. When her lips separated, his tongue slipped inside her mouth.

God, he tasted good. Like cinnamon and whiskey. The taste of him in combination with his hands sliding up her sides was an onslaught of sensations. A complete annihilation of the world around her.

She wrapped her legs around his waist, her fingers sliding into his hair, pulling and tugging.

When his hand slipped beneath her top and skimmed up her

side, taking the shirt with it, her breathing stopped. Then he cupped a hand over her bra and palmed her breast.

She groaned deep in her throat as wave upon wave of need and desire rippled from her chest to her core. Cody's hand on her was like a bolt of electricity. And she wanted more...so much more.

Her bra cup was tugged down and suddenly he was palming bare skin, his thumb finding her nipple and gliding over it in a circular motion. She'd thought that was it, that was all she could take, but then his head dipped, and his lips closed over her nipple.

She threw her head back and whimpered, her fingers sliding through the soft locks of his hair as her hips ground against him.

His other hand was just trailing up her inner thigh beneath her skirt when a knock came at the door.

She gasped and straightened.

Cody was slower to move, his head lifting as he carefully slipped her bra into place before pulling her top down. Then his mouth went to her ear, his breath brushing against her skin as he whispered, "This is just the beginning, Storm."

CHAPTER 13

"Uncle Cody, can I ask you a question?"

Cody's lips twitched. He'd picked Avery up from school today and she was helping out before opening by folding napkins, while he got things ready behind the bar. He'd already answered a hundred and one questions, everything from his favorite color to why he didn't have any kids.

"Yeah, Avery?"

"When you and Daddy were growing up, who was bigger?"

Finally, an easy question. "Well, your dad was the fourth born, and I was the third, so me. It worked well because it meant kicking his butt was easy."

"Really? Daddy said he could beat you with his pinky."

Cody threw his head back and laughed. Of course he did. "Maybe one day we'll put him to the test."

"Auntie Nylah always said she could beat up her brothers, but I don't know if I believe her. She's a lot smaller than you and Daddy."

"Auntie Nylah may be a shorty compared to her brothers, but don't let that fool you. She's a tough nut." She'd had to be, growing up with all of them. Hell, he and his brothers were often scared of the woman when she got mad.

"Do you think I'll get a brother or sister one day?"

He paused what he was doing, his gaze rising to his niece. "I'm not sure, Avery. But I do know that you'll always have four overprotective uncles and a badass auntie whenever you need us. Not to mention your dad."

She frowned. Because he didn't mention her mother?

He crossed the room and sat opposite her. "I'm sorry your mom's not here."

Her gaze rose, and in that moment, she looked so much wiser than her eight years. "Even when she *was* here, it kind of felt like she wasn't. Honestly, I miss Sadie more than I miss Mom."

Cody frowned. "Sadie left to get married, right?"

Avery nodded. "Yeah. She's engaged to Scott, and he had to move to Atlanta for his job. But she stopped looking after me even before she left to get married. I think Mom didn't like her. Or maybe Scott didn't like her working for Mom." Her nose wrinkled at the other man's name.

"You didn't like Scott?" Cody had seen the guy but never met him.

She lifted a shoulder. "He was okay. I just thought she could've done better."

Very astute words from a very little person. "I'm sure she'll come visit, especially because her grandmother lives here."

"I hope so. Mrs. Hanley next door is nice, but she's not Sadie." Avery glanced up, mischief suddenly in her eyes. "I like Harper."

Interesting change of topic. "I like Harper too."

"If you marry her, will she be my auntie?"

He laughed. "Yeah, she would, but let's not mention that around her."

"Why not?"

How did he explain to an eight-year-old that some people

scared more easily than others? "Because I need to convince Harper I'm the right guy for her first."

"Mrs. Hanley said women fall all over themselves for Daddy and his brothers."

Well, Mrs. Hanley just became his new favorite person. "I don't know if I believe that, but if it's true, then I've found the one woman who doesn't."

The bar door opened and the second Eastern walked in, Avery's eyes lit up. "Daddy!"

She ran straight into his arms, and he threw her into the air before hugging her. "Hey, princess, you have a good time with Uncle Cody?"

"Yes, he let me fold napkins and eat pretzels."

"Pretzels?"

"Mm-hmm, and he let me drink apple and orange juice mixed together."

Cody rose from the table, grabbing the folded napkins. "We went a bit crazy."

"I'm glad you had fun." Eastern met Cody's gaze. "Thank you."

"Anytime, you know that."

The two of them stayed for a few more minutes, chatting—well, mostly Avery talking—before Cody waved them goodbye. He was stacking the napkins behind the bar when the door opened again. "Forget some—"

He stopped at the sight of a tear-stained Vanessa standing just inside the bar.

Cody frowned. "What are you doing here?"

She crossed the space between them, the tears freely rolling down her cheeks. "Miles and I had a bad fight, and I just…I didn't know where to go."

"Vanessa, you shouldn't be here. You and Miles are not my business."

She didn't stop. She rounded the counter and stopped right in front of him. "You don't understand. The things he said…they were awful! Then he grabbed me. And he…he *hurt* me."

Cody's brows tugged together. "He hurt you?"

Was that even possible? He'd known Miles for a long time, and he didn't think the man was capable of hurting anyone physically, especially a woman. But then…he hadn't thought his best friend was capable of sleeping with his girlfriend either, and he'd done that.

She tugged up the sleeve of her shirt, revealing bruises in the shape of fingerprints on her wrists. "He…he wouldn't let me go. He was so *angry*." Her breaths shortened until she was almost hyperventilating.

Cody ran his fingers through his hair, not wanting to believe it, but the evidence was right there…clearly *someone* had touched her.

When her breathing became more ragged, he forced his voice to gentle. "Vanessa, breathe."

Her chest rose on a deep inhale.

"I'm going to call Eastern and—"

"No!" She cut him off and shook her head vigorously. "I don't want police involved. Definitely not the sheriff. I just…I needed to be with someone who made me feel safe."

She stepped toward him, but he stepped back. "We're not together anymore, Vanessa. I can't keep saving you."

"Cody…"

She stepped forward just as the bar door opened and Barry stepped in. He stopped a few feet inside. "Am I interrupting something?"

"No," Cody answered firmly before Vanessa could speak. "You need to go, Vanessa. And I encourage you to call Eastern at the office if you need help."

* * *

HARPER MASSAGED her temple between customers. God, her head hurt. She wasn't even sure why—she'd just woken up feeling off today. Lightheaded, a bit nauseous. She probably should have stayed home and rested, but the new guy Cody was supposed to train had ghosted him, not showing up for his shift.

"Hey."

She jumped at the feel of Cody's hand on the small of her back. Man, that was how out of it she was, surprised by a single touch in a busy bar.

His brows flickered. "Are you okay?"

"Yeah, just a headache."

Concern laced his features. "Do you need to finish early?"

"No, I'll push through."

She started to walk past him, but his fingers slipped around her wrist. She turned to see he was close. Really close.

He lowered his head. "I don't want you working while you're not feeling good."

"I'm okay, Cody."

Before he could respond, she stepped out of his grasp, grabbed a tray, and moved to the floor. Her mind shifted back to the previous night. To the drunk guy who'd grabbed her.

Immediately, she glanced around. Even though it was a small town, and most locals were wonderful, they got a lot of tourists who came for the Smoky Mountains, so most weeks there were new faces in the bar. Tonight, she didn't see anyone unfamiliar.

She lifted an empty glass and placed it on the tray, but the second she stepped away from the table, a wave of dizziness washed over her and she stumbled. The glass fell from the tray and shattered on the floor.

Shit.

She blinked three times to clear her vision before lowering to the floor to clean up the mess, lifting the largest shard. When she went for another, it sliced her finger. Crap! She really was out of it tonight.

Suddenly, a big body lowered beside her. Cody's gaze fell on her hand. He cursed and lifted it. "You cut yourself."

"It's small. I'm fine." Together, they gathered the remaining pieces. Cody grabbed the tray and rose, placing his free hand on her elbow.

While Cody went to ask Barry to sweep the area where the glass had dropped, Harper went into the kitchen and grabbed the first aid kit. She hadn't even gotten it open before Cody was beside her.

She sighed. "Cody, I can do it."

He didn't respond, just opened the kit and pulled out a Band-Aid. Then, gently, he cleaned and covered the small cut.

"You're not yourself," he said quietly. "Is it the headache, or did Barry mention that Vanessa was here?"

She frowned, the ache in her head intensifying. "Vanessa was here?"

"Yeah. Only for a couple of minutes before I sent her away. She was upset."

And she'd run straight to Cody. Not a surprise. "Barry didn't say anything."

"So the headache's that bad."

"I'm just not feeling well."

He touched her forehead, the frown between his eyes deepening. "You're hot."

"I'll finish the shift and go home."

"Harper—"

"We're busy, Cody. You need the extra hands. I'll finish, then rest when I get home."

"We can manage without you."

She shook her head, stepping away. "I'm finishing my shift. I won't drop any more glasses, I promise."

The hard set of his jaw was the last thing she saw before she turned and walked away.

For the next couple of hours, she pushed her body to keep

moving. But every minute that passed had the ache in her head intensifying and the exhaustion in her limbs deepening. It was almost closing time when Barry pushed a glass of water into her hand.

"Drink. You look like you could use it."

Her gaze softened as she accepted the beverage. "Thank you."

She sipped the water, feeling Cody's intense gaze on her. He'd been watching her all night. Did she look as bad as she felt?

The last few customers were trickling out when Harper went to the office to check her phone. The screen blurred in front of her. At the creak of the door opening, her gaze shot up, but that quick change in focus had her world spinning.

She grabbed the wall to steady herself.

"Harper? Shit! You're not okay."

His voice sounded like it came to her through a tunnel. "I…I think I need to lie down."

The words were barely out of her mouth before she was falling. The last thing she saw was Cody lunging toward her before her world went dark.

CHAPTER 14

*V*oices sounded around Harper. They were hushed, one deep and familiar. Cody. The other she'd never heard before, but it was a woman.

"She has a fever, probably the flu that's been going around town."

The flu…was the woman talking about *her*? Was she a doctor?

"What can I do?" Cody sounded so worried.

She itched to reach out and touch him. Assure him she was okay. But her limbs felt heavy, her body so exhausted that even the thought of moving made her want to fall back into a deep sleep.

"I've given her some pain meds for the headache, which will also help her sleep. Make sure she stays hydrated. You can give her some Tylenol when she wakes up, but what she really needs is rest."

Retreating footsteps sounded, and the voices became muffled. She let exhaustion pull her under. It was only when a warm hand cupped the back of her head that she came around again.

"Storm, can you hear me? I've got a straw for you. I need you to drink some water." She parted her lips and sipped some cool liquid before Cody eased her head back to the pillow. Then he cupped her cheek, and she leaned into the touch. "You scared me."

She peeled her eyes open a fraction. Cody was a blur in front of her, but she didn't need to see him clearly to feel his concern. She didn't know where she was or what time it could be, but it didn't matter. With Cody, she felt safe.

"Stay with me," she whispered.

Her eyes fluttered shut, and the silence stretched so long she wasn't sure if he planned to stay or go. Then the bed dipped beside her, and warmth cloaked her. She snuggled into the heated body, letting it lull her back to sleep.

* * *

HARPER WOKE SLOWLY, the sunlight hitting her closed eyelids. There was still a dull ache in the back of her head and her limbs felt heavy, but when she opened her eyes, she didn't feel the need to slam them closed again.

She frowned. What time was it? From the sunlight streaming into the room, it was obviously daytime, but how many hours had passed? And where was she?

Her gaze moved around the small bedroom. She would have assumed she was in Cody's apartment above the bar, but the bedsheets were a feminine pale peach color. Not only that, but there was a fuzzy clock with bunny ears and a wardrobe with a white robe hanging on the front.

Slowly, she sat up. There was a tinge of lightheadedness, but nothing like what it had been. Swinging her legs to the side, she tested them by applying a little bit of pressure. When her knees didn't cave, she stood. Good. She could hold her own weight.

She walked over to the mirror and grimaced at what she saw. Her skin was pale and her hair a mess, scruffy, with locks twisting every which way.

Argh, she looked terrible.

Quickly, she ran her fingers through the strands, trying to make them semi-presentable, but after a few seconds it was clear this was as good as it was going to get.

Noises sounded from outside the room. The clattering of pans. Maybe the opening of a fridge.

A pile of clothes sat on the dresser. She lifted the top item to find a pale pink T-shirt and, below that, jeans. All female clothes and all about her size.

With some relief, she removed the bar clothes that she'd woken in and changed. What she really needed was a shower, but first, she'd figure out what was going on.

She opened the door to a small living area with a huge window to the right. There was a big leather couch, a coffee table and a TV attached to the wall. To the left of the living room was a dining table, then what she presumed to be the front door.

An apartment.

She moved toward the front door, noticing the small kitchen beside the dining room, and stopped at the sight of Cody. He had his back to her as he worked at the stove. The smell of bacon and eggs tinged the air. But that wasn't what stole her attention.

Cody wasn't wearing a shirt. And every time he moved, the muscles in his back pulled and rippled.

God, who knew a man could have such a sexy back? Even with his shirt on, she'd known he was big and broad, but without it? It still shocked her.

He turned, one side of his mouth immediately lifting when his gaze fell on her. "You're awake."

"I am. Is it morning?"

"No. It's almost six p.m., Storm."

Her eyes about fell out of her head. "Almost six? I slept that long? Why aren't you at the bar?"

"I closed tonight."

She frowned. "You closed?"

"There was no way I was going to leave you while you were so sick."

"You didn't have to look after me."

He took a small step toward her. "I did. You needed someone to make sure your fever went down and you stayed hydrated."

Memories of the last few hours came back to her. Of Cody waking her to put a straw to her lips. Carrying her to the bathroom.

The air stalled in her lungs, and her next words came out more as a whisper. "No one's ever looked after me like that while I've been sick."

The half smile dropped from his lips. "No one? Not even your mom?"

She swallowed. "My mom hasn't been well for most of my life." *All* of her life. "She's an alcoholic."

Something flickered in Cody's eyes. An emotion Harper couldn't place. It wasn't pity. It was softer than that.

He moved closer and his hands went to her hips. "I'm sorry."

She lifted a shoulder. "It was all I knew. This…you…it's *not* what I know."

"But it's what you deserve."

He'd decided that in the short amount of time they'd known each other? "Thank you."

He leaned forward and pressed a light kiss to her forehead. It seeped right into her skin, dulling the last bits of pain in her head. "You don't need to thank me for taking care of you."

She swallowed. "So, it's six at night and you're making eggs and bacon?"

"And bagels."

She glanced up at him, one side of her mouth lifted. "Because you like to eat breakfast for dinner?"

"Because you missed breakfast. Who wants to wake up to dinner?"

This man was something else.

Gently, he guided her to the table. "Rest. It's almost ready."

"How did you know I'd wake up for dinner?" she asked quietly.

"I didn't. But I was hoping the smell of bacon would pull you out here."

She chuckled. "And it did."

He grabbed plates and cutlery, and she moved to help, but he shook his head, placing a hand on her shoulder to keep her seated as he returned to the table. "Nope. You've been sick. I'm taking care of you."

Her eyes softened, and for what had to be the hundredth time, she wondered what planet this perfect man had come from.

* * *

THE HAZEL SPECKS in Harper's brown eyes flickered as she told Cody about her job as an executive assistant. It was the first time she'd willingly talked about her life outside of Misty Peak without prompting. The first time her smile looked easy and her laugh natural when referencing her past.

They'd almost finished eating, but he barely noticed; Harper had taken up all his attention.

"So you enjoyed your job?" he asked.

Her smile softened. "I loved it. But I think a lot of that was the financial freedom it gave me, and Ivy made me feel…important. And good at what I did. Two things I hadn't really felt before."

The familiar anger edged his vision. He wanted to learn about Harper's life, but every piece she revealed made him angrier, to the point he was ready to go out there and find this so-called family and give them a piece of his mind.

He'd felt the pain of losing both his parents, but the reason it had been hard was because they'd given so much of themselves. They'd sacrificed for him and his siblings. Made them feel loved and important. Gifts he'd never taken for granted.

"I'm sorry you had to leave the position," he said quietly.

She lifted a shoulder, a small smile on her lips. "The new position I found is pretty good too."

"Really?"

"Mm-hmm. My new boss even cooks me breakfast for dinner."

"He sounds like a *great* guy."

"He is." She chuckled but immediately touched her head. The tightening of her eyes was small, but he didn't miss it.

"You need to rest."

She shook her head. "No, I need to help you—"

"You're not helping me. Your options are to relax on the couch, where we can watch a movie, or in bed."

Her brows arched. "You want to watch a movie with me?"

Why did she ask him that like it was a crazy idea? "I do. But only if you're up to it."

"But…shouldn't I get home?"

Shit. He'd been waiting for that question.

He chose his words carefully. "I'd prefer you to stay here, in the spare room…at least for tonight." If it was up to him though, it would be longer.

When she remained silent, he left his seat and lowered to his haunches in front of her. "You passed out on me, Harper. That scared the shit out of me. I just…I need to know you're okay. For tonight."

Her bottom lip disappeared between her teeth, and for a moment he was sure she'd say no. Or at least put up a fight.

"Okay."

The air whooshed from his chest. "Okay?"

"Yeah."

Without giving her any warning, he slid his hands behind her back and knees and lifted her.

She gasped and grabbed onto him. "Cody! What are you doing?"

"Making sure you're taken care of so you never want to leave." So much damn truth to that statement. He lowered her to the couch but continued to hover over her. "Now, I'm going to run downstairs to feed Tommy. When I get back, I want to see you right here."

"But—"

"No getting up. No clearing the table. No washing any dishes."

"Cody—"

"I need you to promise me, Harper. I take my duties as your nurse very seriously."

Her lips twitched like she was fighting back a laugh. "My nurse? You don't look like any nurse I've ever had before."

"Harper…"

"Fine. I promise I'll stay right here."

"Good." Then, because he couldn't stop himself, he leaned forward and touched his lips to hers. "And think of what movie you want to watch."

Those were his last words before he slipped out of the apartment and moved down the stairs.

He'd tried to get word around town that the bar was closed, but he'd also put a sign on the door. Not everyone would be happy, but he didn't care. He never shut the place last minute, but there'd been no part of him capable of leaving Harper as she was.

No one's ever looked after me like that while I've been sick.

Her words repeated in his head, burning through him like acid. Fuck, what kind of life had she lived? What had she done when she was a kid and sick with the flu? Had she just been expected to look after herself?

The idea made his chest tear in two.

He double-checked that everything was locked up before heading to the back door. He was halfway there when the handle rattled from the other side.

What the hell?

His next steps were slower. When he turned the lock and

opened the door, he stepped out just in time to see the back of someone in a black hooded sweatshirt, running away.

The *fuck?* Was it the same guy who'd attacked Harper less than a week ago? He'd looked about the same size.

He wanted to chase after the asshole, but he was already out of sight—and for all Cody knew, already in a car. Plus, he didn't want to leave Harper inside alone.

Tommy brushed against Cody's legs, and he bent down and petted him. "Do you know who that man was, Tom Tom?"

He got a purr in response.

Once Tommy's bowl was filled, and Cody had given him one last pat, he rose and pulled his phone from his pocket to call his brother.

"Cody, everything okay?"

"A guy just tried to open the back door of the bar. When I stepped out, he ran. He matched the physique of Harper's alley attacker that night."

Eastern cursed. "I'll send some guys to patrol the streets. You make sure your place is locked up."

"Will do. And Eastern, if you find anything, I want to be the first to know."

CHAPTER 15

"*H*ow are you feeling today?" Tilly asked.

Harper sipped her iced coffee. They'd just left Sugar and Spice and were enjoying a short walk before going back to Tilly's car. Harper had quickly discovered it wasn't just cupcakes and cookies that Mrs. Sandler did freakishly well. The cold drinks, the hot drinks, and the donuts were mouthwatering. The shop had become somewhat of a hub for her.

"A lot better," she finally answered. "I think it was some twenty-four-hour flu. I'm just so grateful for Cody."

Tilly gave her a warm smile. "It's nice that he looked after you. He's a good guy."

"He's been so amazing. Last night, after he made me breakfast for dinner, we watched a movie together on the couch and I fell asleep. When I woke up, I was in bed because he'd carried me there and tucked me in, all without waking me. I don't actually think he's real."

Tilly chuckled. "Extraterrestrial?"

"He has to be. I've never met a man like him. He's too...everything. Kind, considerate—"

"Sexy."

Harper laughed. "Uh, yeah, way too sexy."

"Well, I grew up in the same town as him, and I can tell you that unless he came down in a baby spaceship like Clark Kent, he's real." She sipped her shake. "He's always been one of the more relaxed Walker brothers."

"Do you know his other brothers who are still in the military?"

"Lock and Jace? Not well. Although, I know they're polar opposites. Lock's really intense and in some super-secret military program, and Jace is the fearless, fun-loving youngest brother. Not that he's any less dangerous. They're *all* dangerous."

In more ways than one. "So they're all different?"

"Oh yeah. Even their sister is different than the rest of them. Not that I know her that well, either. But they're all intrinsically good…even if they don't all like me."

She frowned. "Have any of them made it known that they don't like you?"

Tilly scoffed. "They don't need to. A lot of people around here don't like me. If certain people in this town ever looked at me with anything other than contempt, I'd probably die of shock."

Harper was pretty sure Tilly had been going for dry humor, but the tone of her voice gave her away. It affected her. Hell, it would affect anyone. "I'm sorry."

The other woman lifted a shoulder.

Okay, they needed a new topic of conversation. "Do you have any siblings?"

Tilly shook her head. "Nope. I'm an only child. My mom and I were close, but she passed away a few months ago…an aggressive form of brain cancer. It felt like she went from a few bad headaches to only having a couple months to live in the blink of an eye."

Harper's heart clenched. "Oh my gosh, I'm so sorry."

"Thank you. I felt kind of lost after she died. She was my only family and my best friend. It's part of the reason I came back here and moved into the house she left me. It's the house she grew up in, then raised me in, and I guess it makes me feel close to her again."

Harper touched the other woman's hand. "Then this is exactly where you're supposed to be."

She still didn't know the details of what had driven the woman away, but she did know that coming back had been hard for Tilly, and she'd done it anyway.

They'd just rounded a corner when they stopped abruptly at the sight of Kayden in front of them.

His eyes hit Harper, and he dipped his chin, then they shifted to Tilly. And even though she was pretty sure he tried to conceal it, there was the smallest tightening of his eyes. "Matilda. I heard you were back in town."

"Tilly. And yes, I am."

"For good?"

"Yes. For now, at least."

Kayden didn't need to say anything for Harper to see the displeasure on his face.

She cleared her throat and touched Tilly's arm. "It was nice to see you, Kayden."

They moved past him, and Tilly all but deflated.

"Hey. You okay?" Harper asked gently.

"Yeah, I just...I tell myself I'm strong enough to deal with people blatantly disliking me, but some days, I don't know if I am." When Harper just frowned, Tilly took a deep breath. "My father was a stockbroker. He invested a lot of the townspeople's savings. Or at least, he *told* them he was investing it...then one day, he took the money and ran."

Harper gasped. "Oh my gosh!"

"Yep. My mother and I stayed for a bit, but we got so much backlash from the community that we left after a month. I guess that probably didn't help clear our names. Mom never sold her house because it was owned by my grandmother at the time, but even after my grandmother died, she kept it."

God, this woman had been through so much. "You shouldn't be paying for your father's crimes."

Tilly looked up and down the street. "Well, now that I'm back, let's hope I can prove to the community that I'm not my father. It will be hard though. One of the people he stole from was Toby Walker, Kayden, Eastern, and Cody's father. He was the most wonderful man you'd ever want to meet, and he trusted my father implicitly. From what I heard, Toby ended up losing the family home and needed to mortgage the bar."

Her heart clenched for Cody and his brothers and the father she'd never met. "That's awful. But still not your fault. Trust me, I know better than anyone that the sins of our parents are not our burdens to bear."

Tilly blinked back obvious tears. "Thank you, Harper. I needed to hear that today."

"Of course."

They'd just arrived at Tilly's car when a figure down the road had Harper's gaze catching.

Wait, was that…

She gasped before quickly yanking the passenger door open and dropping into the Mazda and ducking as low as she could.

Tilly lowered behind the wheel, throwing a worried look her way. "Are you okay?"

"I need you to drive."

"Harper—"

"Please! There's someone across the road, and I don't know if he's seen me, but I need to get away from him."

So many questions ran through her mind. How had he found her? Why was he here?

But none of that really mattered, because the fact was, her father *had* found her, and he was right here in Misty Peak.

* * *

CODY WORKED MECHANICALLY behind the bar. The music was loud and the place busy as he served customers. Despite Harper assuring him she felt fine, something was wrong. She'd arrived a little late for her shift, pale and quiet.

Was she still sick? Or was it something else?

She'd been fine this morning. In fact, before Tilly had picked her up, she'd looked happy and relaxed, an easy smile on her face. She'd even kissed his cheek before leaving, which was huge for Harper. She never initiated contact.

He only dragged his gaze from her when Kayden dropped onto a stool and ran his fingers through his hair.

Cody raised a brow. "Rough day?"

"You could say that. First, I ran into Matilda. She was walking down the street with Harper and… I don't know. You told me she was back, but knowing something and seeing it with your own eyes are two different things."

Cody swung the bar towel over his shoulder. His brother had always taken what had happened to their father the hardest. Likely because he was the oldest and had tried to shoulder a lot of their father's problems, even as their dad had tried to shield him from everything.

"For what it's worth," Cody started, "I don't think she or her mom had anything to do with what Martin did to our family."

"Why'd they run then? If they knew nothing, why'd they high-tail it out of town after people realized what he'd done?"

Cody filled a glass with beer and pushed it across the bar. "Maybe they didn't have the energy to plead their case again and again. Maybe they couldn't look people in the eye who their husband and father had robbed. *Or*, maybe they didn't want to be blamed for what Martin did…exactly what you're doing to Tilly."

A muscle in Kayden's cheek clenched as he lifted his beer.

Trust…it didn't come easy to Kayden. And that wasn't something that always worked in his favor.

Cody leaned forward. "Hey. When you saw Harper today, did she seem okay?"

"As far as I could tell, she was fine." Kayden frowned. "Why? Is she not fine now?"

"I don't know. Something's off with her."

He watched as she filled a glass at the other end of the bar. Outwardly, she appeared fine. But he didn't miss the way she scanned the crowd every few seconds, as if she was looking for someone.

He turned back to his brother. "What else turned your day to shit?"

"Linda told me she's retiring."

Cody's brows shot up. Linda had been running the visitors center since they were kids. She'd made it the tourist attraction it was, setting up the café and the tours. Even initiating work for the skywalk. "Who's taking her place?"

"She wouldn't tell me."

Cody laughed. "Why not?"

"She said she's announcing it at her retirement party."

Ah, that explained the dark mood. Kayden hated surprises, something Linda knew. "It's like she's trying to torture you."

"And she's enjoying the torture. I swear I saw a smile as she turned away from me."

Cody chuckled. The woman had always thought Kayden was too serious. It was why she was so good for him.

The smile slipped from Cody's face when the door to the bar opened and a group of men walked in, and at the back of that group was Miles. The men were his work colleagues, but Miles knew he wasn't welcome here. Cody had made himself crystal fucking clear.

He stepped from behind the bar. Distantly, Kayden calling his name sounded from over his shoulder, but he ignored it. The second he reached his ex-friend, Cody grabbed him by the collar of his shirt and pulled him back toward the door.

"Cody!" Miles growled. He tried to tug away, but Cody didn't ease his hold.

When they stood outside, Cody shoved him against the wall.

"What the fuck, Cody?"

"*You're* saying what the fuck? I told you, Miles. You're not welcome here."

"The guys wanted to go for a drink, and this is the only bar in town. What was I supposed to do?"

"That's not my problem."

Miles blew out a breath. "*Fine.*"

He went to step away, but Cody stopped him. "I need you to answer a question."

His brows flickered. "What?"

"Did you put your hands on Vanessa?"

The guy jerked back as if Cody had slugged him. "Put my hands on her? As in *hurt* her?"

The front door opened and Kayden stepped out. Cody ignored his brother, stepping closer to Miles, crowding him. "There were bruises in the shape of fingerprints on her arms. Bruises she said *you* put there."

He opened and closed his mouth. "*What?* I…I didn't…that wasn't me."

"Who was it then?"

"I don't know! We haven't been in a good place lately."

He didn't know who the fuck to believe. What Vanessa did was none of his business, but when he knew a man was putting his hands on a woman, it was in his genetic makeup to act. She could be lying…but so could Miles.

Kayden put his hand on his arm. "Cody. You need to back off and let him leave."

The door opened again, and this time Harper leaned out, concern on her features. "Is everything okay?"

He forced himself to release Miles and step back. "I told you this last time, and I'll tell you again, you're not welcome in my bar, Miles. Don't come back."

"Cody…come on, man. We were friends. *Best* friends."

"I thought we were." He turned. When he reached Harper, he placed a hand on the small of her back and led her inside.

"Are you okay?" she asked quietly.

They reached the bar, and he stopped in front of her before gently cupping her cheek. "I am. Are you?"

She looked up in surprise. Surprised that he could tell something was wrong? She shouldn't be. He was so in tune with this woman, he felt every shift in her mood.

She finally shook her head. "Not really."

"Why not?" He inched closer, every part of him needing to fix whatever the problem was. "Tell me, Storm. Tell me and I'll fix it."

She opened her mouth, but before she got any words out, her gaze caught on something behind him in the bar—and every bit of color leached from her face. Turning his head, he followed her gaze to an older man by the door who was looking directly at her. A man with brown eyes…

Eyes just like Harper's.

"Who's that?" Even though he asked the question, a part of him already knew.

For a moment, Harper was silent, her pale skin making the hazel in her eyes look almost black.

He gripped her hips, afraid she'd pass out. "Harper?"

"It's my father. He found me."

CHAPTER 16

He'd found her. Harper's father had found her, and not just her town—her workplace.

Her heart pounded, fear crawling through her chest as she moved around Cody's apartment, grabbing all the little things she'd accumulated over the couple nights she'd stayed here.

There was only one thing she could think to do. One word that screamed at her, so loud and so furious it wiped out everything else.

Run.

She needed to get out. Go. Disappear. If her mom and brother hated her for testifying and ensuring her dad was thrown into prison, how did her violent, former drug-addict father feel?

His brown eyes, eyes so similar to her own, flashed in her mind, angry and hate filled.

A whimper tried to escape her lips, but she swallowed it down.

Where was she supposed to go—and how was she supposed to get there? She had no car. It was the only reason she hadn't left hours ago, when she'd spotted her father across the street. She'd come downstairs to work almost on autopilot, going over plan after plan of what she could do. To leave or stay. To hide or run. Maybe a part of her also wanted to be close to Cody, because that was where she felt safe. But after having her father walk inside her place of employment…there was nowhere that would feel safe unless it was far away from him.

Why was he here? What was his plan? To hurt her again? To drag her back to Hamilton?

Her fingers shook as she grabbed her toiletries from the bathroom. Ali had brought some of her stuff over when she'd been sick. It wasn't much, but when you had almost nothing, everything was important.

She returned to the bedroom, grabbed a T-shirt off the dresser, and shoved it into her bag.

A ride. That was the first thing she needed. Someone to take her to the cabin so she could pack the last of her things, then another ride to a bus station. Where *was* the closest bus station? And when would the next bus come? God, where would she even go from here?

Panic welled in her chest. It was so thick and heavy that it pressed down on her, suffocating, making every breath a battle. Every thump of her heart a struggle.

Then more panic bubbled to the surface. A different kind, but one that weighed just as heavily on her chest.

Panic at the idea of leaving Cody.

She paused and pressed a hand over her heart, as if that could somehow stem the pain. She hadn't known him for long, but in their short amount of time together, he'd slipped into her heart and become the first person who'd given her hope for a better future.

She closed her eyes and focused on the air moving in and out of her lungs. It was only the click of the apartment door opening that had her pulling out of her stillness. Quickly, she grabbed her cat nightgown from the bed and stuffed it into the bag.

"Harper…"

His voice… It slipped inside her, making her yearn for a future that felt so far out of reach. A voice that usually brought her comfort, but right now, she only felt heartache.

"Are you going back to the cabin?" he asked.

"No. I have to leave Misty Peak." God, even saying those words out loud hurt. She pushed down the rippling pain in her chest and tried to zip the bag, but it got stuck halfway.

"Harper, I can't let you leave like this."

"It's not your choice." She yanked at the zipper, this time applying more force. "He's not a good person. None of my family are. And if he knows where I am, then so do Mom and Ross. They're *poison*. They just take and take until you've got nothing left. Until you *believe* you're nothing."

She cried out as the zipper refused to budge. *Goddammit!*

Warmth suddenly covered her back, strong arms wrapping around her body before gentle, strong fingers slipped over her hands. "Harper. Stop."

"I can't!" she cried, tears pressing at her eyes. "He's here! I haven't seen him in eight years, not since he…since he hurt me. And he found me!"

Warm breath brushed her neck. "You're safe with me."

Those words whispered inside her, offering just a glimpse of hope. A hint of safety.

Still, she fought it, her chest heaving as rational thought seemed impossible. "He's *downstairs*, Cody! He's—"

"Kayden's sending him away, and he and Barry are finishing the evening. I'm not leaving your side, and I'm not letting him near you—not tonight or any of the nights after this one."

"He'll be back." The words were spoken so quietly, she wasn't even sure they reached him. "They all will."

Warm lips touched her ear. "Trust me to look after you."

She hung her head, wanting to trust this beautiful man. But how did she learn to trust when every person who'd come before Cody had hurt her?

A gentle kiss touched her cheek before he whispered the words, "Don't leave me."

Her heart beat recklessly in her chest, and for a moment she couldn't move. She couldn't think. All she could do was feel. Cody's breath against her cheek. His heat against her back.

A wild panic built inside her, the knowledge that if she left, she'd lose that. She'd lose *him*.

Slowly, she turned and looked up into his ocean-blue eyes. So much strength. But also, under the strength was something else. Something that almost aligned with her own emotions—fear.

It looked so out of place on him. He never looked scared. Because he was on the verge of losing her?

A tear trickled down her cheek. "If I stay, my battles will become your battles. And that's not fair to you."

"Your battles already *are* my battles. And I want to fight them with you." He swiped the tear away. "We haven't known each other for long, and you still have a ways to go with trusting me. But I have this reckless hope for our future. That you were meant to end up here with me. That we were meant to end up together."

The beats of her heart stumbled over each other. "I'm starting to wonder if maybe hope's not as reckless as I thought." Needing more of his comforting warmth, she slid her hands up his stomach, then chest. But it wasn't enough. She needed more. "Kiss me, Cody."

His eyes turned a darker shade, his gaze shifting between her eyes. Then one of his hands slipped through her hair and he lowered his head.

The second his lips touched hers, she felt it. The calm. The release of fear and panic. It was as if his touch, and his touch alone, pulled her away from the ugliness of the world around her and transported her somewhere else. Somewhere just for them.

Almost desperately, she slid her hands over his shoulder and around his neck. When his hands lowered to her ass and lifted her, she gasped at the sudden elimination of any space between them. The cascade of emotions that his closeness brought.

Air whipped around them as he moved out of her room and into another. When he stopped and lowered them to a bed, his mouth never left hers. And the weight of his powerful body over hers…God, it was everything. Her cage of safety. Her temporarily perfect world.

He lifted his head, and she wanted to cry. To tug him back to her and seal them together once again.

She opened her eyes, realizing she was in a room with masculine shades and a dark bedspread. *His* room. But what really stole her attention was the way he looked at her. Like she belonged to him—and tonight, he was taking what was his.

"You sure you want to do this, Storm?"

She traced the lines beside his eyes with her gaze. The flecks of black hidden beneath the blue of his irises. "You're the *only* thing I'm sure of."

His eyes darkened even further, the muscles in his neck flexing. Then his head dropped again, but this time he kissed her cheek. Her throat. His hands trailed down her sides, then taking hold of the hem of her shirt and tugging it over her chest.

She didn't have time to feel self-conscious because his mouth was already returning to her body, his lips kissing the skin above her bra. He pulled one cup down and took her pebbled nipple between his lips.

A cry slipped out, and she arched as his tongue flicked over the hard bud, desire rippling through her core, catching her breath and stalling the rhythm of her heart.

When he switched to her other breast, she arched again, allowing his hands to slip behind her and unclasp her bra before pulling it away. Harper barely noticed as she pushed herself farther into his mouth, weaving her fingers into his hair and pulling at the strands. She wrapped a leg around his waist, grinding against him.

She panted as he released her and his mouth moved down her body, his fingers slipping into the waistband of her skirt and panties and dragging both down. Suddenly, she was naked beneath him. But again, she didn't feel anything but safety and a desire that ran so deep it was a part of her.

His head moved between her thighs, causing her breath to stutter. When his mouth lowered to her core, his tongue against her clit, she cried out, instinctively trying to snap her legs together, but his arms were wrapped around her thighs, his shoulders making movement impossible.

She didn't recognize the sounds that rumbled from her chest as he continued to lick and suck. Or the way her body twisted and arched.

The torture was relentless.

A finger touched her entrance, and she stilled. Then he pushed inside her, his mouth on her clit, tongue moving in circles.

"Cody…" she cried, her body unbelievably close to snapping as he continued to thrust into her. "Please, I need you."

Her breathing was becoming ragged and she was right on the edge, threatening to tip over, when he rose. His fingers went to the bottom of his shirt and lifted it over his head.

Even though she'd seen him shirtless before, her breath still caught. He was the definition of strength and power. Like a gladiator.

When his hands went to the button and zipper of his jeans, she watched impatiently, her blood pumping far too fast in her veins. He shoved the remaining clothes down so that he stood completely bare in front of her…and suddenly she had to relearn how to breathe. So big and formidable. And tonight, he was hers.

He opened the bedside table and pulled out a foil square, but before he could slip it on, she sat up, taking it from his fingers. He growled as she wrapped her fingers around his cock. Slowly, she trailed her hands up and down his length, testing out what he liked.

When she slipped the condom over his tip, she rolled it down slowly, continually playing with him. Once it was all the way on, Cody grabbed her wrists, pulling her hands away from him, and then she was on her back again, and he was between her thighs.

His eyes bore into hers, so intense she couldn't look away. "You're mine, Harper Rain. You know that, don't you?"

His...it felt so right. "And you're mine."

His eyes darkened further still. "Yours." Then he thrust inside her.

* * *

It took every scrap of strength Cody possessed to remain still. To give her some time to adjust to his size. But fuck, it cost him. It felt like his heart was a second away from clawing out of his chest. Like his lungs were so tight from holding his breath, they'd burst.

Gently, he lowered his head and grazed her lips with his own. "So damn beautiful."

She cupped the back of his head and slipped her tongue between his lips, tangling it with his. He groaned at the taste of her. At her sweetness. Her softness.

When her legs wrapped around his waist, pulling him deeper, he barely suppressed the growl.

Fuck, he was fighting a losing battle.

He lifted his hips and lowered. It was fire, so hot and fierce, he could barely think. The desire on her face spurred him to do it again, the sounds emanating from her chest speeding his thrusts.

This woman was *his*. She'd shown up out of nowhere, in the middle of a storm, and nothing had been the same since. She'd changed him. Changed everything.

He cupped her breast, grazing her nipple with the pad of his thumb, loving every little cry and whimper that came from her lips. When he lifted her thigh and began thrusting into her at a new angle, her fingers dug into the flesh of his shoulders, almost breaking skin. He welcomed the bite of pain.

Lowering his head, he latched onto her neck, sucking and nipping at her skin, his thrusts gaining speed.

He knew the exact moment she was close. Her walls started to tighten around his cock, her breaths stuttering in her chest.

He nipped her flesh before whispering, "Let go, Storm."

And she did. She screamed, her back rising from the bed as she shattered beneath him. He kept pumping into her, hard and fast, watching the complete release wash over her features until he couldn't hold himself together anymore. He shouted her name as he broke, his mouth once again finding hers. Taking. Tasting. Consuming.

When he had nothing left, he finally stilled, the only movement in the room the rise and fall of their chests.

It was a few long seconds before he had the strength to lift himself. She gazed back with such open trust and vulnerability that it almost cracked his heart in two.

"You're amazing, Harper. You know that, right?"

Her bottom lip disappeared between her teeth. "You're starting to make me believe it."

Damn straight he was.

He lowered to her side and tugged her against him. Holding her felt like the most natural thing in the world. As if here, with Harper in his arms, was the only place he was supposed to be.

CHAPTER 17

*L*ight flickered in from the crack in the curtains. It was morning, but Cody wasn't ready to get up. Not when Harper's soft breaths brushed his chest as she lay across his body and her legs tangled with his.

Last night had been everything. Not just physical. Something deeper had passed between them. He'd known from the start that Harper was meant to be his—the problem had been convincing her.

The muscles in his forearms coiled at the memory of spotting her father inside the bar last night. When the man looked at Harper, there had been something akin to hate on his face.

He was relatively tall, maybe six-one. And muscular, probably from years of prison workouts. Cody had glimpsed cheap-looking tattoos on his arms and a few more snaking up his neck. The guy looked like the cliché of an ex-con.

But what really gutted him? The fear on Harper's face.

He forced himself to gently untangle his body from hers. Her soft hum almost had him reconsidering his decision to get up rather than staying with her and holding her for just a bit longer. But he needed to get in contact with Kayden to find out how last night went. Had her father put up a fight when Kayden told him to leave?

Cody had wanted to kick the guy out himself, but Harper came first. Always. And he'd needed to make sure she was okay.

Once he was on his feet, he tugged the sheet up to cover Harper's body before pulling on some sweats and grabbing his phone.

He'd just reached the kitchen when his brother picked up. "Cody. I've been waiting for your call."

"Did the asshole leave quietly?" He opened the fridge door and pulled out the eggs.

"He did."

Wasn't a surprise. Ex-cons had certain rules they were forced to live by. If the guy started a fight, it would violate his parole. One call and he'd be headed right back to jail.

"I went up to him," Kayden continued, "told him he needed to leave and he wasn't welcome back in the bar. He said he wanted to speak to Harper, but I told him that wasn't going to happen. There was a moment where he seemed to size me up, maybe trying to decide whether or not it was a fight he could win. He's obviously smarter than he looks, because he turned and left."

Why'd that feel too easy?

"Although," Kayden added before Cody had a chance to respond, "I did see him waiting in a car on the street after I closed up. When the guy saw me, he drove away."

"So the fucker was waiting for her."

"It appeared that way."

Cody lowered the eggs to the counter and gripped the edge. "I need to find out where he's staying."

"Why? So you can go threaten him?"

"So I can tell him to stay the hell away from Harper."

"And if he says no—which is the most likely outcome—what will you do?"

Cody ground his back teeth together. "I'll tell him exactly what will happen if he goes near her."

"And that's why *you're* not going anywhere near *him*. You can't just threaten people when they've done nothing wrong."

"Nothing wrong? He went to prison for *hurting her*. For keeping drugs in their home when she was a child. He shouldn't be here."

"I know that."

"Tell me what the hell I'm supposed to do then. Wait for him to find her again when we have no fucking clue what he wants? The next time, maybe when she's alone and defenseless?"

"No, I expect you to stick with her and make sure she's never alone and defenseless. Then, if he approaches her or threatens her, you're there to protect her and you can make a report to Eastern."

"He's dangerous," Cody ground out.

"Exactly. So let him fuck up, which you know he will, then let Eastern take care of him."

Cody remained silent. He wasn't agreeing to shit, and his brother knew it. Mostly because he knew a man like Harper's father didn't abide by the law—exactly why he'd gone to prison in the first place.

At Cody's continued silence, Kayden sighed. "Just don't do anything to get yourself into trouble, okay?"

"She's important to me. I'll do whatever I need to keep her safe." But Kayden was right—to protect her, he needed to keep his ass out of prison, no matter how much he wanted to search every inch of this town and kick her father's ass.

There was a small pause. "You haven't known her very long, Cody."

"Doesn't matter. I care about her. A lot."

Hell, he'd go so far as to say he was falling in love with the woman. Not that he'd be admitting that to Kayden before he said the words to Harper.

His brother blew out a breath. "Okay. Just…be careful."

"You know I always am."

He hung up and took out the bread to make French toast, his mind never far from Harper. Even though he knew from Eastern that her father had just been released from prison, he wanted Harper to tell him. He wanted her to trust him with her past, even the darkest parts of it.

But if she didn't, he needed to admit to her that he knew. Because otherwise he'd be deceiving her.

He was just cracking the eggs into a bowl when he heard the rustling of sheets from the bedroom.

And he'd just poured some milk into the dish when another noise sounded.

A whimper, followed by a small cry.

What the hell?

He rushed to the bedroom, stepping inside to see Harper still in bed, eyes closed but a deep frown creasing her brows. She was tossing her head from side to side, and the look on her face…

Torment.

* * *

Harper's heart pumped violently in her chest, the small wisps of air barely making their way into her lungs as she drove to her mother's house.

Gone. Her money was gone. She'd been so sure the text to say her rent check had bounced was a mistake. How could it not be? She had money in her account. A lot of money. All her savings, from years of working and barely spending a dime. Hell, she lived on noodles and rice most of the time because saving to buy a home far away from her family was more important to her than eating. She had a dream of a small Cape Cod with a white picket fence. A cat to call her own and a little vegetable patch.

The bank teller's words repeated in her head again and again.

"A Mrs. Margaret Rain withdrew the funds earlier today. She's the joint account holder."

Harper's fingers whitened on the wheel.

How had she not realized?

She'd started working her first job back when she was fifteen, and she'd needed a legal guardian as a joint account holder in order to open an account at the bank. She'd never thought to change that or open a new checking account when she turned eighteen. She'd just...forgotten. Besides, that was years ago, and her mother had never touched her money before. What had changed?

It didn't matter though, did it? Because unless she convinced her mother to give it back, the money was gone. Every dollar she'd worked so hard to save. And with it, her dream.

She'd headed for her hometown the minute she got out of work, the heavy rain slowing what was usually about a thirty-minute drive to the house where she'd grown up. Now, it was almost six when she pulled up outside her mother's rundown home. The wood was rotting on the familiar front porch, and the yard was so overgrown, she could barely see the windows.

Ignoring the rain that pounded against her shoulders, she slammed her door closed and ran to the front door. Her fist hit the wood hard. She had a key somewhere, but it had been so long since she'd come here, she had no idea where it was.

It took long minutes before the door finally opened, Ross on the other side, a smirk on his face. "Hey, sis."

"Where is she?" She didn't wait for an answer, just pushed past him into the house. God, it stunk in here. Like alcohol mixed with stale food and vomit. There was stuff everywhere. Old takeout boxes. Clothes. Dirty dishes.

After a brief pause at the empty living room, she moved into the kitchen, finding that empty too.

"Something got you angry, Harp?"

The way her brother sneered her name as he followed made her want to turn around and slug him. She didn't. She kept moving through the house. The bathroom was empty, but there, in the center of the unmade bed in the master bedroom, was her mother, passed out on her stomach. The image was so familiar that she was thrust back years into her childhood.

She ran straight over to her mother, grabbed her shoulder, and rolled her to her back. "Where is it, Mom?"

Her mother groaned, but her eyes remained closed.

Harper shook her, a new desperation weaving through her limbs. "Wake up! You need to tell me where you put my money!"

"You won't get it back."

She stopped and turned to look at her brother. He stood in the center of the room, arms crossed over his chest, smug smile still on his face. "What?"

"The money. Mom called the bank, asking for a loan. They turned her down...but they kindly reminded her of a joint account she had access to. Told her how much money was in it. She gave me a cut, of course. But I wouldn't be surprised if the rest is already gone."

No. That wasn't possible. That was her house deposit. Her escape!

Slowly, she rose to her feet, a new rage filling her chest. "You let her do that to me?"

"Don't know why you're so upset. We're family. What's yours is mine, right?"

A black fury took over, and Harper ran forward, shoving her brother in the chest. "Haven't you taken enough from me?"

Her brother stumbled back.

"Isn't all the hatred you've shown me, the way you leech every bit of good from my life, enough?" Harper screamed.

She went to shove him again, but he grabbed her arm so tightly, she cried out. Then his fist flew forward, colliding with her cheek and sending her to the floor.

He towered over her. "You've always thought you're so much fucking better than us. You're not. It's your fucking fault Dad went to prison! Your fault the neighbors heard you scream and the house was raided. Because of you, we've barely been getting by for years. We took what you owed us. And we'll keep taking for as long as we damn well like!"

At his words, her rage shifted into something else. Something worse. A deep hopelessness.

It was never going to end. They'd keep taking and taking until she had nothing left...not even herself.

Ignoring the throbbing in her cheek, she rose to her feet and shoved past her brother into the hall. The world blurred around her as she ran through her childhood home.

Rain soaked her as she dashed to her car, but she barely felt it. The second she dropped behind the wheel, the panic expanded in her chest. Choking her. Drowning her.

It kept expanding until one word entered her head. Her only hope.

Run.

CHAPTER 18

"*Harper*? Harper, wake up." The deep, familiar voice penetrated her sleep. Then a warm hand cupped her cheek. "Storm, honey, open your eyes."

It took a few blinks for Cody to come into focus. He sat on the edge of the bed, shirtless, looking so worried she almost forgot everything her subconscious had just dredged up.

"Are you okay?" he asked gently.

Was she? She could still feel the impact of her brother's fist on her cheek. Could still feel the devastating weight of her mother's betrayal like an open wound.

"It was just a bad dream."

A slight frown creased his brows. "Will you tell me about it?"

The idea made a new wave of fear fill her lungs. This man already knew snippets of the mess that was her life, but what happened when he knew all of it? The full worthlessness of her family?

"Could you pass me a shirt?" she asked quietly.

Silently, he reached into a drawer and pulled out one of his own. It drowned her, and even though it was clean, it still smelled of him. Woodsy and masculine.

She took a breath before starting. "That night I showed up here…I'd almost finished work when I got a text that my rent check had bounced. I called my bank and was told—" The sharpness returned to her chest, cutting off the words in her throat. But Cody's hand covered her thigh, allowing a fraction of the pain to ease. "He told me that my mother's name was still on the account—she was a cosigner, from when I was a teenager—and that she'd withdrawn everything."

Cody frowned. "Was there a lot in there?"

"All my savings since I'd started working at the age of fifteen, so…thousands of dollars. I was stupid not to realize she was still on the account and had access to it. And that stupidity cost me." She swallowed. "I left work that night and drove straight to my hometown, to her house. I was so angry and upset. She'd never been a good mother. She was absent a lot of the time, always drunk, and completely ignorant of any pain I'd ever endured. But this was the worst thing she'd done since…"

She paused, not ready to talk about her father just yet. "In years. She was passed out when I got there, which wasn't unusual. She often passed out with an empty bottle of whiskey by her head. My brother was also there, and he informed me that I wouldn't be getting my money back. That I *owed* them, and they'd keep taking from me as often as they liked."

Anger radiated off Cody. "Why does he think you owe them?"

"While my mother's an alcoholic, and my brother's a deadbeat, my…my father was a drug addict. And when he was using, he became violent." Cody's fingers tightened around her thigh. "Usually, he'd just shove or hit me. He did the same to Mom and Ross. But one day, he escalated to the point he ended up throwing me down the stairs. I screamed, and the neighbors heard."

"That's how he was arrested."

Her gaze flashed up, a look of shock on her face. "How did you know?"

A muscle flexed in Cody's cheek. "After the alley attack, Eastern found a report on your father. It revealed that he was out of prison after serving eight years of his ten-year sentence. The details said a neighbor heard someone scream, police showed up, and he was arrested for assault and drug possession."

All this time, he'd known one of her greatest secrets. She shouldn't be surprised. The information was a matter of public record, and his brother was the town sheriff...but for some reason, she'd never allowed herself to consider he'd bother looking into her past.

"Why didn't you say anything?"

"I wanted to wait until you trusted me enough to tell me yourself."

She let that sink in, realizing she wasn't angry. If he'd told her, she'd have been utterly embarrassed, considering they hadn't known each other nearly as well back then. But now? Now she trusted him. "It's true. Police found drugs in his system and searched the house, where they found more. Enough to put him in prison. Despite what a terrible person he was, my mother loved him. He was also the only income earner in the family, so she and my brother blamed *me* for being broke."

"When they should have made sure you were okay and protected you."

She could have laughed, even though there was nothing remotely funny about any of this. "They've never protected me from anything. And when Mom took my money, I just felt so defeated and hopeless...I ran. I realized that unless I disappeared, it would just keep happening. They'd sweep in and destroy any life I tried to build."

"I'm sorry."

For some reason, those two words made her want to cry. Maybe because they were spoken so gently. Maybe because no one had ever cared that her family didn't love her, but Cody seemed to.

"I'm scared." The two whispered drops of truth fell from her lips. "I don't know what my dad wants, but I know it can't be good."

A hard look came over Cody's face. "I promise I will do *everything* in my power to protect you from him."

"I want to believe that's enough."

"It has to be." They both remained silent, and after a beat, he tilted his head. "What were you saving for?"

She smiled sadly. "A small house. White picket fence. Space for a cat. A vegetable garden so I could grow my own food. That felt like security to me. I used to dream about it when I was young and living in a home where I didn't feel safe."

His warm fingers touched her chin, pulling her gaze up to him. "This is a setback. It doesn't mean it won't happen."

"I keep telling myself that, but sometimes it's hard to believe it."

"I'll believe it enough for the both of us."

* * *

CODY MOVED from table to table, filling up the small bowls of nuts that sat on each one. They weren't open yet. After breakfast, he'd driven Harper to the cabin so she could collect the last of her things because she'd finally agreed to stay with him. It was a huge weight off his chest.

Her father would be back. And they still didn't know who this firebug was who'd torched her car, or the person who'd attacked her in the alley. It wasn't safe for her to be on her own, and thank God, she was letting him look after her.

He'd called Eastern, but his brother hadn't seen or heard from Rodney Rain.

Cody's muscles tensed just thinking about the guy. The spineless sack of shit. Hearing Harper tell him in her own words that he'd pushed her down a flight of stairs made him want to go out and murder the asshole.

"We're out of napkins," Barry said from behind him.

Cody turned. "Sorry, I've fallen behind on some of the ordering. I'll do it today."

"Well, that doesn't help us tonight. I'll go get some from the grocery store. Maybe I'll run into Mrs. Sandler on the way."

Cody chuckled. Barry had always had a thing for the bakery owner. He'd encouraged the old man to make a move and ask her out, but that never happened.

Barry stopped at the door and turned. "Is Harper okay?"

The smile slipped from Cody's lips. "Better than last night."

"You said that guy Kayden threw out was her father?"

"Yeah. He's bad news. If you see him again, you don't let him near her."

Anger hardened Barry's expression. "Will do."

He stepped out, and Cody turned to the next table, only to hear the door open again.

"You forget something, old man?" He froze when he saw Vanessa.

She gave him a small smile as the door closed behind her. "Hey. How are you?"

"Vanessa, this isn't a good time. I'm setting up for tonight."

Her heels clicked against the wooden flooring as she crossed the room. "I was hoping to speak to you."

"About what?"

"Can we go to your office or something?"

"No."

Her eyes tightened and she wet her lips as she stopped in front of him. "I made a mistake."

Oh, *fuck* no. "Vanessa—"

"Please, just hear me out. We got together so quickly when you got home from the military. We were good together! I'd never been with someone who made me feel so much and it just…it freaked me out." She stepped closer. "We can be good again, Cody."

He stepped back, keeping the buffer of space between them. "No."

"*Yes*. I miss you! We can have what we did before. We can be happy."

"I *am* happy—with Harper."

Her face screwed up. "Harper? Your new waitress? You've known her for two seconds!"

"We're together, and I want you to stop coming in here. Stop trying to touch me and stop talking to me. Just leave me alone."

"Cody…you don't know what you're saying! I *need* you, especially after Miles! He *hurt* me. I left him, but I'm scared he'll do it again."

"I spoke to Miles. He said he didn't do it."

She flinched like he'd hit her. "And you believe him? Over *me*?"

Right now, he didn't know who the hell to believe, but he knew it wasn't his business. "If you feel unsafe, you need to go to the sheriff and tell him what happened."

"Unbelievable." The word was more of a hiss. "You're just going to let me be a victim of domestic assault, let Miles *hurt* me, so you can have sex with that slut!"

"*Hey!*" Any calmness that had previously been in his voice disappeared. "You do *not* talk about her like that. And in case you forgot, *you're* the one who couldn't be faithful. *You're* the one who cheated on *me* when I was losing my father. Did you really think I could just move past that?"

"If she wasn't here, then yes, I think you'd take me back."

He shook his head. "You don't know me at all, Vanessa. You broke the trust between us, and that's not fixable. I've moved on, and you should too. Now—I want you to leave and *never* come back."

Her chest moved up and down quickly with her angry

breaths, her head shaking like she was in total disbelief. "You'll regret this, Cody. You wait!"

When she stormed out, he ran frustrated fingers through his hair. How he'd ever dated the woman, he had no damn clue.

He turned to see Harper step quietly out of the back room. Fuck, how long had she been there? "How much of that did you hear?"

"Enough." She tilted her head. "Are you okay?"

"Depends. Are you okay with what I said about us?"

"About you moving on with me, and that we're happy?" A small smile curved her lips. "Yeah, I'm okay with what you said."

He crossed the space between them and pulled her into his arms. "I am, you know. Happy. Even though we have a lot going on, when I'm with you, I'm the happiest I've ever been."

Her eyes softened, her hands trailing up his chest. "Me too, Cody."

He lowered his head and kissed her, yet again feeling the tension of the world around them drift away.

CHAPTER 19

"How does it feel to finally have a new account?" Cody asked as he held the bank door open for Harper.

She smiled up at him. "*Way* overdue. I should have done it a long time ago."

"But you're doing it now. Better late than never."

When he slipped his fingers through hers, her skin tingled right up her arm. A few days had passed since her father had been in the bar, and he hadn't made a single appearance since. In fact, she'd almost started to convince herself that whatever Kayden had said to him had chased the man away. Probably wishful thinking though.

She'd tried to call Ivy, her old boss, a few times, but so far the woman hadn't returned her call. She was the only person who knew where Harper was, so she had to have been the one to share her location with her father. Although, why she would do that, Harper wasn't sure.

"So," Cody started, "we have a few hours before the bar opens. Is there anything you'd like to do?"

"Well, I'm always up for a stop at Sugar and Spice." Damn her and her sweet tooth.

He chuckled. "What the woman wants, the woman gets."

When they turned the corner, two men came into view. Harper frowned. "Is that…"

Cody tensed beside her. "Travis and Dayne."

The men who'd worked at the bar, who'd stolen from Cody and warned her off him when she'd first started working there. They stood close together on the sidewalk and appeared to be arguing. Travis, in particular, looked like he was talking at a million words a minute.

"Come on, let's cross the street," Cody said quietly.

But before they could, both Travis and Dayne looked up. Travis's eyes narrowed, and right away he started moving toward them. Well, less moving and more marching. Dayne scrubbed a hand over his face before following.

Immediately, Cody pushed her behind him.

"You're a damn asshole," Travis yelled before he'd even stopped in front of Cody.

Cody kept one hand on her arm as he spoke, his voice calm. "What are you talking about, Travis?"

"It's not enough that you fire me and have me labeled a thief around town, but you also set your fucking sheriff brother on me?"

"I don't know what you're talking about."

Travis shoved Cody in the chest, causing Harper to gasp, but Cody barely moved. "You *do* know what I'm talking about! Your brother dragged me into the station and questioned me about whether I threatened your precious bartender in the alley behind the bar. Hell, he even questioned me about the fires. Was that your doing? Or should I be talking to *her*?"

Travis stepped to the side, but Cody mimicked the action, blocking his line of sight. "Don't even *look* at her. And if you push me again, you better be ready for me to push back. I didn't set

Eastern on you. If he decided you were a possible suspect, that's from *your* actions, and you have no one to blame but yourself."

A scowl crossed his face. "You're a dead man, Walker."

"Is that a threat?" Cody's voice was so dark, Harper almost didn't recognize it.

Dayne grabbed Travis's arm. "Come on, man. Let's go. He's not worth it."

Travis shook his friend off. "Not a threat. Just a warning that I'm not happy. And when I'm not happy, no one is."

He turned and stormed down the street in the other direction. Cody didn't move immediately, instead waiting until they were a good distance away. When he finally faced her again, there was visible anger in his eyes, but it wasn't conveyed in the soft tone of his voice.

"Are you okay?"

She nodded. "You?"

"Yeah. Just ready for the assholes to leave us alone." This time, he didn't just take her hand, he slid an arm around her waist and led her across the road. She didn't miss how his gaze continued to move down the street, almost like he expected Travis to come back.

Sugar and Spice was full of people, with half the tables filled and Mrs. Sandler busy behind the counter, serving customers. Cody led her over to an empty table. She was about to sit when her phone rang, Ivy's name popping up on the screen.

"I've got to take this, Cody. It's my old boss returning my calls."

He nodded, and she moved to a quieter corner of the shop before answering. "Hi, Ivy."

"Hi. Sorry it's taken me so long to return your call. You have *not* been easy to replace. I mean, I've replaced you, but jeez, I'm only just realizing how much you did and how efficient you were."

She cringed. "Sorry. If my situation was different, I would

have stayed and trained the next person."

"Hey. I know you. I know you'd only have left for a good reason. Whatever the family emergency is, I hope it's getting sorted out."

Nope. Not getting sorted out at all. "Family is kind of why I'm calling. Did you happen to share the town I'm in with any of my family?"

"Actually, your mother stopped by. I couldn't believe how much she looked like you, just older! She was quite upset, said there was a big problem and you weren't reachable, but she needed to send you something and asked for your address..."

Harper closed her eyes.

This was all her fault. Illegal or not, in a small southern town like Hamilton, of *course* Ivy wouldn't have hesitated to give her address to her mother. She'd never shared any of her family issues with her old boss, and what kind of person didn't want their own mother to know where they were?

Just her.

"Sorry, I...I know I shouldn't have done that," Ivy hastened to add, after Harper's obvious silence went on long enough to turn awkward. "I just thought—"

"It's fine." Her eyes popped open. It wasn't fine, but what else could she say? "Thank you for being a great boss, and I hope my replacement catches up on everything quickly."

* * *

Keeping his eyes on Harper, Cody pulled his phone out of his pocket and called his brother. Eastern picked up on the second ring.

"Cody—"

"Travis is damn unstable."

There was a small pause. "Did something happen?"

"He just threatened me on the street while Harper was with me. Basically threatened her too."

"Whoa, back up. Start from the beginning."

Cody took a breath to try to calm the rage that coiled inside him. "He saw me and Harper, rushed over, and started spewing shit about how I already fired him and got him labeled a thief, and now I'm the reason he was taken into the station and questioned about the attack on Harper in the alley. His exact words were, 'You're a dead man, Walker.'"

"Jesus. Okay, I'll handle it."

Even though his brother was trying to reassure him, Cody knew there wasn't a lot he could do other than keep an eye out for the guy. Travis hadn't broken any laws. He was just angry and talking shit.

"I just wanted to keep you aware of the situation. I'll talk to you later."

Cody ran his fingers through his hair and turned toward the counter. He met Harper's gaze as she remained on the phone across the room and winked at her, receiving a small smile and a reddening of her cheeks in return.

Damn, she was beautiful.

"Cody, honey, sorry I was busy when you and Harper arrived," Mrs. Sandler said, stopping in front of him. "It's been a crazy day. What can I get you?"

"Just a black coffee for me and an iced coffee for Harper."

"Any cupcakes or cookies?"

"Yeah, that would be great. Surprise us." He held out his card. "How are you doing?" The woman looked tired.

She sighed. "I'm missing Sadie. I have a couple of young girls who work here, but nothing's the same as having my grand-daughter by my side."

"How is she?"

"She's set to marry Scott in a month."

There was the smallest hint of distaste in the woman's expression. She didn't like him. But then, not many people did. Word around town was that the guy was boring as shit and had almost no personality. "Are you going to the wedding?"

"I am. It'll be nice to see her again."

"Well, shout out if you ever need a hand here."

She handed back his card. "Thank you, honey. You've always been so helpful. All you boys have."

He dipped his head before moving back to the table just as Harper sat down with him. His hand immediately went to her back. "Everything okay?"

"It was my old boss, Ivy, who told my mom where I am." She lifted a shoulder. "I never let her in on what went on with my family, and even though she shouldn't have shared that information, I can't really be angry at her. She thought she was helping."

Regret tinged her words… She was blaming herself for her father finding her and showing up like he had. "Hey. He could have chosen to stay away. You ran. You blocked your brother's number. They knew you wanted nothing to do with them, yet still he came here. That's on him."

She swallowed, then nodded. "Yeah."

"You know what will turn this day around?"

"What?"

"Copious amounts of sugar."

The corners of her lips tugged up. "Really? That's all it takes?"

"Well, that and some Cody time."

This time she threw her head back and laughed. "You know what, I think you're right."

Mrs. Sandler came to their table and set down a donut and a double chocolate chip cookie. "Good surprise?"

Cody grinned at her. "Great surprise." Then he looked at Harper. "I've had a few of them lately."

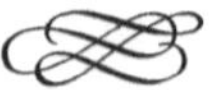

CHAPTER 20

"So, this is the Misty Peak Sunday Market," Harper said as she took in all the stalls. Some were set up with fruits and vegetables. Others sold hot food. There were even some pre-loved clothing canopies and a couple that sold home-made craft items, like bee and bird houses.

Cody's fingers tightened around her hand. "It is. It's very much loved by the locals, exactly why you see so many people here on a Sunday morning. Mrs. Sandler even comes and sells some baked goods that aren't on her usual menu."

Harper's belly growled. "You mean I can have some Sugar and Spice goodness without even going to the store?"

"Yep."

"God, this town's dangerous for my waistline."

He lifted her hand and kissed the back of it. "Eat the cupcakes. You'll always be beautiful."

Oh, Jesus. Every time she thought he couldn't get any better, he said sweet things like that.

Her smile was short-lived though, because when she looked up, it was to see Vanessa standing a few stalls away with a group of women. Her friends were talking around her, but her attention was fixed on her and Cody.

For some reason, Harper felt the urge to tug her hand out of Cody's. Maybe because she didn't want to attract any more trouble. Maybe because she felt neither Cody nor herself had the energy for a confrontation when so much else was going on. But when she tried, Cody's fingers tightened, preventing her from going anywhere.

He frowned at her. "Hey, you okay?"

"Yeah, I just…I don't want to cause any trouble with Vanessa."

He stopped and faced her to cup her cheek with his free hand. "Harper, I don't care about Vanessa or what she thinks or does. I care about *you*. Touching you is as natural and necessary to me as breathing. And more than that, I *want* to touch you."

More sweet words that made her pulse race. "Can I tell you something? Every so often a part of me still wonders if you and I are a good idea…if falling for you will just make it hurt worse if things don't work out. Because things *never* work out for me, Cody. But then you go and say something like that."

He lowered his head, his lips grazing hers before his mouth moved to her ear. "There is no part of me that *ever* wonders if you and I are a good idea. I *know* we are."

She sucked in a sharp breath, no idea how to respond to that. There was a part of her that was glad he was so confident. She needed that because it wiped away some of her own hesitation.

She opened her mouth, not exactly sure what words were about to come out. But someone else spoke first.

"Maybe you two lovebirds should get a room."

They both looked up to see Kayden grinning at them, Eastern by his side.

Cody straightened. "What are you guys doing here? You never come to the market, Kayden."

He lifted a shoulder. "Decided to change things up."

"It's good to see you both." Eastern shoved his hands into his pockets, his gaze returning to Cody. "I got a call from Nylah last night."

"Really? She still loving life in Cradle Mountain?" Cody asked.

"Yeah, I don't think she's ever coming home."

As the three men spoke, Harper's gaze wandered to a vendor who sold small handmade wooden houses. One of them in particular caught her attention. The details...they were exactly like the home she'd always envisioned she'd buy one day. A white picket fence. Adorable shutters. It even had the charming feel of a country cottage.

The crowd kept blocking her view, so she took a step away from Cody. "I'm just going to look at the stall over here. I'll stay within sight."

She ducked under the pop-up and lifted the small house, tracing the intricate details. It was beautiful. Whoever made it had even gone to the effort of adding details inside. Beautiful furniture. Wall art. It must have taken hours.

"That's my favorite too."

She glanced up at the lady behind the table. There were half a dozen people around her, also looking at the houses. "It's beautiful. For a long time, I dreamed about buying a home just like this one."

Her smile was soft. "Maybe one day, you will."

"Maybe." She set the house back down, and the woman turned to another customer.

Harper looked for Cody, but the crowd had thickened and she could no longer see him or his brothers. She inched to the end of the stall, maneuvering around locals, and took a step in the direction she'd last seen him.

Suddenly, she was violently yanked around the canopy. She opened her mouth to scream, but a hand clamped over her lips and she was half carried, half dragged toward a border of trees.

She fought the person's hold, but they continued to drag her along, the trees offering enough coverage that if anyone was nearby, they didn't notice a woman being abducted in broad daylight. Then she was shoved hard against a wall. It had to be the back of a public restroom. It was the only building in the area.

Every other thought left her head when she looked up, her heart pounding in her chest...

Dad.

Her breath stalled, and she was instantly thrust back to the last time he'd stood this close to her. When he'd been high on whatever drug he was taking, vicious and angry, and she'd been a defenseless fifteen-year-old, so scared she'd barely fought back.

"I see you're avoiding me, Harper."

His deep, familiar voice slid into her veins like ice, causing the fine hairs on her arms to stand on end. "What do you want?"

"I spent eight years in prison because of you, and you dare ask me what I want?"

Because of *her*? Suddenly, the familiar fear shifted into something else. Something that hardened her voice and steeled her spine. "You mean because *you* pushed me down the stairs while you were high and the neighbors heard me scream?"

She didn't even see him move before his fingers wrapped around her throat, choking her. "You ungrateful bitch! I'm your *father*. If it wasn't for me, you wouldn't be alive."

Panic seized her chest as the air cut off in her throat.

"You think you can take all those years from my life and not pay for it?" he growled.

She tried to scream. To claw at his wrists. His arms. But every second that ticked by had more black dots hedging her vision—until a new voice sounded.

"Hey! Let her go!"

Harper barely heard the shout over the buzzing between her ears. She was sure she was going to pass out when suddenly her father grunted loudly, his fingers loosening around her throat.

When he grunted a second time, his fingers finally released

her and she slipped to the ground, gasping for air and grabbing her neck.

"Get away from her or I'll hit you again!"

She forced her eyes up to see Tilly standing there, a long, thick metal pole in her hands.

"I've already called the police," Tilly said. "They won't—"

Before she finished speaking, Rodney ran.

* * *

"What about Lock and Jace?" Cody asked, his gaze on Harper as he asked the guys if Kayden or Eastern had spoken to their other brothers recently.

Eastern nodded. "I spoke to Jace last week. He's doing well. Upbeat as ever. Lock's a bit harder to get in contact with."

While Jace was an Air Force Combat Controller, Lock was part of an Army Ghost Ops team. You never knew where he was or when he'd be reachable. "As long as they're both safe."

As his brothers continued to talk, a large crowd passed the stall.

One second. That's how long she was out of his sight. One damn second—and when the crowd cleared, she was gone.

Fuck! Where was she?

He looked at the vendor beside it, and the one beside that. She wasn't at either.

"Everything okay?" Eastern asked.

"Can either of you see Harper?"

As his brothers searched their surroundings, Cody pulled his phone from his pocket and called her number. She didn't answer.

He rushed over to the canopy while his brothers searched the area.

"Excuse me."

The woman looked up. "Yes?"

"Did you see where the girl went who was looking at that house?" He pointed to the one Harper had lifted.

She frowned. "Um, no, I'm not sure. Sorry."

Dammit! He found Eastern just as his brother's radio mic sounded.

"Call received from a Matilda Taylor reporting an attack on a woman at the market."

Cody's skin chilled.

Eastern lifted his mic. "I'm on the scene. Location?"

"Northern restrooms."

Cody was moving before the dispatcher had finished speaking, weaving through the crowd, ignoring the questioning looks from people around him. Something inside him told him it was her. Harper was the woman who'd been attacked.

Who had attacked her? Travis? Her father? The person from the alley? Goddammit, he should have kept her within reach at all times! The crowd was dense and he knew she was in danger.

When he saw her behind the building, his heart jumped into his throat. She sat on the ground, fingers on her neck, with Tilly crouched beside her.

He crossed the space between them and lowered to her side. "Storm! Are you okay?"

She glanced up, and when her fingers dropped, he saw deep red marks on her neck—bruises in the shape of fingerprints.

Fury washed over Cody's skin, sinking deep into his bones.

"It was my father," she said, as his brothers reached his side. "He grabbed me when I was at the stall and pulled me into the trees. I was in shock and didn't fight back as hard as I should have. He shoved me against the wall. He was so…so *angry*."

Eastern crouched in front of her. "Did he say what he wanted?"

Fear glazed her eyes, and Cody wanted to kill the asshole.

"He said it was my fault he went to prison. That I needed to pay. He started to choke me, but then Tilly hit him with a metal pole."

"I parked on the other side of the trees and saw them as I was entering the market," Tilly explained softly. "I yelled at him to leave her alone, but he wouldn't. The pole was sitting behind a tent, so I picked it up and hit him. Twice."

Harper gripped Tilly's hand. "Thank you. If you hadn't walked past when you did..."

Cody's hand fisted at her unfinished sentence. What would the asshole have done? Inflicted more injuries? Worse?

He helped Harper to her feet as more officers arrived. Harper took them through what had happened a second time, and Tilly answered questions the officers asked. Cody could barely keep his rage in check. The man had *touched* her. *Hurt* her. His own fucking daughter.

And it had happened because Cody hadn't kept her within arm's reach.

Kayden approached, anger rolling off him as well. "You okay?"

"No. I want to find the guy and make him pay for what he's done."

"Eastern will find him," Kayden said quietly. "And in the meantime, you and I will also be keeping our eyes out for him."

Right now, that didn't help. He hadn't kept a close enough eye on Harper today, and he sure as hell hadn't seen her asshole father.

When the police were done, Cody slipped an arm around Harper's waist and led her to the car, continually scanning the market.

He helped her into the passenger seat before moving behind the wheel.

When her fingers wrapped around his arm, her touch was soft. "Hey. Are you okay?"

His brows tugged together. "You're asking *me* if *I'm* okay?"

"You seem quiet."

He forced his features to soften as he looked at her. "I hate everything about this. That he got to you today. That he was already a shit father, but now he's trying to hurt you again."

"Me too. But Eastern said he's out on good behavior and what he did today is reason to lock him up again. That's good. As soon as they find him, he'll go back to prison."

"Storm…nothing about what happened today is good." He reached out and cupped her cheek. "I'm sorry I lost sight of you."

Her brows flickered. "Nothing that happened today is your fault."

"It is. Protecting you is my job now. And today, I failed you."

"Cody—"

"But next time I'll do better. I promise." He had to do better, because losing her when they'd barely begun wasn't an option.

CHAPTER 21

"How are you?" Tilly asked. "And I want an honest answer, because after what happened a few days ago, I know you'd have to be rattled."

Harper wrapped her fingers around her glass. The bar wasn't open, but they sat in a booth, quiet music playing over the speakers. "I don't actually know. On one hand, I hate that my father attacked me. And in the quiet moments I swear I can still feel his fingers around my neck." Feel his breath on her face…

She shuddered, and Tilly reached across the table and wrapped her fingers around Harper's hand. "I'm so sorry."

"Thank you. But on the other hand, I'm so relieved that you walked past. And Cody and his brothers have been watching me so closely since it happened. It's crazy that I haven't been here for very long, yet I have so many people looking out for me in this town."

"And we'll continue looking out for you." Tilly shook her head. "I still can't believe that was your father."

"He's…not a good guy." She looked up, the words coming easier than she thought they would. "He's been in prison for years for assault and drug possession. The assault was against me while I was a teenager."

Tilly gasped. "Oh, Harper…"

"I knew the time would come when he'd be released. I guess the optimistic part of me had hoped that if he ever found me, he'd be a changed man and repentant about what he did. Maybe even want to make amends." She scoffed. "It was probably more delusional than optimistic because it definitely has not been the case. Men like him don't change. Once evil, always evil."

"I understand crappy people. You know what I've learned these last few years?"

"That dads suck?"

"Yep, that, and also that having a bad parent is no reflection on us. If anything, we should be commended for our strength in not following in their footsteps."

Harper frowned. "Have you seen your dad since he stole from the people in this town and left?" She wanted to cringe at her wording, but she didn't know how to say it any other way.

"Nope. My guess is he wanted all the money to himself. That, and he knew my mother and I would want no part in what he did. She was the kind of person who did the right thing just because it was the right thing to do. She was an amazing woman."

"I wish I'd had a chance to meet her."

"Me too." Tilly blinked a few times. "What about your mom? At least tell me she's better than your dad."

"Not much. She's a drunk who stole my life savings. And my brother's pretty terrible too."

Tilly's mouth dropped open. "God. How did you turn out so well-adjusted?"

Harper laughed. "Well-adjusted? Uh, no. Insecure? Sure. Slightly dysfunctional? Definitely."

"Hey. I'm dysfunctional too. We can bond over it."

"Sounds like a hell of a friendship."

They both laughed, and Harper lifted her glass of juice. "To new beginnings."

Tilly lifted her glass. "May they be better than the crap we left behind."

They clinked their glasses and sipped. She remained with Tilly for another hour, chatting about anything and everything. The woman was easy to talk to and even easier to like. It was nice to just talk without having to censor what she said. How anyone could believe Tilly had a bad bone in her body, Harper had no idea.

When her friend rose and said goodbye, Harper locked up after her before heading to Cody's office. The door was ajar, but she still knocked. He glanced up from behind the desk, and she grinned at his reading glasses.

"I like the sexy glasses."

He leaned back in his seat. "Yeah? Like them enough to come over here?"

"And what would I do over there, Mr. Walker?"

His smile widened, showing one perfect dimple. "Come and see."

She took one step toward him, only to stop when her phone rang. She pulled it out, frowning when she saw it was an unknown number. Jesus Christ, was it her brother again? Better question, did he know their father was here?

Probably.

For once, she wanted to answer it. Tell him just what she thought about him even though it would likely achieve nothing.

"Everything okay?" Cody asked.

"Yeah, I just want to take this. I think it's Ross."

His eyes narrowed. "You sure you want to talk to him?"

"I need to ask him something."

Cody nodded, never taking his gaze from her. Instead of turning away, she crossed to his desk and lowered her head until her mouth touched his before whispering, "Keep the glasses on."

He growled, and she chuckled as she straightened and headed out of the room, only answering when her feet hit the stairs. "Ross?"

"What the fuck? I've been trying to call you for days."

She could have laughed at the irritation in his voice. "Don't tell me you're actually surprised I haven't answered. Ross, Mom stole from me and *you* hit me. Then the first call you make is to tell me Dad's out of prison."

He scoffed. "We had every right to that money, and I hit you because you were being fucking annoying."

This was her brother. This was her *family*. Unbelievable. "Well, as fun as this is, I only answered because I want to know if you knew that Dad was coming after me."

Ross laughed. Actually laughed. "I figured as much. He wanted to know your address, so I assume he wanted to find you."

"And you and Mom just up and got it for him? Not caring about what he'd do to me?" She shouldn't be surprised. But God, it still hurt. It always hurt.

"Mom would do anything for him. Actually, Mom's the reason I'm calling. She's in the hospital. Dad hurt her. She needs you to come home and take care of her."

Harper frowned. "Is she okay?"

"A few broken ribs. A black eye and a fractured wrist. Dad wasn't happy with the state of the house...or the state of *her*."

Ross didn't even sound disturbed by the fact his father had put their mother in the hospital.

She dropped her head into her hand, massaging her temple. "Did you file a police report about what he did?"

"No. Mom doesn't wanna get him in trouble."

Oh, sweet Jesus. She sucked in a deep breath before straightening. "I'm not coming home, Ross."

"Fuck, Harper—"

"If Mom doesn't want this to happen again, she should report the assault. If she doesn't, then no one can help her." Harper hung up before her brother could respond. There was no helping either of them.

* * *

CODY'S LEGS itched to get up and go to Harper. To make sure she was okay. Since the attack at the market, he'd barely left her side. And he wouldn't. Not until they found her father. He'd briefly wondered if the attack in the alley had also been her father, but realized that was before Harper had shared her address with her old boss.

The last few days had been quiet. He didn't even want to open the bar, but both Barry and Harper had convinced him he had to. And they were right. This was the only bar in town. People relied on him being open.

He was just finishing some paperwork when his phone vibrated with a call.

He leaned back in his seat, a smile tugging at the corners of his mouth as he answered. "Nylah Walker, I was starting to think you forgot you had a twin brother over here in Misty Peak."

His sister scoffed. "Forget you? The twin brother who didn't let me so much as breathe without watching? There's no forgetting you, Cody."

Yeah, he'd always been a protector. All his brothers had. And he didn't regret it for a second. "Is Liam still filling my shoes and watching out for you?"

"Uh, yeah. Yesterday, he demanded I take him with me to the *grocery store.* I think it will take him a while to get over what happened after I moved here."

Cody's muscles tightened. An internet-based militia group had gone after Nylah in Cradle Mountain just days after her arrival, when she'd unknowingly IDed one of their leaders. And they'd gotten too close.

"Good. I know you can look after yourself, Ny, but having someone watching your back is never a bad thing."

"Funny, that's kind of why I'm calling. I haven't been receiving my daily texts. It wouldn't have anything to do with your new bartender, would it?"

Cody rolled his eyes at the teasing inflection in her voice. He'd mentioned hiring Harper to work behind the bar, but he hadn't told his sister what had developed between them. "Who told you?"

"Told me what?"

The innocent tone didn't quite come off. "Nylah…"

"Fine. Eastern *may have* mentioned that you're dating Harper…and that she's in trouble. Is everything all right?"

Eastern…of course. Kayden was better at keeping things under wraps. "Yeah, we're dating. And she's found herself in a bit of trouble, but we're looking out for her."

"Is she okay?"

"Yeah, she's okay." For now.

"And she's living with you?"

One corner of Cody's mouth lifted. "Yeah, she's living in the apartment over the bar…for safety reasons." Although, it wasn't all for safety for him. In fact, she'd moved into his room—meaning, he got to hold her every night. Wake up with her in his arms every morning.

"Living together, working together, and you still like her. She must be special."

"She is."

There was a small pause, and when his sister spoke again, her voice was softer. "That makes me happy, Cody. You deserve special, particularly after the mess that was Vanessa. Is she leaving you alone?"

Nylah had never been in favor of that relationship, and when it had come out that she was cheating on Cody, his sister's dislike of Vanessa had only deepened. "No. But I'm working on it."

"Argh, I *hate* that woman. The day you parted ways was a good day."

"Yeah, I should have ended things before she showed me her true colors." Hell, he should have never dated her.

"But it sounds like everything's worked out the way it was meant to. I knew it wouldn't be long. You're too much of a catch. Who do you think will be the next to partner up out of our brothers?"

Cody laughed. "Kayden and Eastern don't seem close." Especially Kayden. The man never dated. He had brief flings here and there, but he'd never once dated anyone long term.

Nylah sighed. "The day Kayden settles down will be the day the moon turns purple."

Cody laughed.

"What about Avery? Is she okay after her mother *left* her? I still can't believe that. I mean, I never liked Jaime, especially because she barely let me see my niece, but I never thought she'd leave Avery."

"She's strong. And Eastern's doing a great job of filling the role of both parents, even while being town sheriff."

"I'm not surprised." They spoke for another few minutes before Nylah sighed. "Well, I've got some studying to do, so I'll let you get back to the bar."

"Okay. Love you, Ny."

"Love you too, Cody. Look after yourself and Harper."

"Will do."

When he hung up, he couldn't hold off any longer. He headed up the stairs and into the apartment to find Harper standing by the window, her back to him. She wasn't on the phone anymore, but she also didn't move as he stepped into the room. Had she not heard him?

Slowly, he crossed the space between them and slipped his arms around her waist. She jolted at his touch, but then her gaze shot up and she softened back into him. "Sorry, I didn't hear you come in."

"Are you okay?"

"Not really…my mom's in the hospital after my dad beat her."

The muscles in Cody's arms tightened. The fucking asshole. "Did she file a report?"

"Nope. Apparently, she doesn't want to get him into trouble."

"What the fuck?"

"I know," Harper said softly. "It doesn't make sense. But then, not many of my family's decisions do."

Slowly, she turned, her hands slipping up his chest and cupping his cheeks. "Have I mentioned how grateful I am to have you?"

"I'm grateful to have you too."

She shook her head. "No, I mean *really* grateful. If I hadn't stumbled across this town, upon you, in the middle of that storm—"

"But you did. And I have a feeling you were always going to."

The corners of her mouth lifted a fraction. "Kind of like fate?"

"Exactly like fate." He lowered his head, and he kissed her.

CHAPTER 22

Harper moved quickly and efficiently behind the bar. She couldn't believe she'd only been working here a month and she already felt so confident serving drinks. Of course, the customers made it easier. The majority were locals, and by now she knew most by name. There were the occasional rude people, usually tourists, but you got that anywhere, and somehow Cody seemed to have eyes in the back of his head, always ready to swoop in.

Not that she needed saving from rude customers, something she'd told Cody more than once. Although, it did feel good to have someone on her side.

"I have a question, Harper."

She glanced up at Archie as she ran a dishcloth over a clean glass. He was probably the first customer Harper had learned the name of just based on his frequency here. "Yes, Archie?"

"How did Walker get such a pretty bartender to work for him?"

He was also a sweet talker. "He just got really lucky, I guess."

"Nah. No such thing as luck." He lifted his beer to his mouth.

"You don't believe in luck?"

"Nope. We work for what we have. I work really hard to be your best customer, and you must work really hard at being so beautiful."

"You're gonna make me blush, Archie."

"You hitting on my staff, Archie?" Cody's arm curved around her waist, causing her to jump.

Archie lifted his beer again. "Just trying to figure out how you got her to work in this dump."

"Must be the Walker charm."

Archie scoffed. "Keep dreaming."

Harper shook her head with a smile as she moved down the bar.

Over the next half hour, the crowd finally thinned out. She glanced at Cody from beneath lowered lashes, already anticipating sliding into bed with him. He was still talking to Archie, that lopsided, dimpled grin on his face. Her heart thumped. It was almost criminal how easy he was to look at.

Doubts still crept into her mind every so often. Doubts from past hurts that she had little to no control over. Was it dangerous how quickly they'd entered into this relationship? Could you really know a person in such a short amount of time? And what if this was all just because of heightened emotions from the danger around her?

Stop, Harper. Don't overthink the one good thing in your life.

Blowing out a breath, she grabbed a tray, then collected glasses and dirty napkins from tables. In the kitchen, she set the glasses in the sink. She was just rinsing them when heat pressed against her back.

"I cannot wait to be in bed with you tonight."

Her breath caught at Cody's words. At the way his hands slid around her body, his mouth touching her neck.

She bit her lip to stop the groan. "Cody, there are still customers out there."

He pressed a kiss behind her ear. "You're right. Let's get these people out first."

This time she *did* groan when he stepped away from her.

They returned to the front, and as Cody started to clear the last customers, Barry rounded the bar and stopped at her side. "How are you doing?"

She lifted a shoulder. "As good as I can be, I guess. I'm grateful for Cody and you and this town, but after the few incidents, I'm still a bit rattled."

"As anyone would be. But you know, even though I give Cody his fair share of shit, he protects those he cares about."

She glanced at Barry, a soft smile on her face. "I've seen that. I'm lucky he cares about me."

"He's lucky too. Trust me." Barry reached for something beneath the bar, then set a small box with the Sugar and Spice logo on the surface. "Here. I picked this up for you today."

Her lips pulled into a smile. "You got me a cupcake?"

"Yeah, but don't tell boss man. I like him to believe I'm a tough nut."

She didn't hesitate, she just pulled Barry into a hug. *This* was the type of kindness she was grateful for. This was what got her through the hard times. "Thank you."

"You're welcome, Harper."

He stepped into the kitchen just as Cody moved back behind the bar. He spotted the box immediately. "What's that?"

"Nothing."

She slipped it off the counter and moved it behind her back. Cody, of course, didn't let it drop. He moved over to her, his steps slow. "Is it a cupcake from Sugar and Spice?"

"Maybe."

"Did Barry give it to you?"

"I'm not at liberty to say."

He stopped in front of her, his mouth moving to her ear. "I

need to watch the men in this town. First Archie calls you beautiful, then Barry gives you a cupcake."

"People are nice."

Cody's mouth trailed down her neck, then across her cheek. "Maybe. Or maybe they're trying to take what's mine."

"Yours?"

"Mm-hmm. *Mine.*" One more kiss, and he stepped away. But then he frowned. "Do you smell that?"

She took a deep breath in, and her entire body went taut. "Smoke."

Suddenly, Barry ran back into the bar. "There's a fire in the alley dumpster."

Harper started to rush toward the back, but Cody shook his head. "Stay inside and lock the door."

"Cody, I can help!"

"No. Barry and I will handle it."

She opened her mouth to argue, but Cody was already running down the hall toward the back door.

Her legs shook to go after them. She wasn't helpless. She could be useful. But instead of running after them, she walked toward the door as Cody requested.

She was just reaching for the lock when the door was shoved open from the other side.

She gasped when a man barged inside. "Travis! What are you doing here?"

"It's a bar. I'm here to have a drink, Harlow."

"It's *Harper.* And we're closed. You need to leave." She held the door open for him, but he didn't step back toward it. Instead, he continued toward the bar.

"No soldier boy? Does that mean I have to get a drink myself?"

He moved as if to step behind the bar, but she ran in front of him. "I'll say it one more time before I call the police. *Leave.*"

He leaned in close, his breath—which already reeked of alcohol—brushing against her face and making her gag. *"No."*

"Fine. I'll get Cody." She took off toward the back door, but strong fingers wrapped around her wrist, pulled her back, and shoved her against the bar.

"Hey. Hold on, babe. Let's not go doing anything crazy."

She tried to move around him, but his hands went to either side of her body, caging her to the bar. "You're drunk. Leave now before you do something you'll regret."

"Something I'll regret?" He laughed. "Do you know what it's like to live in a town where everyone looks down on you? I can't even walk into my local fucking *bar* without being kicked out."

There were very good reasons for that, and Travis knew it. "Coming in here like this will just make it worse."

"Nothing could make it worse." He leaned closer. "Wanna tip?"

"No. I want you to step back before I make you."

She was a second away from kneeing this asshole between the legs when his mouth neared her ear. "Here's my *tip*—if you were smart, you'd leave. This town won't be kind to you."

* * *

Flames danced in front of Cody's eyes. *Goddammit.* Who the fuck set a damn dumpster ablaze?

"I've already called the fire department," Barry said as he carefully attempted to close the nearest lid. Cody ran to the other side of the dumpster to pull the other lid down. The fire was contained to the dumpster and they technically didn't need to call the department, but being safe was smart.

Barry pulled out his phone. "I'm calling the sheriff."

Eastern wasn't on tonight, and Cody didn't want to call him personally because he'd be home with Avery. "Good, I'll check on Harper."

He'd just stepped in when he heard voices down the hall,

coming from the bar. What he saw when he entered made fury slip into his veins and spread like wildfire.

Harper, pushed against the bar, with Travis looming over her.

Cody was across the room in a second, grabbing Travis off Harper and throwing him into the pool table. "What the fuck are you doing?"

The asshole laughed, but the sound came out more as a scoff. "I'm talking to your new piece of ass. I see you haven't labeled her a whore or a thief yet, like you did Vanessa, me, and Dayne. Waiting for the perfect time?"

Cody's hands fisted, and he itched to throw a punch. "I told you to stay away from her."

"And what the mighty Cody Walker wants, he gets, right?"

"Did you start the fire in the alley?"

"Someone set a fire in the alley? Shame it wasn't the bar. If it was me, I would have burned this place to the fucking ground."

Cody stepped forward, but Harper grabbed his arm. "Cody, don't. He's drunk and trying to get a reaction out of you."

"Yeah," Travis said quietly, voice condescending. "Listen to your woman…while you still can."

"What the fuck does that mean?"

"Well, from what I hear, she was attacked in the alley. Her car was torched. And wasn't there something about someone grabbing her at the market?" Travis leaned forward. "Don't worry, I've got your back. I told her to leave. I mean, it's probably best, right? Just look at how easily I got to her tonight. Imagine all the things I could've done to her while you weren't here."

Cody swung, nailing the asshole in the face.

There was an audible gasp from Harper behind him, drowned out by the sound of sirens from the street.

"That's the *second* time you've threatened her," Cody growled. "Do it a third time, and I'll give you more than a black eye."

Two officers rushed inside the bar, the first guy's eyes narrowing on Travis, then Cody. "What happened here?"

"I was trying to lock the door while Cody and Barry worked on the fire out back," Harper rushed out before Cody could get a word in. "Travis forced his way in. He trapped me against the bar, then Cody came inside and pulled him away."

The officer switched his gaze back to Cody. "You hit him?"

"He *threatened* her," Cody snarled.

Travis groaned as he leaned on the pool table, clutching his face.

"His timing is also damn questionable," Cody continued. "He showed up seconds after the fire started."

"Fuck you," Travis groaned from behind his hand.

The officer sighed as he and his partner lifted Travis from the table. "Come on, time for some questions."

"You're taking *me* in?" Travis growled. "He *assaulted* me!"

Travis fought the officers but didn't have much success. Not only was he drunk, he was outnumbered two to one.

Cody stepped up to Harper, his hands skimming her arms and waist. "Are you okay?"

"I'm fine. You didn't need to hit him."

His back teeth ground together. "What he said—"

"Was wrong. But hitting him is just going to make it worse."

Fuck, she was right. He knew she was. He scrubbed a hand over his face before meeting her gaze again. "I'm sorry."

"Come on, let's check the alley."

The next hour was a rush of firefighters putting out the blaze and Barry, Cody, and Harper answering questions. When it was finally time to go upstairs, it couldn't have been soon enough. Harper went up first while Cody locked up the bar.

He'd just secured the front door when Eastern called.

"Hey."

"Cody. Is everything okay? I got the alert that there was a fire at the bar, but I fell asleep in Avery's room so didn't have my phone with me."

"Fire was in the dumpster. It's been put out."

"Any suspects?"

Cody ran his fingers through his hair. "Travis was here. Forced his way inside while I was out back and Harper was by herself in the bar. She's okay. I hit him though, and police took him in."

"Shit. What a mess. You think the fire was his doing?"

"He says it wasn't...but I don't know. There's too much going on right now, and I don't like it."

"I know, brother. We'll get it sorted out."

Yeah, but when? "Thanks for checking in, Eastern."

"Always."

When he reached his apartment, it was to find Harper already in bed, the lights dimmed. He took a quick shower before sliding in behind her and pulling her against him.

"Still mad?" he asked quietly.

"I was never mad. Just...tired."

Tired...of what was happening? Or more? "You know what we need?"

"What?"

"A date."

There was a small pause before she spoke. "We've been on a date."

"Not to Sugar and Spice or to the mountains. To dinner. Just you and me. Let me wine and dine you."

She looked over her shoulder, a slow smile curving her lips. "I'd like that."

"Good." He kissed her. "Sleep."

CHAPTER 23

The Italian restaurant was busy, particularly for a Monday night. But that wasn't what had her attention transfixed. It was the white collared shirt Cody wore, with the top two buttons undone and showing just a bit of skin. It was the way that even though the shirt was loose, there was no denying the muscles beneath.

Man, he looked good.

"You know I don't need fancy, right?" she finally said, almost wanting to squirm under his watchful gaze across the table.

His blue eyes twinkled in the dim lighting. "What *do* you need?"

That was a good question. Not much. "A smile in the morning. Someone who sees me as an equal. And a surprise cupcake here and there wouldn't be terrible."

"I'll buy you all the cupcakes in the world if it makes you smile."

She grinned. "That would be very dangerous." But hell, she wouldn't say no.

"Did your previous partners see you as an equal?"

Her brows shot up at his question. She hadn't been expecting it. "I don't think so. They weren't the best boyfriends." Understatement of the century. "I've been cheated on. I've been broken up with via text. One guy told me that he might stay if I got some work done. I think he was referencing my breasts."

Cody's brows flickered. "You have beautiful breasts, Harper. And I think that every man who came before me was crazy."

"Is that right?"

"Well, they'd have to be to not have realized what they had when you were together. To not care if they lost you."

"You're a bit of a charmer, Cody Walker."

"Either that or honest."

She shook her head, a smile she couldn't stop spreading across her lips.

He leaned forward. "So…can I ask you something?"

"Why do I feel nervous about that?"

"Why didn't you put more distance between you and your family earlier? They're awful people. And the guys you dated were dicks."

"I should have." She fiddled with the napkin in front of her. "While I was in high school, a friend's mother got me an after-school job. Then, when I graduated, I had to move out as soon as possible because I couldn't stand living in the same house as Mom and Ross. I got the cheapest apartment the farthest I could get from my family, while still close enough to my job. I cleaned offices until an assistant job came up in the building, then a couple years later, I worked my way up to executive assistant."

She lifted a shoulder. "I guess I got comfortable. I felt lucky to have the job. I was able to save money. Dreamed about the day I'd have enough to buy the house I wanted, far away from my family. I think I got so caught up in the dream that I didn't realize I should have left a long time ago."

"Your story kind of reminds me of my mother's. She came to Misty Peak after leaving a family that didn't treat her right. Met my dad, and the rest was history."

Harper tilted her head. "I wish I could have met her."

"She would have loved you. Losing her was the hardest thing I'd experienced up to that point. They didn't find the breast cancer until it was too late, and we didn't get nearly enough time to say goodbye."

She reached across the table and weaved her fingers through his. "It must have been so hard."

"It was. My dad though…he fought the lymphoma for years. Gave it hell. Best decision I ever made was leaving the service before he passed so I could spend those last few months with him."

"What was your best memory of him?"

He laughed. "I have so many. He had the best sense of humor, and he just doted on us kids, especially Nylah. He was also our greatest protector."

"Ah, so that's where you get it from."

"That's where we all get it from. All my brothers are the same."

When their drinks were set in front of them, she didn't miss how the server's gaze lingered on Cody a beat too long. She couldn't blame the woman. He always looked good, but tonight he was on a different level. A can't-take-her-eyes-off-him level.

"So," she started softly as she lifted her drink to her lips. "Tell me the truth, am I your best hire at the bar?"

One side of his mouth twitched. "You sweep the floor with the other four."

Her brows rose. "Four? So Travis, Dayne, the guy you hired who never showed up, and…?"

Something she couldn't identify flickered across his face before he answered. "Vanessa."

"Vanessa worked at the bar?" Why hadn't he mentioned that before now?

"*Very* fleetingly. I'd just gotten home, and she was between jobs, so her working behind the bar helped both of us."

That shouldn't make her feel uncomfortable, right? So why did it? "Is that how you started dating?"

"Yes. I knew it couldn't last. We were too different, something I should have paid more attention to. But I didn't listen to my gut."

"You and I are different." The words slipped into the air before she could stop them.

"We're not different in the big ways. We both have the same ethics and morals. And we both want to make this work."

He was right. Of course he was. Maybe she just needed to stop questioning things and bringing her past insecurities into play.

The waitress stopped at their table again, this time setting down their meals. Immediately, Harper leaned forward to smell her ravioli. The pasta was filled with ricotta cheese and drowning in a luscious cream sauce.

She groaned. "Oh, God, I take it back. You can wine and dine me here whenever you want."

At Cody's silence, she opened her eyes to see him staring at her with the most intense look in his eyes. "I'll bring you here whenever you want, Storm."

She could feel herself blushing, and when she couldn't think of a witty reply, she looked at Cody's plate. It wasn't just *her* food that looked amazing, his tagliatelle with pork ragu looked and smelled just as good.

"So, how do you feel about sharing food?" he asked, as if reading her mind.

"I'm not opposed to it."

Without another word, he put some pasta on his fork and placed it in front of her. She opened her mouth, another groan slipping from her throat when the delicious flavors hit her tongue. "My God, food in this town is out of this world."

"That's not the only thing that's out of this world."

She blushed again, tilting her head. "Stop being such a charmer."

"Never."

The conversation was lighter throughout dinner, but for some reason, the little fact that Vanessa had worked at his bar kept playing on her mind. Why, exactly, she wasn't sure. Because he'd admitted to not listening to his gut and dating her anyway? Because that story was all too similar to theirs?

Halfway through her meal, she pushed her chair back. "I'm just going to pop into the bathroom."

He nodded, and she felt his gaze on her the entire way. It was hot and way too intimate for the busy restaurant.

In the bathroom, she was just about to come out of the stall when the door opened and the voices of two woman sounded.

"Doesn't Cody Walker look hot tonight?"

"Just tonight? That man always looks good."

The first woman's voice lowered. "And he's with that bartender of his. The one who's had trouble following her around town. Man, he just loves to save people."

Harper frowned. What were they talking about?

"Has he saved someone before?"

"Don't you remember Vanessa? She started working at the bar when she had that really aggressive ex who wouldn't take no for an answer. I'm pretty sure that's how her and Cody got together. He was protecting her from the guy and she was bragging all around town how safe Cody made her feel."

"Oh, I *do* remember that."

"She actually told me it was a double-edged sword though. Cody likes playing protector, so when she didn't need one anymore, he started pulling away. Especially emotionally. Like, of *course* she shouldn't have cheated on him, but it probably got to a point where she just wanted someone to dote on her and love her again."

So Vanessa had not only worked at the bar but she'd needed protecting...just like Harper?

And that's what Cody was good at. What he'd openly admitted time and time again.

Everything these strangers said played into Harper's every fear. That Cody's affection toward her was temporary. That she wasn't meant to have a forever kind of love. That eventually, he'd leave her or hurt her…or both.

* * *

CODY SHOT a glance toward Harper in the passenger seat. She'd been quiet since returning from the bathroom, barely saying a word other than asking if he was ready to go.

He wondered if it had something to do with the women who'd gone in after her. He vaguely recognized one of them as a friend of Vanessa's. He also remembered how much she liked to gossip.

His fingers tightened around the wheel. "Is everything okay?"

There was a small pause, and he could almost hear her thinking before she answered. "Did Vanessa have issues with an ex?"

His brows slashed together. The woman had told Harper about Vanessa's ex in the bathroom? "Yeah. He came into the bar a few times while she was working there and caused trouble. I let him know he wasn't welcome, and Eastern kept an eye out for him. He still does. He's bad news."

She nodded, seeming to consider his every word. "Can I ask you something?"

"Anything."

"Do you see *us* as long term?"

Did she *not* see them as long term? Or had he not been obvious enough about the depth of his feelings for her?

When the corners of her mouth turned down, he realized he'd taken too long to answer.

Goddammit. "Yes. I see us as long term."

The silence between them stretched, and fuck it was loud, buzzing in his ears and thickening the air around him. When he pulled into a parking spot outside the bar, he turned toward her, but she was already climbing out.

He bit back a curse and followed her out of the car and into the bar. He waited until they were inside with the door locked before gripping her arm. "Harper, wait."

She stopped, but it was a moment before she turned. And when she did, his heart clashed against his ribs at the vulnerability on her face. The way she wrapped her arms around her waist in a defensive gesture.

He stepped forward, but she immediately inched back like she wanted space, and that small move shattered him. "Tell me what's going on in your head, Storm."

At the use of his nickname, her eyes widened a fraction like they always did. "I don't know. My emotions are all over the place."

His were too…because right now, he had no idea what was going on and all he wanted to do was touch her. "Try."

"It's stupid, but first you mentioned Vanessa worked with you, just like me. Then these women in the restroom said you like playing protector and get bored when you don't need to anymore. And…I don't know…I guess that just feeds into the part of me that feels undeserving of a happy ending to my story."

"You don't think you deserve a happy ending?"

"Life just keeps reminding me that it may not be in my plans. And every time I look at you, I wonder why you're with me. Because surely men like you aren't interested in women like me."

He could have laughed. "Intelligent women? Beautiful? Smart? Empathetic?"

"Women who were born on the wrong side of town. Women who have alcoholic mothers and ex-con fathers and a brother who has no problem with violence."

The familiar rage still slipped to the surface whenever she

mentioned that. "Harper, the family we're born into does not define who we are. You are *nothing* like the people who raised you, and that just makes me want you more. Because it shows your strength. Proves that despite your adversity, you still ended up here."

"I'm a mess," she whispered.

"No. You need reassurance that I'm in this for the right reasons and that I'm here to stay. And that's okay." This time when he stepped forward, she didn't step back. He slipped his arms around her waist, and God, touching her felt good. "I *am* a protector, and whether there's no one after you or an entire army of people, I will *still* be your protector. I won't get bored when things die down. In fact, I'm waiting for that day."

"Really?"

"Yeah, Storm. The day you walked into this bar, I felt something I'd never felt before with anyone. And those feeling have just grown every day since. They have nothing to do with who's gunning for you...although, yeah, that pisses me the hell off."

A hint of tears shone in her eyes.

"And when you asked me if I saw us as long term, I only hesitated because I was surprised you needed to ask. I thought my desperation for you was written all over my face every time I set eyes on you."

Her chest rose on a deep inhale. "Cody...I'm sorry. I—"

"Don't. Don't ever apologize for needing reassurance. It means I haven't done my job in making you feel secure in us."

A single tear slipped down her cheek, and he wiped it away with the pad of his thumb. She turned her head and kissed his palm. "Thank you."

She was quiet for a moment, the pain in her eyes shifting into something else. Something hotter. Her fingers grazed up his chest before settling on the top button of his shirt. Slowly, she undid it.

"Storm...what are you doing?"

"I've been wanting to undo these buttons all night."

Another popped open. Then a third. His fingers tightened on her hips. "Is that right?"

"Mm-hmm. It's actually been driving me a bit wild."

Five more popped open, then she pushed the shirt aside, her soft fingertips grazing his bare skin. She inched forward, her warm breath brushing over his flesh before she dipped her head and kissed his chest.

His breath stalled. "Harper…"

"That almost sounds like a warning, Mr. Walker." She continued to kiss his chest as her fingers went to the button of his jeans.

His fingers dug into her hips. "There's no almost about it."

The sound of his zipper going down was loud in the quiet room. Then, she reached inside his briefs and wrapped her fingers around his cock. He groaned deep in his throat, his chin dropping to his chest.

Her mouth continued to move across his chest, kisses like small flames burning his skin. When her hand started to move against the length of his cock, he lost the last scrap of restraint, growling as he lifted her and turned to place her on the pool table.

CHAPTER 24

Cody lifted Harper so quickly, she barely had time to grab him before she was planted on a hard surface. Then his mouth crashed to hers, his tongue sweeping straight inside.

She moaned, widening her thighs and wrapping them around his waist. She reached for his cock again, continuing to play and stroke. His groans were loud and primal. That, in combination with the feel of him in her fingers, sent the blood rushing between her ears. He was thick and long, his tip pushing against her core.

For a moment there, she'd pushed him away. Almost let the fear inside her win.

"I only hesitated because I was surprised you needed to ask. I thought my desperation for you was written all over my face every time I set eyes on you."

She nipped his bottom lip as his fingers went to the edge of her sweater, tugging it and her shirt over her head in one swift move. Then he kissed down her neck and slid his hands behind her back, unclasping her bra.

The second her breasts fell free, he cupped them, his lips

wrapping around one straining nipple as he grazed the other with his thumb.

She cried out, her fingers slipping into his hair, pulling at the strands. Every stroke of his tongue made a new ripple of desire burn through her. She was barely aware of it when one hand left her breast and moved down her body, stopping at the top of her jeans.

The button popped, the zipper glided down, and he whispered, "Lift for me, honey."

Her head was such a fog of desire that she had to play his whispered words over in her mind a couple of times before they made sense. With her hands on the table, she pushed up and kicked off her heels as Cody pulled her jeans and panties down her legs.

Then he was back between her legs, his mouth once again on her neck as his hand dipped between her thighs.

The air in her lungs stalled as he swiped her clit. Then did it again and again.

Oh, God, she was on fire.

She gripped his shoulders, digging her nails into his flesh. His thumb continued to move against her core as a finger touched her entrance. He slid inside.

It was an onslaught of sensations. Possession and desire and urgency rolled into one.

He found a spot behind her ear with his mouth and nibbled while his finger thrust in and out of her, and his thumb worked her clit.

"Cody…" she gasped, tightening her legs around his waist and tugging him into her. Telling him with her body what she needed, she reached between them, wrapping her fingers around his cock once again and positioning him at her entrance.

He growled as he withdrew his finger, and she nudged him inside her. Heat flared in her belly as he found her lips again. He'd just pushed in another inch when she pressed at his chest.

He stopped immediately, his mouth separating from hers. "Are you okay?"

"You're not wearing anything."

His muscles bunched beneath her fingertips and he cursed under his breath before reaching into the pocket of his jeans and pulling out a condom. He tore it open with his teeth before slipping it over his cock. Then he was back between her thighs, his tip pressing at her entrance.

This time, his kiss was gentler. More of a graze. One swipe. Two.

"I need to tell you something, Harper."

He expected her to understand words when he was inching inside her? "What?"

Another kiss, then words whispered against her skin. "I'm falling in love with you."

Her heart slammed against her ribs, any remnants of calm splintering. The action was so sudden and violent it stole her breath. "Love?"

His gaze bore into hers. "Yeah, Storm. Love."

Three breaths, each as shaky as the last. Then, "I'm falling in love with you too, Cody."

The words were so easy to say out loud. Like they'd been there at the surface for a while, waiting to be released.

His eyes darkened to an almost black shade, then his mouth slammed to hers again as he thrust inside her. Her scream was silenced by his mouth. By his tongue melding with hers.

He began to thrust, his hand returning to her breast, kneading. Palming.

Everything burned. Her limbs. Her skin. Even her lips felt like they were alight at the way he kissed and devoured her.

When his thrusts became faster, she tugged her mouth from his and threw her head back. The sounds spilling from her chest were so primal, she almost didn't recognize them as her own.

His head dipped and he once again wrapped his lips around

her nipple and sucked, his tongue sweeping her bud back and forth.

She was so close to the edge she could feel the foundation crumbling beneath her. Then his hand returned to her clit and swiped, and she fell, her walls clenching his cock as she broke around him.

* * *

THE SWEET SOUND of Harper's orgasm shot straight into Cody's chest, piercing his heart. He released her nipple and lifted his head, watching the array of emotions play over her features. The complete relief and vulnerability.

Fucking gorgeous. Every inch of her. And his. She was all his.

He kept thrusting as her walls pulsed around him. As her desperate moans pierced the air. He wanted to stretch this moment. To stay inside her for endless minutes. But too soon, he reached that cliff edge, and he couldn't hold on. He fell. Shattered so fiercely and violently that he barely knew how his legs kept him upright.

He thrust into her until he had nothing. Nothing but her.

When he finally stilled, the silence slipped around them, beating over his skin and holding him in place.

Both their breaths came quickly, and on every inhale, Harper's breasts grazed his chest.

He touched his forehead to hers. "You're unbelievable, Harper."

Her eyes closed, fingers slipping behind his neck. "Only when I'm with you."

She still didn't get it. She was the sun, the moon, and every damn star in the sky. She was everything, all the time, regardless of who she was with.

Gently, he slipped out of her. Then, with an arm around her back and waist, he lifted her from the pool table. His jeans were undone, his shirt unbuttoned, while her clothes lay strewn over the floor of the bar, but he ignored all of that as he carried her up the stairs toward the apartment. Instead of going straight into the bedroom, he went into the bathroom and gently placed Harper on her feet as he reached around her and turned on the shower.

She just looked up at him, still naked, complete trust in her eyes. Damn, she undid him.

Quickly, he removed the remainder of his clothes before lifting Harper once again. This time, she wrapped her legs around his waist and her arms around his neck. She fit so well against him. Like this was exactly how they were designed to be. Together. Connected.

He stepped under the warm spray of water, and immediately she tightened her hold on him, her head lifting as her gaze bore into him.

"Did you mean what you said? About falling in love with me?"

Fuck yes, he meant it. If he was honest with himself, he'd probably been falling in love with the woman since the day he set eyes on her.

"Yes."

"No one's ever said that to me before."

Some of the warmth in his chest cooled, an icy anger taking its place. But he made sure to keep it off his face.

"Never?"

She shook her head. "My family never said it. And my relationships never got to that point."

The anger coiled in his gut. This woman should have been told every day, multiple times a day, that she was loved. That she was easy to love. That she was *made* to be loved.

He lowered his head, his mouth grazing her lips. "I'll tell you every day, Storm. Every. Damn. Day."

CHAPTER 25

$\mathcal{H}$arper climbed out of the car, and Cody was immediately by her side, his hand slipping to the small of her back. She glanced up at the Misty Peak Visitors Center. It looked different at night. The windows of the building were illuminated with light while the moon cast a dim glow over the trees and mountains that surrounded the center.

"This place is beautiful," Harper said quietly as they made their way toward the building. "I can see why Kayden likes to come here every day."

"He likes the peace and quiet. Not so much the tourists. I'm honestly not sure why he works with people. He's too low on patience and I think he'd be better suited to a job where he worked on his own."

"Maybe he just pretends he doesn't like people when really, he enjoys the company."

Cody laughed, a full belly laugh. "I'm not sure that's it. I always suspected my brother could live on his own in the mountains and be perfectly happy."

Harper shook her head, not believing that for a second. Of course, there were some people who'd suit that lifestyle. But most people needed at least *some* company, and by the amount of time Kayden spent visiting Cody at the bar, she suspected he was one of them.

"Will many people be here tonight?"

"Yeah, I think quite a few locals from around town were invited. Linda made it more of an open invitation so that anyone who wanted to celebrate her retirement with her could."

"When does she finish?"

"A couple weeks. I hear she's going on a big vacation after."

She nodded as they stepped inside the building. Sure enough, the visitors center was filled with people. A table of food sat against the back wall, including a giant cake, with a banner hung above that read Happy Retirement Linda. Music played throughout the room from ceiling speakers, with chairs and a few tables positioned around the space.

Cody's hand slid around her waist, tugging her into his side. He'd closed the bar for the night so they could attend, but despite his smile, he'd been tense most of today. Possibly because a roomful of people meant threats could come from any direction. But surely they were safe when he and his two former special ops brothers were also in attendance?

He guided Harper toward Eastern and Avery. The small girl immediately ran over to Cody. He lifted her into his arms and threw her up in the air. "Hey, beautiful girl."

"Uncle Cody, have you seen the cake? It's vanilla and strawberry!"

"What? Vanilla and strawberry? That's my favorite."

Avery giggled. "No, it isn't. It's *my* favorite."

"Can't it be both of ours?"

She shook her head. "You like chocolate. That's what we got you for your birthday."

"Oh, yeah, I forgot."

She laughed again. "You forgot your favorite cake flavor?"

"Yeah, silly Uncle Cody. Luckily, I have *you* to remind me." He touched Harper's arm. "You remember Harper?"

Avery turned her intelligent eyes on Harper. "Hi. What's *your* favorite cake flavor?"

"Have you ever had Nutella cheesecake?"

Her little eyes lit up. "No. But I like Nutella."

Harper leaned forward and lowered her voice. "It's *amazing*."

Immediately, Avery wriggled out of Cody's arms and tugged on Eastern's top. "Dad, can I have a Nutella cheesecake at my next birthday?"

He sipped his beer, a knowing smile on his face. "Sure."

"There's Mrs. Sandler. I'm gonna tell her!" Avery ran across the room toward the bakery owner.

Harper cringed. "Will there be a problem if Mrs. Sandler doesn't do Nutella cheesecake?"

Eastern shook his head. "Nah. Her birthday's not for a while. She'll change her mind at least a dozen times before then."

"Oh, good." She shifted her gaze to see Tilly standing on her own, wineglass in hand, several feet away. Harper frowned. The other woman hadn't mentioned she was coming tonight. But then, neither had Harper.

She touched Cody's arm. "I'll be back in a second. I'm just going to say hi to Tilly."

His gaze landed on the woman before he nodded.

Harper crossed the room. When she touched Tilly's arm, the other woman jumped, then touched a hand to her chest. "Harper, sorry, I was in my head for a moment."

"That's okay. Is everything all right?" She was holding her wineglass very firmly and she didn't look...comfortable.

"Yeah, I'm just a bit nervous to be here. So many people and all."

"Has anyone said anything to you?"

"No. But starting a conversation with anyone is like pulling teeth." She shook her head. "I'm probably being too sensitive."

"Not at all. Your feelings are valid. I'm sorry people are making you feel uncomfortable."

"I'll get used to it. Anyway, how are you? I'm sorry, I don't think I've checked in enough since Travis barged into the bar. Has he made another appearance? Or your father?"

"Actually, no. Neither of them have. Which is good, I guess."

Tilly frowned. "You don't sound certain."

"Not seeing or hearing from my father in particular makes me nervous, because I don't know where he is or what he wants." Well, other than to seek some form of revenge on her for his jail sentence because the guy couldn't take responsibility for his actions.

"Eastern and the other officers haven't spotted him?" Tilly asked.

"Unfortunately not, but Cody keeps reassuring me that if he's here, they'll find him."

Tilly touched her arm. "Eastern's good at his job, and Cody's good at looking out for people. If they say you're safe, I'd trust them."

"I'm trying. Trust doesn't come as easily to me as it should. Anyway, I didn't ask. Are you here because you're close to Linda?"

Tilly's brows rose. "Actually, I'm—"

Her words were cut off by a small commotion near the entrance. Harper turned her head to see a beautiful woman with thick auburn hair and ice-blue eyes throw her arms around Cody's shoulders. Behind her stood a tall man with light brown hair and gray eyes.

Harper shifted her attention back to the woman. There was something oddly familiar about her. When she released Cody, she moved to Eastern and wrapped her arms around him before Avery's small arms wrapped around the woman's legs. That's when it clicked.

Tilly leaned into her. "That's—"

"Nylah," Harper finished with a smile. "Cody's twin sister."

* * *

"WHAT THE HELL are you doing here, Ny?" Cody asked, unable to wipe the smile from his face as his twin lifted Avery into her arms. He hadn't seen his sister in months.

Nylah frowned at him. "You thought I was going to miss Linda's party? That woman's family. I had to come."

Liam stepped forward and held out his hand. "It's good to see you again, Cody."

"You too, Liam. You doing well after everything?"

Cody had left Cradle Mountain shortly after the office of Liam's security company had been blown up and his team almost killed. It was a crazy mess.

"Yeah, we're doing really well, actually," Liam said with a nod. "Working from a new office and happy to not have any assholes targeting us."

"Good. I'm glad." After everything he and his team had gone through, they deserved to be safe and happy.

Nylah was just setting Avery back on her feet when Kayden stepped out of the crowd. He grinned before Nylah threw her arms around him. He swore his sister was the only person who could make their grumpy oldest brother smile.

"What are you doing here?" Kayden asked as they parted.

"I can't believe any of you need to ask that. It's Linda's retirement party." She shifted her gaze to Cody and lowered her voice. "And I need to meet Harper. Is she here?"

Of *course* his nosy twin sister would want to meet Harper.

He lifted his gaze to see Harper watching both him and Nylah from across the room. He smiled at her and immediately, she headed toward them. When she reached his side, he slipped an arm around her waist. "Harper, this is my twin sister, Nylah, and her partner, Liam. Nylah and Liam, this is Harper."

Liam dipped his head. "It's nice to meet you."

"You t—"

Harper's greeting was cut off when Nylah tugged her into her arms. "It's so nice to finally meet you! I've heard so much about you."

Harper chuckled. "Good things, I hope."

"The best." Nylah pulled back. "Is my brother treating you right?"

"He is."

"Good. Otherwise, I'd have to beat his ass." She thumped his shoulder before turning back to Harper. "You don't have a drink. Come on, let's get a drink and you can tell me everything."

Cody frowned. "You're just taking her?"

"Yep." That was all Nylah said as she dragged Harper away.

Liam stepped closer. "Can you tell how excited she's been to meet Harper?"

"Should I be worried?" Hell, why was he even asking? His twin had a million embarrassing stories at her disposal.

"Yes," Eastern answered for Liam. "Be very worried."

Kayden held out his hand to Liam. "It's good to finally meet you in person rather than over video calls."

Cody had almost forgotten that he was the only one who'd met Liam in person.

"You too," Liam said as he shook Kayden's hand, then Eastern's.

"So, you said things in Cradle Mountain have been good?" Eastern asked.

"Yeah. Quiet."

"Great, otherwise we'd have to drag Ny back," Kayden said.

They all smiled at that, because everyone knew Nylah had a strong mind and did what she wanted, not what others dictated.

"How's it been here?" Liam asked.

"We could use a little quiet," Cody said before he could think better of it.

The easy expression slipped from Liam's face, and his brows tugged together. "Nylah mentioned something. What's going on, exactly?"

"Just had a bit of trouble with Harper's family, a town firebug, and a drunk guy I can't seem to shake." So, plenty had been going on. Certainly more than usual.

Liam's frown deepened. "Anything my team can help with?" Liam's security business, Blue Halo, was one of the best. Although, they were based across the country in Idaho.

Cody shook his head. "Not at the moment. Eastern and his officers are watching things, but we'll let you know if that changes."

Liam dipped his head.

The next hour was a mix of catching up with Nylah and chatting with locals. When the music quieted, everyone looked toward the front as one of the employees at the center gave a speech about Linda. Harper leaned into his side, and Nylah stood at his other, her hand in Liam's.

When it was Linda's turn to speak, visible tears shone in the older woman's eyes. "Thank y'all for coming. I'm not going to speak for long because you all know I'll become a blubbering mess. But I will say that it's so nice to see so many familiar faces here tonight. You've all become like family to me. I'll be sad to leave my position as the manager here—it's been rewarding and challenging and I've met the best people. I'll still be around town, bothering everyone and getting into your business…after my big vacation, that is."

The crowd laughed before Linda continued. "What makes this move easier though, is knowing that this place will be in good hands once I'm gone. I'm so excited to announce my replacement —Matilda Taylor."

There was a collective silence, only broken by a couple of gasps. The smattering of applause from the crowd came later than it should have, and it wasn't as loud as it should have been.

Linda hurried to continue. "Tilly has a business and marketing degree and special interest in the Smoky Mountains, as this is where she grew up. I trust her to run the visitors center with care and passion, and I know she will take it places I never could."

Cody shot a look at Kayden to find his brother's jaw locked and his knuckles white around his beer. The man did not look happy.

CHAPTER 26

"Um, no, he absolutely *was* afraid of lizards," Nylah argued from across the bar. "I loved reptiles and got one for my tenth birthday. Cody wouldn't go near it for the first year."

Harper grinned at Cody. It was the middle of the day, and she sat on a stool beside Nylah, while Liam and Cody stood behind the bar, Cody with his eyes narrowed on his sister.

"Is that true?" Harper asked, surprised that the seemingly fearless man in front of her had ever had a fear in his life. "I thought you weren't scared of anything?"

"First of all, I was ten," Cody began. "Secondly, I'm pretty sure that phobia was caused by Nylah putting the thing on my face while I slept and having to wake up to this creature crawling over my nose and mouth."

Oh, God. She'd probably have a fear of lizards too if that happened to her.

Nylah bit her bottom lip, probably to stifle the grin. "The things we do to our brothers when we're ten."

"That story almost makes me glad I'm an only child," Liam said, shaking his head.

Cody bumped his shoulder. "Don't fall asleep around her and any reptiles, man."

They all laughed. It was the day after the retirement party, and Nylah and Liam had stayed over in the guest room upstairs. They were only here for one more night, so Harper was sucking up the time she got to spend with Cody's twin and her partner before they left. The morning had been slow, with a late wake up and everyone preparing breakfast together. Nylah had been sharing so many stories of her and Cody's life growing up, and they all made Harper laugh.

"I like these stories," she said with a grin as she lifted her coffee to her lips. "I feel like I'm getting to know the real Cody."

Nylah leaned closer. "I have a lot more where they came from."

Cody groaned. "When did you say you were leaving?"

"Not as soon as you'd like, brother."

A knock sounded at the bar door, causing both men to straighten.

"Expecting company?" Liam asked.

"No." Cody moved toward the door, with Liam not far behind. When he pulled it open, Harper could just see Tilly on the other side.

When Tilly saw the two large men looking down at her, her mouth opened and closed before her gaze shifted around them to Harper. "I'm sorry. Is this a bad time?"

Harper rose to her feet and moved toward the door. "No. Is everything okay?"

"Everything's fine. I just wanted to check if you were free for a visit. I texted but…"

Harper cringed. "Sorry, I left my phone upstairs." Guilt slithered down her spine because the woman really looked like she needed a friend, and after last night, Harper wasn't surprised. The news of her replacing Linda had not exactly been met with overwhelming joy. She'd hoped to talk to her again at the party, but Tilly had left too quickly after the announcement.

Cody stepped back. "Come in. Liam and I will head upstairs. I need to put him to work to help me fix a cabinet, anyway."

"Are you sure?" Tilly asked.

"Absolutely."

Harper gave Cody an appreciative smile as Tilly stepped inside. He closed and locked the door before leaning down and pressing a kiss to Harper's cheek. "Yell if you need me."

"I will."

When the men disappeared, Nylah stepped forward. "Hey, Tilly. How are you? I haven't seen you in years." Her voice was gentle, probably perceiving that was what Tilly needed at the moment.

"It's been a rough few weeks, but I'm getting there."

"Would you like me to leave too?" Nylah asked.

Tilly shook her head. "No. Stay. Please." She lifted a box. "I brought way too many Sugar and Spice cupcakes, and Harper and I will definitely need help finishing them."

Nylah's mouth dropped open. "You are a literal angel. Do you know how much I've been dreaming about those cupcakes since I left?"

"Can't be as much as me," Tilly laughed.

They moved to a booth, and Harper waited until they were seated with the box of cupcakes open in the middle of the table before asking, "How are you doing after last night?"

Tilly hesitated, and that hesitation told Harper everything. "A couple of people approached me to congratulate me, which was nice. Mrs. Sandler. Ali. But if I'm honest, it was really disappointing. I intentionally got to town weeks before the announcement to get people used to the idea of me being here. I guess a part of me was hoping I could convince everyone that I'm not the bad guy." She laughed, but there was no humor there. "Make them like me."

Harper reached across the table and placed a hand over hers. "I'm sorry. Maybe it will just take a bit more time."

"For what it's worth," Nylah started slowly, "I never blamed you for what your father did. His actions are not your burdens to bear, and I'm sorry others don't think the same."

Her smile softened. "You've always been so kind, Nylah. Cody and Eastern, too."

They all heard the name she'd failed to mention.

Nylah's expression turned sympathetic. "Kayden will come around. He'll have to, seeing as you'll be working together at the center."

"I don't know." Tilly picked at her cupcake. "I tried to talk to him last night, and it was so frosty that I could almost feel the ice forming between us."

"He has trust issues," Nylah said quietly. "As the oldest brother, he always took on extra responsibilities to take care of the family. Especially after Mom died."

Tilly nodded. "I get it. I do. My father stole a lot of money from a lot of people. I knew moving back here would be hard. I just didn't realize it would be *this* hard."

"What can I do?" Harper asked.

"You're already doing it. You're being a friend."

"And I'll *keep* being a friend." A mischievous grin spread across her lips. "And as a friend, I think I know what we need."

"A shotgun for all the closed-minded townspeople?" Nylah scoffed under her breath.

Harper laughed. "Well, that and…margaritas. We just got a new shipment of triple sec, and it's a really good one."

Tilly groaned. "Yes, please. I would die for a drink right now."

"Do you need help?" Nylah asked.

"Nope. I've got it. You two catch up." Harper rose from the table and went into the back room to find the still-sealed box of liquor.

She'd just lifted the box onto a table when something covered her mouth from behind and a strong arm slipped around her waist.

For a split second, shock rendered her still. Then the chemical on the cloth began to fill her nose. She tried to kick the person behind her. Tug her arms out of their hold. But they held her too tightly, and a strange heaviness began to filter through her limbs, making it so she could barely move.

Oh God! What was on the cloth?

The person turned, and the last thing she saw was the open window, then her world turned dark.

* * *

"ARE you sure you don't want us to stay a bit longer?" Liam asked as he held the wooden plank in place at the top of the cabinet. "Just in case you need an extra set of hands?"

Cody nailed the plank in place. "I appreciate the offer. We've actually been struggling to find a location for where her father might be staying. If Callum could look into it…"

"Done."

Callum was their tech guru at Blue Halo Security. He was able to find a lot of information that others couldn't.

"Thanks." Cody grabbed another nail. "I'm glad my sister found such a great guy. A bit surprised you're former military, considering she left here to get *away* from her overbearing military brothers, but then, also not really. I always knew she secretly loved our overbearing nature."

Liam laughed. "As I hope she secretly loves mine."

He secured the final nail in place before stepping back. "Thanks for your help. It's one of those jobs I've been meaning to get to for a good year."

When he'd moved into the apartment, there were a few things that needed repairing. He'd been working on them slowly, one at a time.

"Anytime." Liam frowned. "Everything okay with the woman downstairs? Tilly, was it?"

Cody walked into the kitchen and grabbed two beers from the fridge. "Depends what you mean by okay. Her father was a broker, and a lot of people in town trusted him with their money. Unfortunately, five years ago, he took the money and ran, putting people in very bad situations…including our father."

"Shit."

Cody pushed one of the beers across the counter. "I don't think Tilly had a part in it or knew what was going on, but it didn't help that she and her mother left town a month after her father."

"Maybe they just couldn't take what their father had done, and being here was a constant reminder."

Cody's thoughts too.

Liam sipped his beer. "I can say that though because I'm separate from the situation. I imagine that her returning would have reminded locals of what her father did, and because he's not here for them to blame…"

"They blame her," Cody finished. "Exactly."

Which was wildly unfair to Tilly but also not entirely surprising. "Let's go back down. With everything going on, I like to have eyes on Harper as often as possible."

"You got it."

They jogged down the stairs and into the bar. Cody frowned when he noticed Harper wasn't with the women. He stopped beside the booth. "Hey. Where's Harper?"

Both women looked toward the kitchen, but it was Nylah who answered. "She went into the back room to make margaritas, but now that you mention it, that was about ten minutes ago."

Cody set his beer on the table and checked the kitchen. His heart slammed against his ribs.

The previously locked window was wide open. Someone had broken in.

Fuck!

He ran forward and wrenched open the kitchen door—which should also be locked, but right now, it wasn't.

Nothing. No car at the mouth of the alley. No people.

Gone. Harper was *gone*!

A mix of rage and panic burned through his veins as he pulled out his phone and tried her number. When ringing sounded from the dumpster, Cody's skin went cold. Liam entered the alley next and was moving before Cody could, jumping into the dumpster and climbing out of it a second later—with a cell in one hand and a cloth in the other.

Liam lifted the cloth to his nose. His eyes narrowed. "Chloroform."

A fear like none he'd ever experienced hit Cody so hard that he almost fell to his knees. With muscles that felt like they were about to snap, he made another call. His brother answered on the second ring. "Cody—"

"She's gone, Eastern. Someone took Harper."

CHAPTER 27

*H*arper groaned at the pounding in her head. God, it was intense. It traced around from the back of her skull, across to her temple. She tried to push up to a sitting position, but immediately her arms gave out and she dropped back down to a soft surface.

What was wrong with her? Was she sick?

Wild panic coiled in her belly, but she forced it down.

Breathe, Harper. Just breathe.

It took repeating those words in her head three times to finally gain the strength to roll from her side to her back. She scrunched her eyes as the pounding intensified.

Maybe this was what a migraine felt like? She had no idea. She'd never had one, but her mother used to complain about them a lot after a heavy night of drinking.

Slowly, she peeled her eyes open.

The first thing she saw was a wooden ceiling with an old single globe light centering the space, casting a dull glow over the room.

She forced her head to turn, ignoring the throbbing pain in her skull. The room was almost bare, with no windows, a bucket

213

in a corner, and the single mattress she was lying on. There wasn't a door that she could see, just a set of stairs against the far wall.

What the hell? Where was she? And how did she get here? The last she remembered, she was at the bar with Cody, Nylah, and Liam. Tilly arrived. They sat at a booth. Then…

What happened next? Why couldn't she remember?

Slowly, she tried to sit up for a second time. Again, her elbows threatened to give way, but she refused to let them, using all her strength to get up. She was taking in the room again when she heard something above her. Heavy footsteps.

Something cold and uncomfortable slid over her skin. When the creak of a door opening sounded next, that cold turned to ice. Suddenly, part of her wanted to run, but even if she could… where would she go? Where was she?

The other part of her knew she needed to stay calm. Needed to find answers. Why was she here, and who'd brought her?

A man walked down the stairs, and when she saw his face, her heart stuttered in her chest.

Dad…

For the first time since she'd seen him that day on the street in Misty Peak, he didn't have an angry scowl on his face. In fact, he looked pleased with himself.

The last memory suddenly hit her. The cloth over her mouth as she'd struggled with someone in the kitchen of the bar—it was him.

"You," she whispered. "You drugged and kidnapped me."

He raised a brow. "Surprised?"

No. And wasn't that the saddest part? That she wasn't surprised her own father would do something so horrific? The man who was supposed to raise her. Love her. Protect her.

Straightening her spine, she let the old hurt shift into anger before slowly forcing herself to her feet. Her head ached and her knees threatened to crumple, but she ignored it all, refusing to let whatever her father had drugged her with keep her down. She needed to be on somewhat of an equal level with him for this conversation.

"Why?" The word was quiet but strong. "Because you still can't take responsibility for your actions? You still can't acknowledge that it was *your* fault you were arrested all those years ago? That you wouldn't have been arrested had you not hurt your daughter or had those drugs?"

The smug expression slipped from his face, the scowl she'd grown so familiar with once again returning. "You were always an ungrateful little bitch. Even growing up, you didn't show one ounce of gratitude for what your mother and I did for you."

"What you did for me? You did nothing but hurt and disappoint me! Make me feel like I was a burden on you both. What exactly should I have been grateful for? The fact that you had no ability to regulate your emotions? Or maybe for beating your family whenever you lost your temper? The only thing I was ever grateful for was your arrest."

Her father was across the room in a flash. She barely saw his fist coming before it slammed into her face. Pain cascaded through her skull as she fell back to the floor. It was so intense that bile rose in her throat, threatening to break free.

"How about being grateful that I didn't fuckin' end you when I could have?" Her father growled as he towered over her. "That I didn't starve you. That I allowed you to go to school."

Despite the pain, she could have laughed. So she was supposed to thank him for letting her exist? She probably should have kept her mouth shut, but the need to get her long-unspoken words out was greater than any self-preservation.

"You're a sad excuse for a human being."

The kick blasted through her ribs so hard that it stole her breath and caused her to curl into a ball. "No. That's *you*. Eight years. You took *eight years* off my life! Now I get eight years of *yours*. That's how this works."

She turned his words over in her head a few times before they finally computed. Did he mean…

"You plan to keep me here for eight years?"

"Yep. Not so cocky now, are you?"

She shook her head, the pain barely registering now, white-hot panic taking its place. "You can't do that."

He crouched in front of her, his face blurring before her eyes. "Who's gonna stop me?"

"I'm not on my own anymore. I have people in Misty Peak who care about me. They'll search for me, and they won't stop until they find me."

"Let them try." He rose to his feet and moved toward the door.

She tried to push up, but the pain in her ribs and head had her groaning and falling back down. "What are you going to do with me?" The words were supposed to be yelled, but she wasn't even sure they reached him.

He stopped on the stairs and turned his head, that ugly grin back on his face. "Whatever the hell I want." His eyes raked over her from head to toe. "You turned out decent looking. I'm thinking you can make me a pretty penny."

Nausea welled in her belly.

"But for now," he continued, "I'll just let you lose your mind down here."

Then he kept walking, like he hadn't just revealed he was going to let his daughter rot in a basement while selling her body.

The panic rippled in her chest, gnawing at her insides and pulsing in her throat.

Don't panic, Harper. Panic won't get you out of here. You need a plan.

She was struggling to focus on her breathing when something poking into her hand caught her attention.

She glanced down to see a protruding nail in the floorboard. A *big* nail.

She grabbed the top and twisted. It didn't move. But that didn't stop her. She kept pulling and twisting.

Even when her fingers began to ache. Even when beads of blood slipped from the tips.

She needed a weapon, because there was no way she was letting this asshole keep her here without a fight.

* * *

CODY COULD BARELY KEEP STILL. His blood was rushing violently in his veins, and his skin felt tight enough to rip right off his bones.

She was gone. And he had no idea how to get her back.

The car had barely stopped in front of the sheriff's station when he was out and moving. Liam followed closely behind. Nylah was staying back at the bar to take care of the place with Barry. He couldn't think about anything but Harper right now.

He stepped inside and went straight into Eastern's office. His brother looked up from behind the desk.

"You find anything?" Cody asked before he'd even reached the desk.

"I know who took her."

Cody's feet ground to a halt. He was pretty sure he knew too, but if his brother had evidence... "How?"

"After the fire in the alley, especially considering it followed the attack on Harper, I made the decision to put surveillance cameras back there." He turned his laptop screen and hit a button on the keypad.

At first, the alley behind the bar was still and quiet. They could see Tommy sleeping beside the dumpster, his food bowl not far away. Then a car parked down at the far end, just in view of the frame.

Cody leaned toward the screen. When a man climbed out of the car with a bag over his shoulder, it wasn't until he was

217

halfway down the alley that Cody's suspicions were proven correct—Rodney Rain, Harper's father.

Fucking asshole!

The older man stopped outside the window to the kitchen. Eastern sped up the playback and they watched as he used tools to break the lock and gain entry.

Cody growled when the man exited the building through the door not long after, dragging a limp Harper with him. The asshole threw the white cloth into the dumpster before skimming her body with his hands. He found her phone and threw that into the dumpster as well, then swung Harper over his shoulder.

"I'm gonna kill him," Cody growled under his breath. "Tear him apart with my bare hands."

The door to the station opened, and Kayden stormed into the office, rage on his face. "You find her yet?"

"No," Eastern answered. "But we know it was Rodney Rain who took her."

Cody scrubbed his fingers through his hair. "We've already looked into the guy. We don't know where he is."

"What are his circumstances?" Liam asked. "Any other family?"

"A wife and son who live in Hamilton, Alabama. He put his wife in the hospital about a week ago."

Liam's eyes narrowed. "Okay. Maybe she knows something and, because he's hurt her, she'll talk."

He doubted it, but he'd try anything. He lifted Harper's phone and searched through her contacts for her mother, then hit her name. He was sure the call would go to voicemail when she finally picked up.

"Harper?" The woman's voice was raspy, like she'd just woken up.

"My name's Cody. I'm Harper's partner."

There was a short pause before she spoke again. "What do you want?"

"Your husband kidnapped Harper, and I need to know if you have any information that could be useful to help us find them."

"He wouldn't—"

"He *did*. We have the kidnapping on video."

There was a heavy pause.

Cody ground his back teeth. "He could kill her, Mrs. Rain. Your *daughter*. I know you two haven't had the best relationship, but surely you don't want her to die. Just one piece of information could help. Anything."

The silence stretched so long that Cody was on the verge of giving up, when Harper's mother finally spoke. "When Rodney heard she was in Misty Peak, he mentioned something about a friend he'd met in prison who has a place out your way. I assume that's where he's been staying. If he *did* take her, maybe she's there."

"Where?"

"I don't know."

Cody cursed. "What about a name for the homeowner?"

"Timmy? Or Tony? I don't know. It was something like that."

If it was all she had…

"Let's hope that's enough." He hung up and turned. "We need to find someone Rodney befriended in prison by the name of Timmy or Tony or something similar, who owns property near here."

Eastern started tapping keys on his laptop, while Liam put his cell to his ear, no doubt calling his team at Blue Halo Security.

Too many seconds ticked by as he waited, and every one of them bled slowly into the next.

Kayden clamped a hand on his shoulder. "We'll find her, brother."

Cody could only nod, because in the moment, words felt too fucking hard.

Ten minutes later, Liam hung up and turned. "Rodney shared a cell with a man by the name of Timmy Cellar, who owns an old farmhouse a few miles out of Misty Peak. I have the address."

Cody's heart thudded against his ribs. That was it. It had to be. "Let's go."

CHAPTER 28

*H*arper breathed through the ache in her ribs and head. She wasn't sure how much time had passed—it could have been minutes, or it could have been hours. Everything felt skewed and blurry.

Her fingers ached from digging the nail out of the floorboard, but she'd done it. The nail sat in her hold, and she wasn't letting go.

The thought of using it as a weapon made her feel sick to her stomach, but her father hadn't been lying about keeping her captive for years. If there was one thing she knew about him, it was that he didn't dish out empty threats. If he said he was going to do something, he did it. And she couldn't just sit and wait, hoping someone saved her.

She curled into a ball, trying to warm herself. Christ, the basement was cold. The chill had seeped beneath her skin, almost distracting her from the aches of her injuries.

He couldn't have given her a sheet? A thin blanket or a pillow? He expected her to sleep on this old, ratty mattress with nothing else.

He was an animal. And when he was locked up again, which *he would be*, she hoped they threw away the key.

Closing her eyes, she pictured Cody. The heat of his chest against her cheek. The strength of his arms around her.

She would return to him. She had to. She'd never told him she loved him. Sure, she'd said she was *falling* in love, but that wasn't the same. She needed to tell him that her heart belonged to him. That he'd changed everything. Given her hope for the future. Allowed her to trust in the good of people for the first time in her life.

A shudder rocked her spine, and she curled tighter into herself.

Was it nighttime? She was tired but she wasn't sure if that was because of the stress of the kidnapping or because it was late. She didn't want to fall asleep here because that made her vulnerable, but if her father didn't return, she'd have no choice.

When footsteps thumped against the floorboards above, she held her breath. Was her father coming down? Steps had sounded a few times since she'd woken up, but her dad had yet to return.

Then the click of the lock unlatching rang through the room, and Harper's body tensed. She remained on her side, eyes half-closed as she saw the bottom half of him from the top of the stairs. She watched as he slid the key into his right pants pocket.

Her heart started to beat faster in her chest, nerves trickling down her spine. One chance. That's all she'd have. And if she failed...God, she didn't know what he'd do. Hurt her again? Tie her up? Worse?

She watched as her father made his way down the stairs, his footsteps loud. He held a bowl and a glass in his hands.

"What? You're not even gonna get up and greet me?"

She remained silent, just watching.

"I brought you dinner." He lowered it beside the mattress. She gave it a quick glance, her stomach turning at the sludge-looking mix. No way was she eating that.

"Say thank you, Harper."

She could have laughed. He really expected a thank-you after kidnapping her and feeding her God knows what?

She remained silent, and as she knew he would, he crouched, his face red with visible anger. He grabbed her hair and wrenched her up, causing her to cry out in pain. "You still don't get it, do you? *I'm* in charge. I could let you starve if I wanted, so when I bring you food, you say *thank you.*"

"Sure. I'll thank you for making my life hell. When you thank me for *this.*" In one swift move, she swung her arm and thrust the nail into the side of his neck.

Her father howled as she pulled the nail out, blood spurting from the wound. As he grabbed his neck and rolled to the floor, she lunged for the key and tugged it out of his pocket. Ignoring the pain to her head and ribs, she ran toward the stairs. Her fingers shook as she attempted to push the key into the lock.

She missed. *Dammit!*

She tried again. It was on the third go that the key slotted into place. She'd just pushed the door open when strong fingers wrapped around her ankle and yanked her down to her stomach. She cried out when her already aching ribs hit the stairs.

She kicked her foot out hard, but he didn't let go. Instead, he pulled her down a few steps, her ribs colliding with each one before she was flung onto her back.

Her father reared his arm back, but she threw her head to the side at the last second and his fist collided with wood. He cried out, and she quickly fisted the nail in her grip and jammed it into his shoulder.

His face crumpled, his shout loud. She took advantage of his pain and used both hands and legs to push him off her. He tumbled down the stairs, but she didn't wait to see him hit the floor at the bottom. She turned and ran up the steps and out of the basement to find herself in a wide hallway. The basement door sat beneath the staircase to the second floor. An open entry to a sparse living room sat opposite the basement, with what she guessed was the front door at the far end. A few closed doors lined the rest of the hallway.

Quickly, she turned and locked the basement door before sprinting toward the front door. She turned the knob—but it didn't budge. She searched for a dead bolt, only there wasn't one. There was an old chain, but other than that, there was only a key lock.

No… She needed another key to get out. A key she didn't have.

A loud shout sounded from the basement, followed by heavy steps on the stairs.

Shit, shit, shit!

She ran back through the living room and into the kitchen. The space was old, with barely any furniture. Quickly, she tried the back door, but again it didn't open. Neither did the windows.

Panic started to drown her, tugging her under, but she took a moment to breathe. She'd locked the basement door. She had a little time.

She turned and ran back to the hall, keeping her steps as quiet as possible. When she passed the basement door, she gasped and flinched when it rippled with the force of what had to be her father throwing his body into it.

The wood groaned, the lock clearly struggling. A few more shoves and he'd break through.

Hide! the voice in her head screamed.

There were three doors that led off the hall. She chose the second one, quietly dashing inside.

A bedroom.

First, she tried the window, but after three tugs she knew there was no opening it. He'd sealed the home so she had no escape.

She turned and opened the old wardrobe that sat against the wall beyond the bed, next to the window. Empty.

She'd just slipped inside and closed the door when the

commotion of wood breaking and heavy footsteps sounded in the hall.

* * *

CODY FLUNG his head back against the headrest. They were speeding to the location, but it felt too slow. Kayden was driving, and Eastern and Liam were in a car behind them, with backup not far off. But every second she was away from him, every second she was in her father's grasp, was an opportunity that man had to hurt her.

His pulse beat fast and angry against his temple.

"Don't lose hope." Kayden's words penetrated the fog in Cody's head.

"I fought hundreds of battles in my time as a Delta Force operator, and I learned to switch off the part of my brain that felt fear. I learned to keep a calm head. But right now, I feel the fear like a burning in my lungs. A fist around my heart, squeezing."

The feeling was indescribable. Like he was helpless to soothe the pain and panic.

"Because this is personal," Kayden said quietly. "This is the woman you love."

Yeah, he *did* love her. Somehow, in such a small amount of time, she'd burrowed into his heart, and now losing her felt like losing a part of himself.

"But when we get there," Kayden continued, "you need to keep a clear head. If that's not possible, leave it to us. Eastern's already breaking enough rules by letting us come along."

Cody's hands fisted. There was no way he was leaving the task of finding Harper up to others. "I'm going in."

"Okay, but—"

"Kayden—I'm going in. I'll be fine."

"Fine, as in you'll let Eastern arrest her father, rather than point-blank shoot him?"

His fingers tightened around the butt of the gun in his hand. "As long as Harper's okay."

Kayden sighed as he pulled into a dirt driveway. An old two-story clapboard house came into view. The paint was peeling and the plants outside were either dead or overgrown. It looked exactly like what it was…an old farmhouse that hadn't been lived in for years.

The car hadn't come to a complete stop when Cody was out and running. Before he could reach the door, Kayden grabbed his arm and tugged him to a stop. "Don't be an idiot! We wait for backup and we enter through different points. Got it?"

Eastern's sheriff's car pulled up in the drive, and he and Liam climbed out, both armed with Glocks.

"Cody, you enter through the back," Eastern directed. "Liam and Kayden, through the sides. I'll go through the front. If we don't immediately find anyone, Liam and Kayden take the second floor, and Cody and I will search the first floor."

Cody nodded and moved around the side of the house. When he reached the back door, he wasn't surprised to find it locked. He pulled the small picks from his back pocket, something he'd always carried with him on missions and still kept in his wallet. It didn't take him long to pick the lock. Then, silently, he entered a kitchen.

He systematically moved around the space, opening all the cabinets that were big enough for a person to hide. Every one of them was empty, bar a few cups, plates, and food items.

When he stepped into the hall, he saw Kayden and Liam silently making their way up the stairs, as Eastern stepped through a busted door below the staircase that was barely hanging on by its hinges. He guessed it led to a basement.

Cody turned and walked down the hall quietly. The first room seemed to be storage. Boxes were scattered around inside, all closed and sealed. Keeping his gun raised and back to the wall, he cleared the room, checking behind the stacked boxes.

When the space proved empty, he entered the next one. A bedroom with a big double bed in the center and a wardrobe against the far wall, next to the window.

The bed frame went all the way to the floor, so there was no way anyone could hide underneath. He circled the bed, stopping in front of the wardrobe. Weapon raised, he quickly pulled it open…

An arm swung out, the hand holding a bloody nail pointed right at his chest.

Cody grabbed her wrist before she could make contact. "Harper!"

Her eyes widened, tears filling them before the nail slipped from her grasp and she flung herself against his chest. "Cody!"

He gripped her so tightly, he wasn't sure she was capable of taking in air. He breathed her in, both of them shaking.

She was here. And she was alive. *Thank God.*

When they finally parted, he growled at the dark bruising around her left eye. "Where is he?"

Fear tightened her expression. "I don't know! He locked me in the basement, but I found a nail and stabbed him before running."

Cody opened his mouth to respond when a flicker of movement from the doorway caught his attention. Immediately, he dove over Harper's body, sending them both to the floor behind the bed.

A bullet hit the wardrobe, right about where they'd been standing.

He cursed and covered Harper's body more fully with his own.

Bullets continued to spray the room, giving him no chance to rise and fire back. Loud footsteps sounded throughout the house, no doubt his team coming after hearing the gunfire.

"I'm gonna kill all of you!" the man growled.

Cody waited one more heartbeat before rising just enough to shoot.

He fired almost simultaneously with someone else from the hall, Cody's bullet catching the man in the chest, and the other hitting Harper's father from behind.

The man dropped, and Eastern stepped forward. His brother's round had been the kill shot. One bullet to the back of the head.

CHAPTER 29

$\mathscr{H}$arper watched the moon as it glimmered into the hospital room through the large window. It was late. Or early, depending on which way you looked at it. All she wanted to do was go home and sleep for a million hours, but both Cody and the paramedics had pushed for her to come to the hospital and get some x-rays and checks.

She could just hear Cody's deep, raspy voice from the hall. He was on the phone, possibly with Eastern or Kayden. It was the first time he'd left her side since he'd found her in that room.

Dread pitted in her belly at the memory of everything that had happened in the last twenty-four hours. The panic at waking in that basement. The fear of running and hiding from her father, who would no doubt have punished her for what she'd done.

Even as a kid, when she'd heard her father from the other room, angry and high, and knowing he could easily turn that anger on her, the fear hadn't come close to what it was tonight. Because tonight, she'd known that there was a very real possibility he'd kill her once he'd found her hiding spot. And it wouldn't have taken him long to find it. There were only so many places to hide in the old farmhouse.

There had been, of course, the slim chance she could have fought him off. He'd already been weak after she'd stabbed him in the neck and shoulder. But as she'd found out when he'd shown up in that doorway, he'd had a gun, and her single nail wouldn't have done much against that.

The hand on her arm caused her to jump, then cringe at the sharp pain in her ribs. She'd been given pain meds, but they must have started wearing off.

Cody cursed under his breath. "Sorry. I thought you heard me come in."

"It's my fault. I was somewhere else."

He wrapped his fingers around her hand. "How are you feeling?"

"I don't know. I'm not sure if I should feel good because my kidnapper's dead, or sad because that kidnapper was my father."

"You feel whatever you feel, Harper."

"I feel relief. But also a bit sad. Because after everything, I think I was still holding out some hope that he could change. Or at least learn to take responsibility for his actions. It was stupid."

"No, it was human. He never deserved you."

"No, he didn't." That was something she could say with utmost certainty. "I can't believe that after finally getting his freedom, all he wanted to do was make me suffer."

"He was sick in the head and incapable of manning up to any situation."

Cody was right. That was exactly what her father was. She squeezed his hand. "How did you find me?"

An emotion Harper couldn't place crossed Cody's face. "We actually called your mother."

Shock had her brows shooting up. "My mother?"

"Yeah. At first, she denied your father would have had anything to do with your disappearance. When I told her we had proof in the form of video surveillance in the alley, she told us about a man your father met in prison, who owned property not far from Misty Peak."

She nodded slowly. "I should probably be surprised that she denied my father's involvement. But I'm not. I'm surprised she helped you. And you know what…that *doesn't* make me sad. Because family isn't always blood. It's the people you find who love and support you the most. The people you choose."

He lifted her hand to his mouth and kissed the back of it. "We're all your family here in Misty Peak, Harper. And we always will be."

Her eyes teared up. "I'm learning that."

"I was so scared when I realized you'd been taken. And I'm so damn sorry that you weren't safe in my bar."

"It's not your fault."

"It won't happen again. That's a promise I'm making to you right now."

She tightened her fingers around his hand, noticing he didn't agree with her about it not being his fault.

A knock sounded at the door. They both looked up as a middle-aged doctor stepped into the room. He wore a white coat and had black-rimmed glasses pushed up on his nose.

"Hi. I'm Doctor Vass. I'm just letting you know I've looked over your x-rays and you don't have any broken bones, just a very bruised abdomen and some facial bruising."

She'd suspected as much. She'd experienced broken ribs as a teenager, thanks to her father, and this didn't feel as painful. "Thank you."

"You're free to go, but make sure you rest. The combination of the chloroform, the physical assaults, and the emotional stress will have taken a toll on you."

Oh, she definitely felt that toll right now. "I will."

When he stepped out, Cody's gaze bore into hers. "Ready to go home?"

Home…because Cody's home was *her* home. "Yes. Past ready."

* * *

CODY SLIPPED his arms around Harper's knees and back and lifted her out of the car. She'd fallen asleep within the first five minutes of the drive home, but then, he'd suspected she would. It was late evening and after everything that had happened, in combination with the pain medication, he wondered how she hadn't fallen asleep at the hospital.

He'd already unlocked and opened the bar door while Harper was asleep in the car, so he stepped straight in and kicked the door closed with his foot. He'd return to lock it once he got Harper to bed.

He still couldn't believe how close he'd come to losing her today. The pain and fear of having her out of his reach...fuck, it had nearly killed him. Wounded him to a point he was certain those scars would always be with him.

But she was safe. It was something he needed to continue to remind himself.

In the bedroom, he lay her down and slipped off her shoes and jeans. When he got to her shirt, he clenched his jaw. Specks of blood stained the material. Whether it was Harper's blood from the punch to the face or her father's from either time she'd stabbed him with the nail, Cody wasn't sure. Maybe both.

He tugged the shirt over her head, and she made a little humming noise.

He'd just pulled the sheet over her body when her eyes peeked open. "Cody."

"Yeah, Storm. I'm here."

She swallowed and rolled to her side, setting her hand on his. "Don't leave me. I need you tonight."

He wasn't going anywhere for a long damn time. "I just need to lock up and I'll be right back."

"Promise?"

"I promise, honey. I'll always return to you."

When her eyes closed, he lowered his head and touched a light kiss to her cheek. Another soft hum. The sound slid into his chest, piercing his heart.

For a moment, he just sat and watched the slow rise and fall of her chest. Safe. She was safe. It was something he'd be repeating in his head a hundred times before the sun came up, and he'd need to keep repeating it tomorrow, and the day after that, to truly believe it.

When he finally gained the strength to leave her, he rose from the bed and moved back downstairs. He'd just locked the door to the bar when his phone rang, Eastern's name popping up on the screen.

"Hey, you get home okay? Is Avery all right?"

"Yeah, Avery's asleep in her bed. Nylah had already sent Mrs. Hanley home when she got here after closing the bar." Both Nylah and Liam were staying with Eastern tonight, to give him and Harper some space. "How are you and Harper?"

Cody ran his fingers through his hair. "Better now that we're home."

"So, doctors cleared her?"

"Yeah. No broken bones, just a lot of bruising." His mind involuntarily flicked to the black and blue discoloration on her ribs, and his fingers tightened on the phone to the point he was afraid he'd crush it. When he'd first lain eyes on the bruises, images had flashed through his head of her father kicking her while she was down. If the asshole wasn't already dead, Cody would murder him.

"Good." Eastern cleared his throat. "As well as checking in, I'm also calling to let you know that while we were at the farmhouse tonight, there was a fire set at Vanessa's house."

Cody paused halfway across the room. "At *Vanessa's* house?"

"Yep. And Travis was found just down the street, passed out in a neighbor's front yard with matches in his pocket and reeking of gasoline."

"So this entire time it's been Travis?"

"The evidence is pointing to that being the case. We need to wait until he sobers up so we can question him, but it seems like an open-and-closed case."

Cody shook his head. "It doesn't surprise me. The asshole isn't a good guy."

"Yeah, he has a drinking problem and anger issues. Those two things are not a good combination. The only thing we need is a motive for him targeting Vanessa. You don't worry about that though. I plan to do a thorough investigation." Eastern sighed. "Get some sleep."

"You too. And thank you again for your help."

"I've always got your back, brother."

Didn't Cody know it.

When he hung up, he went straight upstairs and had a quick shower before slipping into bed behind Harper. The second his arms wounds around her waist and he pulled her close, she sighed and whispered his name. "Cody."

Something flickered in his chest. It was hot and territorial and all for Harper. He kissed her bare shoulder. "Yeah, Storm, it's me. Sleep. You're safe."

CHAPTER 30

*H*arper moved down the bar, serving drink after drink. A week had passed since her kidnapping. Nylah and Liam had left a few days ago, staying a bit longer than they'd intended, and she'd only returned to working in the bar last night. Fortunately, a lot of her bruising had healed...well, mostly healed. Nothing a bit of makeup couldn't cover.

It was crazy, but she was actually starting to feel safe for the first time in her life. Not to mention excited for her future. Her future here in Misty Peak with Cody.

Yes, her brother and mother were still out there, but neither of them had made contact with her. Eastern had assured her they'd been notified about her father's death, and she was grateful that burden hadn't fallen on her. She was also sure her mom and brother were probably less than happy about the news...but now they knew she had people watching her back in Misty Peak, so she was hopeful they'd both stay away.

She nibbled her bottom lip, glancing around at the familiar faces as she filled a glass with beer before pushing it over to a customer.

To most, the idea of settling in a new town for good wouldn't be a big deal, but to her, it was everything. She'd lived her entire life physically in one place but mentally somewhere else. Dreaming about her forever home. And even though she didn't have her little house, what she had was better. The house had signified safety. Security. And Cody was both those things and more.

She'd just taken money from the customer and popped it in the till when strong, warm arms wrapped around her waist and heated breath brushed over her neck.

"You doing okay, Storm? Need a rest?"

She turned in his arms, slipping her hands around his neck. "I'm doing great. I'm safe and I have you. What more could a girl ask for?"

A small smile stretched his lips, but it didn't quite reach his eyes, and Harper knew why. Even though Travis had been arrested for the fires, he adamantly denied they were his doing, and there didn't seem to be any motive for him targeting Vanessa. He also denied that he'd assaulted Harper in the alley that night. All of that had been playing on Cody's mind, and Harper felt helpless to do anything about it.

She wasn't worried, because it had to be him, right? Hell, if he was drinking as much as people said, maybe he didn't even remember everything.

She reached out and smoothed the lines furrowing Cody's forehead. "Don't worry so much. It'll be okay."

"With you, I'll always worry." He lowered his head and kissed her.

"Hey. Can I get some help over here?" Barry yelled, humor in his voice.

Cody sighed. "Save me a kiss for later?"

"I'll save you a hundred."

He growled gruffly as he slipped away from her.

Chuckling, she grabbed a tray and headed out to the floor to collect glasses. She'd just cleared the first table when the door opened and Miles walked in.

Harper's brows tugged together. What was he doing here? Cody would flip if he saw him.

She hurried over. "Miles, maybe you shouldn't be here." Heck, there wasn't any maybe about it. Cody was already on high alert—he didn't need his former best friend in the bar.

Dark circles shadowed Miles's eyes. "Please. I just need a beer, and I need to drink it somewhere I'm not by myself."

She studied his face, noticing how pale he seemed. Not only that, but his shirt was wrinkled and he looked exhausted.

She might regret this, but… "Sit over there in the back corner. I'll get you a beer." She'd also let Cody know and cross her fingers that he didn't cause a scene.

Relief passed over the man's face. "Thank you."

She cleared a couple more tables before returning to the bar. After she'd set the glasses in the kitchen, she poured a beer and stepped over to Cody.

He turned—and immediately, his brows tugged together. "What happened?"

What was he, a mind reader? "Nothing happened."

"Then why do you look nervous?"

"I'm not nervous." Okay, maybe she was a little nervous. "Miles is here."

Cody's gaze lifted, tracking around the room, his jaw tightening.

She gripped his arm. "He looked like he needed to be surrounded by people. I don't know what happened with him and Vanessa, but I think it really messed with him. I told him he could sit in the back and I'd bring him a beer."

Cody's gaze lowered to her, his eyes softening a fraction. "I'll take it to him."

"Cody—"

"I'll be nice…ish."

Nerves trickled down her spine as she watched Cody cross the bar. When he stopped at the table, she wasn't sure what she expected to see, but after Cody set the beer on the table, a few words were spoken before he just…walked away.

The air rushed from her chest. Good. She didn't have the energy for a bar fight tonight, and by the look of him, neither did Miles.

Cody returned to the bar and as he passed behind her, he whispered, "Now who's worrying?"

She shook her head, the corners of her lips twitching as he moved away to serve a customer.

The next couple hours passed quickly, with people filtering in and out, drinking, playing pool. By closing time, her ribs hurt, but it was almost a welcome ache after all the resting she'd done over the last week. Moving felt good.

Finally, every customer was gone except Miles, who still sat at the back table. His head was in his hands. God, he just looked so sad. Because of Vanessa? She barely knew the man, and he probably didn't deserve her sympathy after what he'd done to Cody, but she couldn't help but feel just a bit bad for him.

Cody took a step toward him, but Harper set a hand on his chest. "I'll go talk to him."

Even though Cody hadn't kicked the guy out earlier, she didn't quite trust him to be calm if Miles proved hard to remove from the bar. Her gentle approach might be more effective.

She crossed the room and stopped beside Miles's table. "Hey, we're closing up. I'm sorry but I'm going to have to ask you to leave, Miles."

He mumbled something under his breath that she didn't quite catch, so she stepped closer. "What did you say?"

"I should've known better."

"Known better about what?"

"She cheated on Cody with *me*...I should've known she'd cheat on me with someone else."

Harper frowned. "Vanessa cheated on you?"

He looked up, pain darkening his brown eyes. "I loved her. Like *really* loved her. And I thought we were it. I'm not the type who gets involved with a woman who's already in a relationship. I didn't want to do that to Cody, but...I really believed that she loved me too."

"Sometimes we think we know a person when we don't." When he didn't respond, she touched his arm. "I'm sorry, Miles, but you're the last customer, and we really need to close up." She felt awful making him go, because she could just about feel the pain cascading off him, but she barely knew the guy. She wasn't in a position to help him.

Miles sighed and shuffled to his feet.

Harper turned to see Cody was on the phone, frowning, his voice loud enough to hear across the quiet room. "Yeah, he's here at the bar. Harper's just seeing him out."

Who was he talking to?

Cody's muscles visibly tensed. "Someone *beat* her?"

Her breath caught. Eastern. He had to be talking to Eastern. Who'd been beaten?

Cody's gaze moved to Miles. "I won't let him leave."

Something cold and uncomfortable slid over Harper's skin. Was he talking about *Vanessa*? And Miles was a suspect?

Her eyes swung back to Miles, and she took a quick step back, suddenly wondering if he really was a victim...or if he was a perpetrator.

* * *

"Grip those beer bottles any tighter and they'll explode in your hands, son."

Cody shifted his gaze from Harper and Miles to Barry. "I'm still thinking about Travis."

"Why?"

"Eastern said they put a lot of pressure on him to admit to the fires and the alley attack on Harper, but he never caved."

Barry frowned. "What are you thinking?"

"That my brother's good at what he does, and Travis is weak and should have admitted to everything by now."

There was a moment of pause before Barry stepped closer. "Travis was found passed out on the lawn three houses down from Vanessa's place. He had matches and stunk of gasoline."

"I know that. But doesn't that seem too easy? And based on how drunk he was, how could he have set that fire so carefully? Eastern said he was so wasted he blew off the charts, yet whoever set that fire broke in through the back door, threw gasoline all over Vanessa's couch, and set it ablaze—without leaving any evidence. Not even fingerprints."

Barry was silent for a moment, as if turning over what Cody said in his head. "So, you're suggesting someone else set those fires, and is possibly responsible for Harper's attack, and that person is framing Travis."

"Travis would be an easy target. The town troublemaker. Not liked by many. Always drunk."

"Okay, but who would—"

Barry's words were cut off by the ringing of Cody's phone. He pulled it out to see his brother's name on the screen. "Eastern?"

Wind blew over the line. "Hey. I'm looking for Miles Whitley. You seen him?"

"Yeah, he's here at the bar. Harper's just seeing him out."

"Don't let him leave." There was an urgency to Eastern's words that had Cody's muscles locking.

"Why? What's going on?"

"Vanessa went back to her house to pack a few things and she was beaten up."

"Someone *beat* her?" His fingers tightened around the phone.

"Yeah. Pretty badly, too. She was found unconscious and rushed to emergency. A neighbor heard her screaming and called the police. They also reported seeing a man who fit Miles's description leaving her house."

Motherfucker. His gaze rose to see Harper and Miles standing close together. "I won't let him leave." Then, he lowered his voice. "Stay on the line."

Barry stepped forward. "What's going on?"

"We can't let Miles leave. The asshole may have hurt Vanessa." He may not like the woman, but no man had the right to touch a woman that way. *Ever.*

He was coming around the bar, toward Miles, when the door opened and Dayne stepped in.

Cody frowned, taking in the man's bloodshot eyes. His disheveled appearance. The small drops of red on his white shirt. Blood?

Dayne wobbled on his feet. Drunk. The asshole was drunk.

"Get out of here, Dayne." It was Barry who yelled the words from behind the bar.

But Cody was still watching the man closely. There was something...unhinged about him. And it wasn't just his intoxication.

Dayne laughed, but the sound was all wrong. When he lifted a hand to run his fingers through his hair, Cody's eyes narrowed on his knuckles. Bruised and bleeding. He'd been in a fight. Had clearly hit someone more than once.

Cody took a step toward the guy. "What are you doing here, Dayne?"

"You always thought you were the fuckin' king of the town, Walker," Dayne slurred. "Bossing me around. Thinking you run the fuckin' show."

What the hell did that have to do with anything? "I'm gonna ask you one more time. *What* are you doing here?"

When the asshole didn't answer, Cody took two more steps toward him…

Only to stop when Dayne pulled a pistol from behind him and aimed it right at Cody's chest.

CHAPTER 31

Cody's muscles locked, outrage rising inside him that this asshole was pointing a weapon at him in his own bar.

"Dayne," Cody growled, voice low and dangerous. "What the fuck are you doing?"

His smirk only made Cody's blood coil in his veins. "What I should've done a long time ago." He stepped forward and stumbled, making Cody's muscles tense. The guy could easily pull the trigger without even meaning to, that's how fucking wasted he seemed.

"You're drunk," Barry said firmly from behind the bar. "Don't do something you'll regret."

"Something I'll regret?" He laughed, and the sound made Cody's skin crawl. "I do a lot of dumb shit. The fires, for instance…those were pretty stupid. Started because I was bored in this shitty town. And I like the rush of power."

Cody's hand fisted…the other still holding his phone. "That was you?"

"Sure was!"

"You lit my car on fire?" Harper asked.

Another low laugh from Dayne. "I did. That *wasn't* so smart though. I was kind of drunk that night, just wanted you to leave. Attacking you in the alley didn't work, so drunk Dayne thought settin' your car on fire might scare you the fuck away. Didn't think about the fact you wouldn't have a car to leave in."

Harper gasped, and Cody cursed himself for not carrying his Glock on him.

Suddenly, details from his conversation with Eastern came back to him. His gaze flew to Dayne's bloodied knuckles. "Did you beat Vanessa tonight?"

Pain crumpled the other man's expression. "I didn't wanna hurt her! I told her she wasn't allowed to leave me—and she was gonna do it anyway!"

"You…" Miles rasped. "You're the guy she's been cheating on me with?"

"I'm ten times the man you are!" Dayne shouted before shifting his gaze back to Cody. "And I gave her *everything*. But she kept making me so angry! Always visiting *you*. Talking to *you*. Goin' on about *you*. And tonight, she was screaming at me to leave her house. Saying she didn't love me. That I was never *permanent* for her."

Cody watched Dayne carefully, muscles tightening every time he swung the weapon around.

"We were fine!" Dayne yelled. "Everything was fine between us until *she* got to town and ruined us." Suddenly, Dayne switched his aim from Cody to Harper.

Cody growled. "Put the fucking gun down, Dayne."

"No. It was after *she* came to Misty Peak that Vanessa switched her attention back to *you*, Cody. Someone else caught your eye, and she just couldn't fuckin' stand it. I knew if I could get rid of Harper, things would go back to how they were."

Cody's mind was struggling to understand. Dayne had put Harper through all this over *Vanessa*? A woman who pitted men against each other basically for her own amusement and didn't really love anyone but herself?

"I set the fire at Vanessa's house to get her back, but it didn't work," Dayne continued almost desperately. "I thought it would scare her straight back into my arms, but it drove her further away!" His face contorted. "And now I've done something I can't come back from. I don't even know if she's alive!"

Harper's face paled. "You killed her?"

"She was so still when I left… If she'd just *listened* to me!"

"You didn't kill her," Cody said quietly, inching forward, closing some of the space between them. "A neighbor heard her scream and called the police. She's unconscious but alive and in the hospital. You haven't killed anyone. Don't start now."

Dayne's eyes narrowed. "Maybe I *want* to kill someone."

Without warning, the gun went off.

Even as Dayne pulled the trigger, Cody shouted and lunged for him and Miles threw Harper to the floor. Cody and Dayne hit the ground hard. Dayne attempted to swing the gun around, but Cody grabbed his wrist and smashed it to the floor, sending the weapon sliding across the room.

"I'm gonna kill you!" Dayne howled, attempting to get a knee up and pull his wrists out of Cody's grasp.

Cody immobilized the man easily. "Don't think so. And just so you're aware, that was Eastern on the phone when you arrived. I never hung up. He heard *everything*. Your entire confession. He's probably almost here."

The outrage on Dayne's face deepened, and his struggle got more aggressive.

When Cody heard a cry from the side of the room, his head whipped up to see Harper hunched over Miles, blood covering them both.

Fuck!

Barry rushed over, gun in hand and pointed at Dayne's head. "Go to Harper, Cody. Make sure she's okay."

He'd just stood when the door flew open and Eastern burst in, officers behind him.

Cody ran across the room and lowered beside Harper. "Are you okay?"

"He saved me!" she cried. "He lunged and took the bullet. Cody...there's so much blood!" Her hands were pressed to the wound, attempting to stem the blood.

He looked up to see his brother already on the phone to the paramedics, eyes on Miles.

One of the officers lowered beside her. "I'll take over."

She shook her head. "I can't move!"

"You can, Storm," Cody murmured. "Let's step back."

A few silent beats passed, and finally, she lifted her hands. The second she was on her feet, Cody tugged her into his arms, not caring about the blood on her skin or the chaos around them. He just held her.

Another close call...too damn close. Again.

The next hour was a mix of paramedics and police. Miles was taken to the hospital, while Dayne was arrested and taken to the station.

"You sure you're both okay?" Eastern asked as his officers left the bar.

Harper nodded, but her eyes were too wide and her face too pale.

Cody's arms slid around her waist. "I think we're just ready for this night to be over."

"Understandable." Eastern's eyes remained on Harper for another beat, as if he was thinking the same thing as Cody—that she was far from okay. But she didn't look at him. Eventually, he shifted his gaze back to Cody. "Okay. Call if you need anything."

Barry said goodbye and Cody turned toward Harper, but she slipped out of his arms. "Harper—"

"I just...I need to clean this blood off my hands."

He looked down at the dried crimson on her skin. "I'll help you."

"You need to lock up. Join me when you're finished." Then she was gone before he could stop her.

* * *

HARPER'S CHEST heaved with her panicked breaths as she jogged up the stairs. Her heart raced in her chest, and a million different emotions competed inside her. Relief that Dayne had been arrested and taken away. Comfort in knowing that Cody and Barry were okay. And shock and guilt. God, so much guilt.

Miles had saved her. Jumped in front of a *bullet* for her.

Her. Someone he barely knew.

He was still breathing, but was that enough? Would he make it through the night?

Her chest pulled tight, sharp pain cutting through her. It should have been her. Dayne had been aiming for *her*.

She stepped into the apartment and went straight to the bathroom. Immediately, her gaze ran over her reflection, and she saw everything she was feeling. The way the blood had drained from her face. Eyes that were wide and disbelieving.

She glanced down, hating the sight of the blood. She'd given her hands a quick rinse before being questioned by the deputies, but there was still so much red. Under her nails. Etched into the fine lines of her fingers.

She turned on the taps and scrubbed her skin.

The distant click of the apartment door sounded, but she didn't look up as the footsteps neared or when warm arms wrapped around her.

"Storm...are you okay?"

"I'm fine." It was a partial lie. Physically, she was fine. Mentally, she was struggling to come to terms with what had happened.

Cody's finger trailed down her arms before wrapping around the backs of her hands. Then his breath brushed against her ear. "He's alive. He's alive, and thanks to him, so are you. It's a debt I'll owe him forever."

She blinked away the tears in her eyes. "I feel so guilty."

Gently, he applied some pressure to her hips and turned her. She gasped when he lifted her to the counter and stepped between her thighs. Then his forehead touched hers. "Don't feel guilty. He made a choice to save you. I'm sorry I couldn't get to you in time to save you myself."

She glanced up, a tear spilling over. "We need to visit him as soon as possible. And take him food. Lots of food because the hospital food sucks. And books in case he gets bored."

A hint of a smile curved his lips. "I'm not sure he's much of a reading guy, but I'm sure he'll appreciate the food."

She nodded, a semblance of calm returning to her. "This is it, right? It's over? The attacks. The fires. The constant worry."

"It's over." He swiped the tear from her cheek. "But you and I are just beginning, Harper Rain."

Another speck of calm returned to her, and suddenly she needed to get words out that she'd been keeping inside her for too long. "I don't know if this is the right or the wrong time to tell you this, but I love you, Cody Walker. And each time something happens, the thing I fear most is that I'll never get a chance to tell you. So I'm telling you now. I love you."

His intake of breath was sharp, his fingers tightening on her waist. "You love me."

It wasn't a question, yet she answered like it was. "So much that I feel that love everywhere. From my toes to my heart."

Both his hands came up to cup her cheeks, and with closed eyes, he leaned forward, touching his forehead to hers once again. "You have no idea what those words do to me, Harper." He eased back, his eyes boring into hers. "When that gun was pointed at you tonight, I felt everything stop. Because that's what happens when I think about losing you. My world stops, because I love you too."

A new wave of tears pressed at her eyes. "You love me?"

"So damn much it hurts." Then his mouth crashed to hers, and she let his kiss heal her.

ody laced his fingers through Harper's as they drove back to the bar from visiting Miles in the hospital.

Just over a week had passed since Dayne's attack, and in that time, he'd confessed in the sheriff's office everything he'd admitted to them. That he was the one who'd set the fires around town, partly because he was bored, partly for the rush. That he'd framed Travis just because he could. And he was the one who'd attacked Harper in the alley, wanting to scare her into leaving town in some sick attempt to fix things between him and Vanessa.

Not only did they have Dayne's confession, but Vanessa had woken up in the hospital and confirmed that it was Dayne who'd caused her injuries.

He shot Harper a quick glance. "How are you feeling?"

She smiled at him, and the smile was so genuine he felt like he'd been kicked in the gut and all the breath had been forced out of him. "Relieved that Miles is okay and being discharged soon."

He was relieved too. Not just because he wanted Miles to be okay, but because it lightened the guilt that had been pressing on

Harper since the attack. She hadn't spoken about the guilt again, but she didn't need to—he saw it.

"Do you think you'll ever be friends again?" Harper asked softly.

He frowned as he took a right turn. "I'll always owe him a debt I'll never be able to repay for saving your life. And I believe that he really thought he loved Vanessa, that he thought they were meant for each other, and that's why he did what he did. I'm not saying it was right, because it wasn't. But I *do* think he became a victim of her...charms." He lifted a shoulder. "I guess that's my long-winded way of saying maybe."

She nodded. "Even though I don't like Vanessa, I'm glad she's going to be okay."

Cody shook his head, thinking about the injuries Dayne had inflicted on her. Broken ribs. A concussion. A fractured wrist and a ton of bruising. She'd made some shit decisions—cheating on him, blaming Miles for bruises obviously inflicted by Dayne in a bid to win back Cody, then cheating on Miles—but that *still* didn't mean she deserved what had happened.

"I'm glad she'll be okay, too." He lifted her hand and kissed the inside of her wrist.

"What was that for?"

"Do I need a reason to kiss you?"

"I guess not."

Another kiss, and he turned onto the street where the bar was located. He frowned when he saw a woman sitting on the curb outside the bar. Who was—

Harper gasped and straightened, eyes on the woman. "Oh my God."

"You know her?"

"That's my mother."

What the *fuck*?

He pulled up close to the bar, but neither of them moved to

get out of the car. Harper's mother saw them and rose to her feet, but she didn't approach.

He turned to Harper. "Do you want me to send her away?" Because he would. Hell, he'd cut out his right kidney if this woman asked.

Her chest rose with a deep breath. "No. It's okay. I'll see what she has to say, then she can leave. My mother was never physically abusive."

Even that made Cody's blood boil, because he knew she was abusive in other ways. They both climbed out, and when he rounded the car, he slipped an arm around Harper's waist.

"Mom. What are you doing here?"

The woman wrung her hands together in front of her. "I was wondering if I could talk to you. I don't need long."

Harper didn't immediately respond, and her mother started shuffling her feet, clearly uncomfortable.

Finally, she nodded. "There's an apartment over the bar. We can talk there."

Cody stepped forward and unlocked the door. Before Harper could head toward the stairs, he slid his fingers around her wrist and pulled her close, keeping his voice low. "Do you want me to come?"

She shook her head. "I'll be okay. I need to do this alone."

"Call out if you need me."

She nodded, and he leaned down and kissed her. It was damn hard to watch her walk away with a woman he knew had hurt her, maybe not physically, but in every other way. His feet itched to follow. Protect her. But she wanted to do this on her own, and he needed to respect that.

He ran his fingers through his hair and headed behind the bar. He was just getting things set up for the evening when the door opened.

Kayden entered and dropped onto a stool in front of Cody. "I need a whiskey."

"Rough day already?"

"You could say that."

Cody pulled out a glass and poured a shot. "Wanna talk about it?"

"Linda's been training Matilda this week."

His brows rose. "Okay. And why is that terrible?"

His brother threw back the drink and thumped it down onto the counter. "Because I don't trust her, and now she's running the visitors center. Because the sight of her reminds me of Dad when he told us he'd lost the family home and was re-mortgaging the bar."

Cody's chest clenched. Yeah, that had been a kick in the gut. "Like I've said before, her *father* wronged a lot of people in this town, not her."

"You really think she had no idea? Even if that's true, you don't think she knows where he is?"

"Why would she—"

"She and her mother left too quickly after her thieving father skipped town. Where's she been all this time? And you know damn well that while Dad lost *our* family home, her mother kept hers. That's where Matilda's living."

That still didn't sound like something that was Tilly's fault.

Almost on cue, a knock sounded at the door just before it opened, and Tilly took half a step in, a smile on her face when she saw Cody. Then Kayden turned his head, and the smile dropped. "Oh. Sorry. I thought I'd stop in and see if Harper was here."

Kayden turned back to the bar, his knuckles whitening around the whiskey glass.

"She's upstairs but a bit busy at the moment, Tilly. I can let her know you stopped by?"

"That would be great." She shot one more quick, almost nervous glance Kayden's way before giving Cody a tense smile and stepping out.

Cody's eyes narrowed on his brother. "You gonna be a jerk to her at work every day?"

"When am I a jerk?"

He almost laughed. "A lot of the damn time, and you know it."

Kayden opened his mouth to respond, but Cody's phone dinged with a message. He looked down to see it was a text he'd been waiting for.

She's ready for you. Key's under the mat.

Cody's heart thumped in his chest. She was ready. Finally.

"What has that shit-eating grin on your face?" Kayden asked, pulling Cody's attention.

"That was confirmation that my big gesture to woo Harper is ready and waiting."

* * *

HARPER BARELY LOOKED at her mother as she walked into the small apartment kitchen. "Would you like tea or coffee?"

"Just some water would be nice."

Water? When had she ever seen her mother drink just water?

She turned to the fridge and pulled out a bottle, then pushed it across the counter. Her mother simply touched the cap of the bottle without actually removing it and taking a sip.

Harper folded her arms, repeating the question she'd asked when she spotted the woman outside the bar. "What are you doing here, Mom?"

Still, her mother didn't look up. "I...I wanted to see if you were okay? Your... Cody...he said your father kidnapped you."

Did she actually care? "He did. He locked me in a basement and told me he intended to keep me hostage for eight years. Payback for his time in prison."

Her mother's eyes widened, her gaze finally meeting Harper's. And for the first time possibly ever, she thought she saw emotion in their depths instead of the blank, drunken look she was used to.

"When he asked me to find out where you were, I didn't know that was his intention."

Harper's brows rose. "Really? And what *did* you think his intention was? To finally be the father he should have been all those years ago? To love me the way he was supposed to?" She shook her head. "Or maybe you didn't put any thought into it at all. You were so drunk that you just skipped on over to my boss to find out where I lived to get his approval."

The old Harper may have felt the sting of that theory. The pain of knowing she'd never have the family she once so desperately wished for. But now, having Cody and a life here in Misty Peak, it didn't hurt so much. The family she was born into was something she had no control over. But her future with Cody, that was something she *did* have control over.

"You're right. I didn't think." Her mother dipped her chin to her chest, and when she looked up again, tears filled her eyes. "I'm sorry."

"For what?" She was genuinely interested to know. For giving Rodney her location? For more?

"I'm sorry that I didn't protect you from your father or your brother. I'm sorry that I dulled my entire life with alcohol and wasn't the mother you needed or deserved. And I...I'm sorry that I took that money from you."

For a moment, Harper was so shocked that words didn't come to her.

Never in her life had she expected an apology from the woman who'd made so many mistakes. Now that she had it, she wasn't sure how she felt. It didn't change anything. But it did make a heavy part of her feel just a tiny bit lighter.

Harper swallowed. "I appreciate you saying that. Are you okay?"

"Not really." She sniffed. "I know your brother told you what your father did to me. Then your brother got angry because I wouldn't give him more of the money I took from you, and he left me." She straightened, scrubbing a tear from her eye. "Hearing that your father kidnapped you was...I guess it was the wake-up call I needed. I haven't drunk anything since I went to the hospital, and I don't intend to. I don't expect your forgiveness. But I did put the money I had left back into your account."

A sharp puff of air escaped Harper's lungs. "You returned my money?"

"Some of it's gone. Mostly to alcohol, some to your brother. But most of it's still there." She straightened. "I, um, I'm gonna go now. I just...I needed to right at least one of my wrongs."

Her mother was halfway to the door when Harper finally found words. "Mom."

Her mother stopped and turned her head.

"Thank you. For coming here and doing what was right. I hope you can stay sober."

"Me too."

When she left, Harper just stood, arms wrapped around her waist, taking in what had just happened. The change should have come a long time ago, but it was more than Harper had ever expected.

The apartment door opened and Cody stepped in, his eyes intense as they moved over her face, probably trying to determine what had passed between her and her mother.

He stopped in front of her and gripped her hips. "Is everything okay?"

"She, um, returned what's left of the money she took from me. She also said my brother left her and she's trying to remain sober."

Cody's brows shot up. "Wow."

"Yeah. Wow. It doesn't change anything, but it's nice to know she has a conscience and finally wants to be better."

He slipped his arms around her waist and tugged her to him. "I'm sorry it couldn't have come earlier."

"I'm starting to realize that things don't come when you want them. They come when you need them." She slipped her hands around his neck. "I mean, if everything hadn't happened the way it did, I might not have met you."

He growled softly. "No, Storm, we were always going to meet."

"Oh, I remember. Fate."

His head lowered so his mouth hovered over hers. "Yeah, fate."

He kissed her, and she leaned into him, loving his strength and warmth. When he pulled away, it was far too soon. She groaned, wanting to tug him back.

"I have something to show you," he whispered.

"Really? What?"

"Come and see."

She frowned but he just gave her a lopsided grin before pulling her out of the apartment and down the stairs. When they climbed into his car and started driving, curiosity got the better of her. "You're really not going to tell me where you're taking me?"

"Nope. You'll see soon enough."

Ten minutes later, Cody pulled up outside a small cottage-looking house. There was a navy-blue picket fence and shutters. It was gorgeous. So gorgeous, she was still staring raptly when Cody climbed out and came around to her side. He helped her out before leading her toward the door. They were inside the fence and halfway down the path when she pulled at his hand.

"Wait, Cody. I need you to tell me what we're doing here."

He stopped, his gaze brushing over her face. "Well, it just so happens that this house came on the market a short while ago. I've been communicating with the listing agent...and we're at the contract stage. But, before I buy it for us...I need to know it's the one you've been dreaming about."

Her jaw dropped open. "For us?"

"Yeah. Both our names will be on the deed. It'll be ours. Yours and mine. We can paint the fence white. It has space for the vegetable garden. There are little things that need fixing, but I can do that. And maybe we can even convince Tommy to come live with us."

She just continued to stare at him, her heart beating too fast and her fingers shaking. He was out of his mind, right? He wasn't actually talking about buying them a *home*? "You're serious? You're really buying the house I've always dreamed of?"

"I am. For you. For us. For our future." He stepped closer, swiping away a tear from her cheek. "Because you *are* my future, Harper. You're not mine for a moment. Or a few years. You're mine forever. And I'm yours. And I want us to be perfect."

A few more deep breaths and it finally clicked—she'd been right all along. He *was* perfect. Perfect for her.

She jumped into his arms, and he caught her easily. "I love you, Cody Walker. God, I love you so much!"

"You have no idea, Storm. My love for you is like an obsession." Then he kissed her, and she felt it all. Safety. Strength. And all the love she'd ever dreamed of possessing.

CHAPTER 33

Kayden negotiated his way down the mountain. His morning tour group would be here soon, so he was checking that the path was clear. He was employed by the National Park Service, so the tours were an add-on to his SAR job.

This was his favorite part of his profession. Being out here in the early morning, on his own. There was something so calming about the mountains when the sun was just rising. When he only had the sound of the wind in the trees to keep him company. The feel of the morning mist on his skin.

Some days, he missed his time as a PJ in the Air Force. He'd saved people from all kinds of hostile environments for years. He was trained as a parachutist, scuba diver, rock climber...he was ready for anything. Hell, he'd even had arctic training in order to endure any environment to save others.

Coming home to Misty Peak had been a shock to his system. It was a much slower pace. Well...bar the last few weeks.

His back teeth ground together at the thought of what Cody and Harper had gone through. At what her father had put them through, then Dayne.

Fucking scumbags.

If there was anything Kayden was grateful for, it was the loving home environment his parents had created for him and his siblings. Losing them had been hard, especially his mother at such a young age, but damn if he wasn't grateful for the love they'd given him while they'd been alive.

He moved up the hill to the visitors center. It was still too early for anyone else to be there. Not that many people worked at the center—three other members of the SAR team, who also conducted tours, as well as a couple of people who worked in the café, and a young girl named Pixie who worked at the desk.

And of course, Linda usually worked in her office, and sometimes at the front desk.

He stepped into the building—only to have his feet grind to a halt. A woman was bent over the desk, back facing him as she rifled through papers. She obviously hadn't heard him open the door, because her actions didn't pause or slow.

"Holy crackers. What kind of a filing system is this, Linda?"

Kayden's muscles locked at the woman's whispered muttering. He knew that voice well. Had heard it many times. Had lectured himself time and again not to be affected by its raspy, sexy undertone.

"God dang it." Tilly rose and turned, a cry immediately slipping from her lips when she saw him. She pressed a hand to her fast-moving chest. "Oh my God, Kayden! You scared me. I didn't hear you come in."

"I didn't expect anyone to be here. What are you doing in the office so early?"

She swallowed. "It's my first day without Linda, so I wanted to get a jump on it."

His brows slashed together. "Today's supposed to be Linda's last day."

"I offered to start early, and she took me up on it." When Kayden remained silent, Tilly lifted a shoulder. "I kind of got the feeling she was already one foot out the door since her retirement party."

Maybe. Or maybe Linda didn't want to have the "why'd you hire Matilda" conversation with him for the tenth time.

"I just came in to check my morning tour details. Would you prefer me to check on this computer or the one in the office?"

Her brows rose. "Whichever you usually use."

He usually just asked Linda to pull up the details, and Linda would do so at whatever desk she was occupying at the time. But he wouldn't be asking Tilly.

He dipped his head and was about to walk past her when she sidestepped, blocking his way. She only came to his shoulder, but she stood so close that he could see the array of freckles that dusted her nose.

"Wait. Before you go, I just want to say that I know you don't trust me," she rushed to get out, almost sounding out of breath. "Hell, you don't even like me. But I'm good at my job. I plan to tidy a lot of stuff around here. Digitalize the center. Get more tourists in, maybe some school groups, and get the skywalk up and running efficiently."

Kayden's mind immediately flicked back years ago, to a conversation he'd overheard while home from a mission, between his father and Tilly's.

"You can trust me with your money, Toby. You know me. You know I'm good at my job."

A vein throbbed in his temple, and he took a step back. There was a flicker of hurt in her eyes, and it took a lot of restraint to not let that hurt affect him. "Regardless of whether I trust you or not, you're here. Linda chose you for the job, and your job has little to do with me. I just do the tours and rescues."

He tried to step around her, but Tilly touched his arm. For some goddamm reason, that touch was like a bolt of electricity running through his limbs. When he looked at her again, her big blue eyes were wide and boring into him, almost anxious.

"Working together doesn't have to be hostile, Kayden." The way she said his name, so smooth like silk, made something squeeze in his gut. "So many things have been hard for me in this town." She looked away briefly, like it hurt to think about. "Sorry. You don't care about that. What I'm saying is, we *can* get along. Maybe even be friends."

There was something about the desperation in her voice that made him want to agree.

When the woman looked at him the way she was right now, he wanted to give her anything she asked for.

But then he remembered his dad's face the day he'd told them he'd lost his savings. He'd just received his cancer diagnosis, and on top of that devastating news, told them he'd had to re-mortgage the bar, sell the family home, and move into the apartment over the bar.

"I think a business relationship would be best." The words came out harsher than he'd intended.

Her expression registered her disappointment, but to her credit, she didn't break down. Instead, she straightened and nodded just once.

He forced himself to move. To step around her and into the office to check the details of his morning tour, ignoring every instinct that told him to go back out there and be the friend she obviously needed. A support person. Maybe even an ally.

He ignored it. Because the truth was, he wasn't sure he was capable of any that…not with her.

Order book two in the series, RECKLESS TRUST, featuring Kayden and Tilly, NOW!

ALSO BY NYSSA KATHRYN

PROJECT ARMA SERIES

Uncovering Project Arma

Luca

Eden

Asher

Mason

Wyatt

Bodie

Oliver

Kye

BLUE HALO SERIES

Logan

Jason

Blake

Flynn

Aidan

Tyler

Callum

Liam

MERCY RING

Jackson

Declan

Cole

Ryker

BEAUTIFUL PIECES

Erik's Salvation

Erik's Redemption

Erik's Refuge

SHORT CHRISTMAS STORY

Hidden Shadows

RECKLESS SERIES

(series ongoing)

Reckless Hope

Reckless Trust

Reckless Fall

Reckless Faith

Reckless Love

JOIN my newsletter and be the first to find out about sales and new releases! CLICK HERE

ABOUT THE AUTHOR

Nyssa Kathryn is a romantic suspense author. She lives in South Australia with her daughter and hubby and takes every chance she can to be plotting and writing. Always an avid reader of romance novels, she considers alpha males and happily-ever-afters to be her jam.

Don't forget to follow Nyssa and never miss another release.

Facebook | Instagram | Amazon | Goodreads